PRAISE FOR STEPHEN M. MURPHY

"*Beneath the Gavel* has the best opening chapter I have read in some time and follows it up with a unique plot filled with fascinating characters."

— PHILLIP MARGOLIN, NEW YORK TIMES
BESTSELLING AUTHOR OF *FALSE WITNESS*

"*Beneath The Gavel* is a compelling and ingenious concoction. It's a page-turning legal thriller, an old-school detective novel, a who-done-it murder mystery, and a family drama pitting three generations against each other. Judge Ferdinand Pitt must fight a corrupt public defender, a Commission on Judicial Performance, the police, and his long-suffering wife to uncover the truth about a brutal murder that implicates duty, kinship, and political conspiracy. All written by an author who knows human nature as well as he knows the law."

— RICHARD DOOLING, AUTHOR OF *WHITE
MAN'S GRAVE*

"What's it like for a judge to look down from the bench and see that the defendant standing before him is his long-lost father? You'll find out in this intricate tale of law and lawyers, politics and dysfunctional families, all set against the background of contemporary San Francisco. Steve Murphy knows his subject and he knows how to keep a reader guessing. Surprise after surprise makes *Beneath the Gavel* one wild ride."

— WALTER WALKER, AUTHOR OF *CRIME OF PRIVILEGE*

"Outstanding. Judge Stephen Murphy has written a deftly plotted, propulsive legal thriller/whodunnit filled with inside knowledge and numerous twists and turns. Judge Ferdinand Pitt is a nuanced protagonist who is worth rooting for. A compelling crime novel. Highly recommended."

— SHELDON SIEGEL, NY TIMES BESTSELLING AUTHOR

BENEATH THE GAVEL

BENEATH THE GAVEL

STEPHEN M. MURPHY

INDIES UNITED PUBLISHING HOUSE, LLC
P.O. BOX 3071
QUINCY, IL 62305-3071

First edition August 2025

Cover design by Christian Storm

ISBNs

Hardback: 978-1-64456-843-9

Paperback: 978-1-64456-844-6

Kindle: 978-1-64456-845-3

ePub: 978-1-64456-846-0

Library of Congress Control Number: 2025915023

A judge shall avoid impropriety and the appearance of impropriety in all of the judge's activities.

— CALIFORNIA CODE OF JUDICIAL ETHICS,
CANON 2

1

Judge Ferdinand Pitt slumped in the thick leather chair behind the bench at the Hall of Justice, San Francisco's tired criminal courthouse, and stared down at the defendant standing in front of him. A man who looked like he'd seen better days. Caved cheeks, thinning hair, a gaunt face, his thin frame lost in the orange pants and sweatshirt he wore. His hands chained behind his back, he stared at the floor, not meeting Ferd's eyes. As the seconds passed, Ferd began to suck small gasps of air through his mouth. Swiveling in his chair, his clerk, Jim, turned to look at him. "Judge," he whispered, "are you alright?"

Ferd cleared his throat and closed his mouth. He had been late to court that morning and never had a chance to review the calendar before taking the bench. Now he was on the last arraignment of the day, an alleged violation of Penal Code section 187—murder. Standing with the defendant was deputy public defender Nicole Smedley, Pitt's opponent in the upcoming judicial election. She had a smug look on her face, which drove Ferd crazy. Ferd turned his gaze back to the defendant, whose shoulders were slouched, his eyes still focused on the floor.

The man's name was Dwight Pitt. *How many Dwight Pitts could there be in the world?* He had known only one, the father who had abandoned him and his twin sister when they were just twelve years old.

This Dwight Pitt seemed older than his father would have been, about 67. *Defendant* Pitt appeared to be in his late 70s. If he were Ferd's father, then the years had done him no favors. Ferd continued to stare, searching for some similarity. It *couldn't* be his father. Though his memories were fuzzy, he knew his father had never hit him, had never been violent toward his mother, wasn't even the kind of guy to get into fights. How could a peaceful man like that *kill* a person? He couldn't fathom it, though a lot could change in thirty plus years.

The man raised his eyes and focused them on Ferd, and the judge felt a jolt of recognition—something about his face. The defendant blinked, swallowed, then said, "Long time, Ferd."

Ferd froze. The gravelly voice left no doubt. He looked down at his father with conflicting feelings of resentment and remembered affection. Still stunned, his eyes fell on Smedley, her squat frame bursting out of a cheap black suit. He found himself staring at her, his thoughts swirling, when Smedley said, "Your Honor, do you know my client?"

Lost in a fog, Ferd ignored her question and gazed at Jim, an African American man who was nearing his thirty-first year with the court. He wore his hair in a big Afro and knew criminal procedure cold. Instead of answering, Ferd stood up and said, "We'll take a brief recess." Without a further glance at his father, he hurried off the bench.

Once in chambers, he immediately dialed the presiding judge. "Carol, I've got a problem. The defendant in one of my murder cases . . . He's my father."

There was silence, then a stuttered, "Oh my." Another long

pause before "You'll have to recuse yourself. Tell the attorneys I'm reassigning the case. You needn't worry. You won't have to touch it again."

He had held his breath awaiting her reply. "I appreciate that, Carol." He paused, trying to make sense of the emotions cascading through him. "Would it be alright if I took a few days off? I need to get a handle on this situation."

"By all means. Just keep in touch."

Before leaving, Ferd called Jim to his chambers and explained the situation. The man's face was the picture of sympathy. "That's terrible, Judge," he said. "Never heard of that happening before."

"You should be getting a call soon on the assigned judge. I'll retake the bench and talk to the lawyers." He rebuttoned his robe and moved toward the courtroom.

Jim turned to follow him, then stopped. "I hope you don't mind my saying so, but you don't look so good, Judge."

"As a matter of fact, I don't feel so great."

The bailiff yelled that court was back in session. After retaking the bench, Ferd gazed at his father who appeared on the verge of speaking. Ferd held up his hand to silence him. "Counsel, I am recusing myself from this case. Another judge will be here shortly to complete the arraignment." Smedley was staring at Ferd, an even smugger look on her face.

"May I ask something, Your Honor?" said Smedley.

"I think it best I do not comment on this case at all," said Ferd as he left the courtroom.

FERD SLOWLY MADE his way to the basement garage, unable to get the image of his father out of his mind. *God, he looked awful. What kind of life must he have led?* He leaned back in the driver's seat staring blankly at his watch. The new judge should've arrived by now.

As much as he resented the man, he couldn't ignore his father. He had to talk to him. There was just too much at stake. He knew it was highly unusual for a judge to talk to a criminal defendant, especially without his lawyer present, but Ferd was anxious to avoid Smedley, so decided convention didn't matter when the defendant was your own father.

As Ferd walked along the drab corridors, up the stairs, and over to the jail, he had no idea what he would say to the man. He was unsure how he would react to being with his father. In his private practice as an insurance defense attorney, he became known for his skill in smoothing out disagreements and resolving conflict. He had applied for a judgeship after getting fed up with young lawyers who viewed the law as a business rather than a profession. They were a pack of cutthroat, rude little boys and girls, prone to sending inflammatory and accusatory emails. As a judge, Ferd knew he could exercise his authority and use his talents to moderate such behavior. But now, in this situation he didn't know if he could call on those talents.

Ferd approached the front desk. "Hi, I'm the son of Dwight Pitt. I was hoping to have a word with him."

The female deputy sheriff brushed a strand of brunette hair from her face and said, "Hello, Your Honor. I'll call for him now." Ferd frowned at the deputy's use of the honorific. In this setting, the county jail, he did not wish to be identified as a judge. She made a phone call and, after hanging up, said, "He's enroute from court. Should be only a few minutes."

Ferd took a seat in the visiting room, the plastic bottom jutting into his buttocks, the ash-grey walls darkening his mood. When the deputy brought his father, Ferd looked him up and down. Dwight was thin, the orange shirt and pants he wore hanging loosely on him. His face was pockmarked, covered with patches of grey whiskers. *He can't even grow a proper beard*, Ferdinand thought with distaste. *Hard to believe this old man is my father.*

The two stared at each other, a couple of feet of scratched metal table between them, neither bothering to extend a hand. Dwight took the initiative. "I didn't recognize you in court at first," his father said as he took the seat across from Ferd. "What a success you've become. My boy, such a big shot."

"No thanks to you," Ferd said, gritting his teeth. "And don't call me 'your boy.' I'm not *your* anything."

"You always were a spunky kid, I remember that. Guess that spunk took you a long way. It probably won't mean much if I say I'm sorry."

"No, it wouldn't. And I wouldn't believe it, anyway."

His father looked away, glassy-eyed, biting his lower lip.

Go on and cry, Ferd thought. He pulled back his chair, glancing at the door. "I want to know why you left."

"Ah, son . . ."

"Don't call me that."

"But you are my son, aren't you?" He stared at Ferd, who didn't respond. "Nothing I could say would change anything. I know it doesn't matter, but I've had a rough life. I'm sixty-seven and look seventy-seven. My health is terrible. I got a problem. Alcohol took over my life. I can't stop drinking. I've tried, believe me, and I'll still try."

"Thirty-four years. And other than a few postcards, *at first*, not a word from you. Not one birthday card, not one phone call, not one *anything* to acknowledge you had a son and daughter."

His father looked down at his shoes. "That's a long time, I know. I've been away. I only came back a few months ago. I'm not proud to say this, but I've been living on the streets."

"The streets? You're a homeless drunk. That's what you've got to show for the past thirty-four years?" Ferd leaned forward, the hard plastic seat aching his buttocks.

Dwight looked away, grimacing.

Ferd stood up and arched his back before resuming his seat. "About this murder."

"I'm innocent. I had nothing to do with it."

"So the police charged you for no reason?" Ferd stared at his father, waiting for his response. But he continued averting Ferd's eyes, remaining silent.

Again, Ferd stood up, taking a step toward the door. "Don't go," his father said. "I'd like to talk to you."

Hesitating, Ferd said, "You're not telling me anything."

"I can't . . . My lawyer, she said to keep my mouth shut."

"That includes your son?" Ferd's frustration at his father's reticence gave an edge to his voice, one he didn't try to hide. "And what about your life? Did she tell you not to discuss that too?"

Dwight Pitt glanced up at Ferd, folded his arms across his chest, and started rocking back and forth. "I was thirty-three when I left home," he said, still rocking. "Before then, I was a good provider for my family, you got to admit that."

Ferd sat back down and put his hands on his father's shoulders to stop the rocking. He looked into his father's eyes and said, "Be still."

Dwight stiffened but stopped. "I need a drink."

"I know you put food on the table, provided us a three-bedroom house in the Outer Sunset."

"You were twelve when I left. Old enough to think for yourself, take care of your mother."

"As if you really cared about her." Ferd made no effort to keep the disgust from his voice. "Tell me something I *don't* know."

"Your mother and I had a terrible fight; I left. Drove cross-country, stopping whenever I had to. That's when I sent you all those postcards. Wound up in New Hampshire, found a job at Manchester Insurance Company and started a new life. Met a woman—Janet—we worked together and hit it off. I tried to live a good life, son. God knows I tried."

"What was the fight about?"

Dwight looked away, biting his lower lip. "You'll have to ask your mother."

"I have. Many times."

His father shook his head but didn't answer. Then Dwight raised his gaze to the ceiling, tearing up. He seemed on the verge of saying something when the deputy knocked on the door. "Time's up," she said. "Got to take him back to his cell."

She motioned for Dwight to stand up, then clicked handcuffs onto his wrists. Dwight turned toward Ferdinand. "Son, don't hate me. Please."

Silent, Ferdinand watched the deputy lead his father away, thinking the man was asking far too much of him.

2

Ferd's front door had barely shut before he started mixing a highball brimming with Jameson's. He sank onto the couch next to Sonya, his wife of twenty-four years, and took a gulp, sighing as the liquor swam into his bloodstream. She had met Ferd when she was an undergraduate and he in law school at the University of California, Berkeley. After earning a master's degree in creative writing from Stanford, she began her career as a children's and young adults' book editor for a small publisher, often working from home. A youthful forty-five-year-old, she went to hot yoga five days a week, sweating and stretching her lithe body, burning off the calories she packed in on weekends when she and Ferd usually dined out.

Sonya's eyes grew wide as Ferd recounted his day.

"Can you believe it?" he said. "My father. After all these years."

"Sounds like he's had a tough life."

"Too bad. Not like it was easy for me, growing up without him."

Ferd swung his hand wildly in the air. "The sonuvabitch!"

He tried to swallow his anger with a gulp of whiskey, but it had little effect.

"But you always said he was a good father."

"When he was around. Helped me with homework, took me fishing, came to my baseball games. He wasn't all that affectionate, but he never hit my sister or me. Not even a spanking. This whole thing makes no sense."

"You and Claire were, what, twelve when he left?"

"Yeah, leaving Mom to raise us alone. No father-son events at school for me. The bastard."

Sonya rubbed his back, trying to calm him. "I know it hurts, Ferd, but you've got to let it go. You're only hurting yourself. And you've got to think about this rationally."

He took a sip of the highball. "I'm going to call Claire. She needs to know."

He dialed her cell number. His twin sister Claire was still at work, inputting information into a spreadsheet. Beside the monitor were photos of her two college-aged children where she could see them whenever she was mired in duties as a paralegal for a personal injury firm.

As soon as she said, "Hello," Ferd blurted, "Claire, you won't believe this. It's Dad. I know where he is."

"*Dad?*" She held the phone away from her ear, staring at it.

"He's in jail."

"How . . .?"

"He was in my courtroom. In handcuffs."

There was a long silence, then an audible sigh. She stared at the framed paralegal certificate above her desk, reflecting her neatly coiffed blonde hair. "This is unbelievable. I've hardly thought about him for years."

"He's charged with murder. He's got that damn Smedley defending him."

Ferd had told her all about Smedley. As he waited for her

reaction, he threw back the rest of his drink, but it did nothing to relieve the tension headache that had formed.

"Ferd, I honestly don't know what to say. Did he do it?"

"How the hell do I know?"

"Ferd, don't yell at me. I'm not the problem here."

"I'm sorry, Claire. It's just . . . he claims he's innocent. I don't know what to do."

"Then let's think about this."

"This is all I need. Who's going to vote for the son of a murderer?"

"*Accused* murderer. Innocent until proven guilty and all that."

Ferd grimaced. "I should be able to remember that."

"Tell you what," Claire said, "let's have lunch tomorrow and talk it out. How about Tadich's at noon?"

After hanging up, he poured himself another highball, a smaller one, and turned on the TV to the news. As he'd feared, his father's case was the lead story at six. "Sonya, come see this," he yelled. Sonya returned to the living room, her eyebrow arching at the refilled glass in his hand. She said nothing and turned her attention to the screen just as the newscaster announced that the father of a sitting judge had been arrested and charged with murdering one of the founders of CAPSLOCK, a software development company in Silicon Valley.

"That's *Josh's* company!" Sonya said, bringing her hand to her mouth. Josh was their twenty-two-year-old son who had been working as a coder for CAPSLOCK for the past year.

"Jesus Christ! What if Josh knew the victim? This is unbelievable!"

As the newscaster reported on the arraignment and Ferd's recusal, a photo of Ferd in a dark suit and blue tie appeared on the screen. Beside Ferd's photo was his father's booking photo, the man swimming in orange, looking disheveled. The contrast was stark. To Ferd's further dismay, the newscaster revealed that his father was a homeless alcoholic who tried to use the victim's credit card at Safeway.

"He looks *awful*," Sonya said. "Nothing like the few photos you showed me."

"I know, but it's him, alright."

The newscaster stated that several phone calls to Ferd's court clerk for comment had gone unanswered. Ferd reached over and pulled Sonya closer to him, holding her for several seconds without saying anything.

"You alright?" Sonya asked. "I'm not used to you being so quiet."

"What's there to say, Sonya? I'm totally clueless here. Have no idea *what* to do." He pulled out his iPhone. "Let me call Josh, see what he knows."

"Good idea," Sonya said. "I'm anxious to know too."

Ferd called his son but got voicemail and left an awkward message. Sonya said, "Tell me when you get ahold of him." She kissed him on the crown of his head as she left the room and returned to the study upstairs.

Ferd scrolled through the internet on his phone, looking for anything he could find about the murder. Several local websites were running articles identifying the victim as Patrick Brady, the chief technology officer at CAPSLOCK. His name sounded vaguely familiar, but Ferd had probably heard it from Josh. Brady was stabbed on the evening of Thursday, January 25th, walking down Jones Street in the Tenderloin. A surveillance video from a nearby hotel had captured a fuzzy image of Brady stumbling down the sidewalk after being stabbed, but no footage of the stabbing. Ferd scoured Google for more details, but there were few.

He entered the search term "Dwight Pitt" and found numerous links to Facebook and LinkedIn and a random assortment of real estate agents located across the U.S. For the next hour, he viewed page after page, but none bore any resemblance to his father. Other than the news stories about the murder charges, none of the entries panned out. His father's digital footprint was nonexistent.

As he had for most of Ferd's life, his father remained a mystery.

THAT NIGHT JOSH returned his call, saying his phone had been blowing up with text messages about the arrest of the father of a sitting San Francisco Superior Court judge named Pitt.

Ferd put the phone on speaker so Sonya could participate. "Hi, Josh," she said. "We were wondering if you knew the victim."

"He was my boss."

"His name did ring a bell," said Ferd.

"Yeah, I've been on his team since starting at CAPSLOCK. I never liked him. He played favorites at the office. Honestly? I thought he was an asshole."

Ferd's grip on the phone tightened as he glanced at Sonya. "Keep that to yourself," he said. "No sense stirring things up, especially since that's not how the media's portraying him."

"Don't tell me *you're* listening to the media."

"Good point.:

Sonya asked, "How're things at work? Have they made the connection?"

"Yeah. Everyone knows my father's a judge, so it was pretty obvious. When the news broke this evening, that's when texts came in."

Ferd was quiet for a moment. He squeezed his eyes closed.

"You okay, Pop?" asked Josh.

"Nauseous. I'm taking a few days off work. I haven't seen the guy in thirty-four years, and this is how he comes back into my life."

"Yeah, that's tough. But I wonder how Grandma feels."

"I called her a little while ago, but she didn't answer. I'll go see her soon."

They were quiet for a few seconds. "Dad, the police were at the office interviewing the team."

"Why? What're they looking for?"

Josh paused. "It's a long story. Look, my phone's ringing. Let's talk tomorrow."

3

The Tadich Grill was San Francisco's oldest restaurant, with wood-paneled walls, waiters in white jackets, and mesquite-grilled swordfish that Ferd thought was the best in the city. He arrived shortly before noon. Though Tadich had a policy not to seat a patron until the entire party was present, Ferd prevailed on Jacques, the maître'd, to seat him in a back corner.

As he waited for his sister, Ferd thought about his situation. The online edition of The Chronicle had run several articles mentioning his relationship to accused murderer Dwight Pitt. The wire services had picked up the story and his name was splashed all over the internet. Most of the stories referred to him simply as a sitting San Francisco judge who had recently taken a leave of absence.

Ferd looked around the restaurant at the other patrons, most staring at their cell phones, ignoring their luncheon companions.

"What're you daydreaming about?" Claire asked as she leaned over to give him a hug, her carefully dyed blonde hair rubbing against Ferd's cheek.

Ferd waved his hand around the room. "Just look at these people, their faces stuck in their phones. Whatever happened to conversation, hell, *eye contact*?"

Claire laughed. "Our kids are the same, and you know it." She sat down across from Ferd.

After the waiter had taken their orders, Ferd said, "I met our father after court yesterday. He wouldn't talk about why he left."

Claire looked away, scratching her cheek. "At this point, who cares?"

She continued looking away until Ferd asked, "You okay?"

"Why?"

"Nothing. Just the way you reacted."

"I don't like talking about him. You know that."

"I thought that was the purpose of this lunch."

She pulled a compact mirror from her purse and traced her lips, evening out the lipstick. "It is. Doesn't mean I have to like it."

"Okay. Fine." He took a sip of his water. "So, what're we going to do about him?"

Before she could answer, the server brought their meals, delicately setting down their plates in front of them. While Claire picked at her halibut, Ferd cut off a piece of swordfish. They ate silently until Claire asked, "What about the murder? Did you find out anything?"

Ferd filled her in on what he had learned.

"Strange it was Josh's boss," she said. "Hell of a coincidence."

"I know. Josh didn't care for him much."

"Of course, our dear father says he's not guilty."

"He sounded convincing, but I'm not sure."

"You have doubts? Why not investigate for yourself?"

"What could *I* do? Besides, I can't interfere in a police investigation."

"Come on, Ferd. You are—or *were*—a trial lawyer. Didn't you investigate every case you handled?"

"Yeah, but this is different. We had formal depositions, written interrogatories, private investigators. It was somewhat civilized."

"So . . . what's the big deal, then? If it's so important to find out the truth, you can suck it up and talk to witnesses, do some legwork, make sure the police are doing their job."

Ferdinand put down his fork. "Easy for you to say, Ms. Tribble. Your name is no longer Claire *Pitt*. No one's going to connect you to him. But I have to live with that name; the media already knows he's my father—if he gets convicted, I can forget the election. I'd be done."

Claire reached across the table and grabbed his hands. "Poor Ferd. Paying the price of success."

He made a face. "I could get in big trouble butting into a murder investigation. You know what they say about a lawyer who represents himself: he has a fool for a client. Same with doing your own private investigation. Besides, I don't plan on being off work that long."

"You think you're capable of returning right now? No offense, brother, but looking at you, I have my doubts."

He narrowed his eyes at his sister's gibe, then stuck another bite of fish in his mouth, chewing it quickly. "Even if I did look into the case, I wouldn't know where to start. My days at the district attorney's office after law school were full of drunk drivers and idiots who couldn't keep their noses clean while on parole. Nothing close to the charges our father is facing."

Claire pushed ahead. "The Chronicle mentioned a video. Why not see if you can watch it? I'm sure there's a lot you could find out, if you put your mind to it."

"We'll see. Maybe I could hire a private investigator. That would be the safer way to go." He looked away, his mind racing. "One thing bothers me though."

"What's that?"

"What if I find out he's guilty?"

LEAVING DOWNTOWN, Ferd pointed the car toward Daly City, just over the San Francisco county line. He parked on the street in front of Saint Philip's Assisted Care Center. His mother, Melinda, had been living there for the past six months, ever since she was forced to use an oxygen tank full-time.

She answered Ferd's knock, then returned to the lounger across from the television, blaring as always. With one hand she dragged the clear tubes across the room, using the other to wheel the cart holding her blue and silver oxygen tank. She positioned the tank carefully beside her and looked over at Ferd, who took a seat on the couch. A lifelong smoker of Camels, a pack and a half a day, she had developed respiratory problems five years earlier at age sixty-two. At first, she only needed the oxygen when she exhausted herself, usually by hurrying through a store while shopping. Five minutes of air seemed to revive her. Over time, her usage had increased until she couldn't breathe without it. Now she wheeled a tank with her wherever she went.

"It's about time," she said, muting the television.

"It's good to see you too, Ma. Sorry it's been a while. With all that's going on, I've been so busy."

"That's my son, always on the move." She removed the oxygen tube from her nostrils and coughed loudly, an extended cough that seemed to shake the small room.

"So, I called you last night to talk about Dad," Ferd said.

"Why would you want to talk about him?"

"Haven't you seen the news?"

"I don't watch that stuff anymore. I either sleep or watch movies on Netflix."

Ferd decided to give it to her straight. "He's been charged with murder, Mom. It's bad."

Her eyes widened. She sniffled then, pulling tissue from her sleeve, blew her nose.

Ferd stood up to embrace her, but she waived him off. "I knew this would be a shock," he said, sitting back down.

"How'd you find out?"

"He appeared in my courtroom. In cuffs. Unbelievable, I know. Apparently, he's been here for a little while, living mostly on the streets. He's . . . well, a drunk."

"I guess it runs in the family."

"Ma, don't beat yourself up." Ferd respected his mother, especially for how hard she had worked while raising him and his sister alone. Working two jobs cashiering in different stores, she was always tired, seeming to relax only when sitting at the kitchen table smoking and drinking coffee. Ferd had excused her vices, even when she turned to alcohol to cope with her loneliness and exhaustion. He would often find a half empty bottle of vodka or whiskey in the laundry basket covered with dirty clothes.

Melinda's face scrunched up as if holding back tears. She stopped breathing momentarily, and Ferd became alarmed.

"Ma, you alright?"

She took a deep breath. "Part of me hoped your father had done something with his life. God knows, he made my life difficult enough, but I didn't wish him ill. Why would your father kill someone?"

"The police say it was a robbery gone bad."

"Do you believe that?"

"I don't know what I believe, but I want to find out."

Melinda removed her oxygen tube from her nostrils and began sobbing quietly. "You'd better go," she said. "I don't feel so good."

"I'm sorry, Ma," Ferd said, standing up and getting closer. "I know it's a lot to take in. I didn't mean to upset you."

He kissed her goodbye. "He was the only man I ever loved. Isn't that sad?"

4

At home, Ferd sat with Sonya at the kitchen table, going over his day. "Your sister wants you to investigate?" said Sonya. "That's . . . *crazy*, Ferd."

"I agree." Ferd sipped a bottle of beer and stared at the wall behind her.

His wife laid a manicured hand on his arm. "What're you thinking?"

"That I should forget all about my father, return to work, let the investigation run its course. Let the police prove their case, let Smedley prove reasonable doubt. That's her job, after all."

"But?"

"But I don't think much of her ability as a trial lawyer and doubt she'd conduct a thorough investigation. *And* she's got a reason to torpedo my father's defense: if he's found guilty, my reputation will be shot and she'll win the election easily."

"You really think she'd stoop that low? Just forget legal ethics altogether? I know how seriously *you* view ethics. You sure taught it to lawyers long enough."

Ferd shrugged. "I just don't trust her, Sonya. You should've seen her in court. So smug." He took another sip of beer.

"And the police have already made up their minds that he's guilty."

"What're you saying?" She leaned forward, her folded hands resting on the table.

"There's an investigator I used, before I got on the bench. Barry Fallino, former lieutenant with the SFPD. I think I'll call him tomorrow."

Sonya sat back. "Good idea. Better than trying to look into it yourself."

Ferd appreciated Sonya's views. He stared at her lovingly, remembering how protective she was of Ferd's judgeship and how proud she was of his accomplishments. When Ferd first broached the idea of applying for the bench, she'd encouraged him to go all out even though a judge's salary paled in comparison to his income from the law firm. "We'll make do," she'd said, tongue in cheek. She pushed him to secure letters of recommendation from several judges and prominent attorneys, all but guaranteeing his appointment. Ferd had taken the bench last April, but under California law still had to run for his seat in the next general election on March 5th, a little over a month from now.

"I've got a lot riding on this election," Ferd said, placing the beer bottle on the table.

"I'd say. Already a hundred grand of our own money."

Ferd grimaced, realizing he had to keep pounding the streets of the city's more conservative west side. This area of single-family homes, bundled side-by-side with patches of lawn in back, formed his base. He appeared before all the neighborhood committees, turning on the wit and charm (for Ferdinand could be charming when he wanted to be). At other times, in a more relaxed mood, with the people he trusted, Ferd was sarcastic and biting, but the west siders never saw this side of him. He even acquired the support of the local Irish American community by hosting events at the UICC, the United

Irish Cultural Center. The builders and tradesmen who composed a majority of the UICC membership flocked to his events; at first because he offered an open bar, but later because he was viewed as a safer choice than his opponent (despite both being registered Democrats).

"Curt says I'm leading in the early polls."

"But the bar association endorsed Smedley, just because she's a lesbian." Sonya shook her head. "From what I hear, though, she's attended several charity events on the arm of a well-known financier of the *male* type."

"I don't care about that stuff. All I know is she wants my seat." Ferd reached over and hugged his wife, happy to have her support.

FERD CALLED Josh again that evening, but had to leave a message. Like much of his generation, Josh rarely listened to voicemails, so Ferd also sent a text. But by the time he went to bed, he still hadn't heard back from his son.

BARRY FALLINO HAD an opening in the morning, so Ferd drove to his office in the over-100-year-old Hobart Building on Market Street. A slim sixty-year-old with thick brushed-back silver hair, Fallino looked every inch the retired senior cop. He greeted Ferd effusively, patting his shoulder and urging him to take a seat at the small table across from his desk. They hadn't seen each other since Ferd had taken the bench, and spent some time rehashing their last cases together. The walls were lined with black-and-white photos of Fallino with local politicians, celebrities, and judges. There was no doubting the man had some connections.

"Sorry about your father. That's a tough one, Judge."

"Yeah, well, there's more to it." Ferd gave him the abbreviated version of his childhood and his father's abandonment.

"Shit, and *this* is how he shows up?!" Fallino ran his hand through his hair. "Christ, Ferd. That's big. So how can I help?"

"I feel it's only fair to tell you . . . I've got my own reasons for proving my father innocent. I have an election coming up; I'm thinking winning would be harder if I'm known as the son of a murderer."

"And?"

"I'm not going to lie. I've got a lot of anger and resentment over this guy. But part of me doesn't want him to suffer any more than he already has. Maybe I'm getting soft. The police seem convinced it was him, but it's hard to believe he is capable of *this*." Ferd looked at his friend. "You should see him, Barry. He doesn't look like he could hurt a dog."

Fallino nodded. "You want me to talk to the investigators?"

Ferd nodded back. "They'll talk to you a lot more openly. They might talk to me as the son, but I doubt they'd be frank."

"I can do that. Give me a couple of days."

ON THE DRIVE HOME, Ferd's phone rang. It was Josh. They exchanged pleasantries but when Ferd asked about the police interviews, Josh went quiet. Rather than press him for information over the phone, Ferd invited him to dinner, anxious to hear what his son had to say.

5

Ferd helped Sonya prepare dinner, a prawns and pasta dish that was one of Josh's favorites. Sonya looked at her watch. "He'll be here in a few minutes." She placed her hand on his shoulder and squeezed. "Try to relax so we can enjoy our time with him."

As soon as their son arrived, Sonya handed him a beer and said, "Dinner's almost ready. Go sit down with your dad."

Josh Pitt was a shade under five ten, a few inches shorter than his father. Even with a scruffy beard, which seemed to come and go with his mood, his resemblance to Ferd was clear. He had the same long nose, sharp chin, and bushy eyebrows, though his tight cheeks and small ears more closely resembled his mother's. A graduate of Boston University, where he'd earned a bachelor's degree in computer science, Josh was more introspective than his parents. He had no love for authority, and was constantly criticizing the government and its minions at all levels.

Ferd and Josh took seats at the round Formica table while Sonya served dinner. They ate quickly, mostly in silence. In the year since he'd been hired at CAPSLOCK, Josh had grown more distant, though Ferd knew it was to be expected. Although he spent the occasional weekend with them, it seemed they'd had more contact when he was in school in Boston. At least there he was quick to use video chat. Now *weeks* could go by without a call from him—they knew little of his personal life. Ferd gazed at his son, proud of how hard he worked, though concerned his health seemed to be suffering. He was too thin, now picking at his food, his face long and narrow with deep circles under the eyes.

After cleaning his plate, Josh turned toward Ferd and said, "I'm guessing you want to talk about the police interviews?"

"I do. Didn't want to press you, though."

"I don't like being in the middle of this thing, Dad." Josh seemed to disappear into his own thoughts for a moment, staring straight ahead at something Ferd could not see. "The police grilled me pretty hard."

"Why?"

Josh shuffled in his seat, looking from his father to his mother. "Don't freak out, okay, but I was with Brady just before he died."

This was news. Ferd shifted in his seat but tried not to show his shock. "Where? *Why?*"

"The Promenade Bar, near Jones Street. It's a long story."

"We've got time." He glanced at Sonya, whose eyes were fixed on Josh.

"Brady was hitting on my girlfriend, Colleen, another employee. I didn't like it and wanted him to stop."

Sonya interrupted. "You have a *girlfriend*?" Josh looked at his dad for support, but Ferd knew better than to get in the middle of his wife and son, and only shrugged.

"It's only been a few months. I don't know if it will last."

"Still..."

"It'd be nice to know things like that," Ferd said. "We are your parents, after all."

Josh shrugged. "I'm twenty-two, not twelve."

"Josh," Sonya said, "we're interested in your life. It's not like we're prying."

"I get it, okay. You want to hear the rest of the story or not?"

"By all means, continue," said Ferd.

"Colleen asked Brady to meet off-site and he suggested the bar."

"In the Tenderloin?" Ferd asked. "Why would Brady want to meet there?"

"He'd been there before and it's a hip spot where they wouldn't run into anyone from work. Colleen wanted to give him the brush off, tell him about us, hoping he'd get the hint and leave her alone. But before she got there, I stopped by and gave Brady a piece of my mind."

Sonya frowned. "Weren't you worried he'd get you fired?"

"Of course, but he was out of control."

"Was he married?" Ferd asked.

"*Oh* yeah. His wife has been to company functions. A real clinger. Like she was afraid to let him out of her sight. One time they got into a huge fight. Don't know what it was about, but she tossed her drink in his face."

Sonya's eyes widened. "She sounds volatile. Any kids?"

Josh shook his head.

"How'd Brady react when you told him off?" asked Ferd.

"Said it was none of my business and I should leave. That's the last I saw of him."

Ferd frowned. His father being involved in a murder investigation was bad enough—now his *son* was being interrogated. *How much worse is this thing going to get before it's over?* "What else did the police want to know?"

"They talked to each member of the team separately, but from what I can tell, they mostly wanted to know if anyone had a grudge against the guy. I guess the attack was pretty brutal."

"I assume you told them about Brady and Colleen?" asked Ferd.

"Of course. I've got nothing to hide."

"Good. Best to be totally honest, son."

Sonya folded her arms across her chest. "I don't like this, Ferd. Nothing but trouble, if you ask me."

Josh wiped his hands with a cloth napkin then threw it on the table. "Got to jet," he said, reaching to hug his mother then turning toward Ferd. "Oh, Pops, before I go, I wanted to see about visiting Grandpa."

That caught Sonya's attention. "Why?"

"Why not? I have a right to know my family, don't I? Everything I've ever heard about him has been negative. I want to know if it's true."

Ferdinand wasn't at all surprised his son wanted to meet his grandfather. Over the years, Josh had asked many questions about him, questions Ferd had been reluctant to answer. Josh had always been close to his grandmother, often spending afternoons after school on her porch, chatting away, though he hadn't seen much of her since her move into assisted living. Ferd feared Josh had built up a romantic image of his grandfather, a tortured soul who was under so much stress he was forced to abandon his family, who had moved east to make a better life for himself. Josh always wanted to know what had caused his grandfather to leave, and Ferd had never been able to give him the answers he wanted. In fact, he *still* couldn't.

"You can visit him at the jail," said Ferd. "I'm sure he'd be happy to see you."

"Does he even know about me?"

"I doubt it. I didn't tell him."

Ferd noticed that Josh seemed hurt. "We had many others matters to discuss."

"Goodbye, Father," he said stiffly, giving Ferd a brief hug.

. . .

EARLY THE NEXT MORNING, Ferd got a call from Judge Bradstein. "I'm sure it's been a hard few days, Ferd. How're you doing?"

"Trying to stay positive." He didn't tell her about hiring an investigator. She might not appreciate his looking into a pending case.

"I don't mean to hurry you, but I wanted to get an idea of when you'll be back."

"I know you've been strapped over there. Perhaps some time next week—will that work?"

Ferd could hear her exhale loudly. *Was she upset about his time off?* He hoped not, but all she said was, "I appreciate it, Ferd."

He tried to take a nap on the couch, but just as he closed his eyes, his phone rang. "Ferd, it's Barry. I've got some news and you're not going to like it."

6

Ferd rose to a sitting position. "Hey, Barry. What did you learn?"

"I met with Sergeant Carla Hinton at the homicide detail in the Hall. She's in charge of the investigation. She told me your father had the victim's credit card . . ."

"I knew that already."

"Hold on, I'm getting there. His prints were on the victim's wallet, and . . . Well, they found a partial on the murder weapon. Both were found in a trash can near the murder scene. There's a video from the Blue Arms Hotel, but it's inconclusive. The police think your father tried to rob Brady, and when he encountered resistance, stabbed him."

"That doesn't sound good." Ferd leaned forward, his elbows resting on his knees. "But there could be another explanation."

"There's more." Ferd had never heard Fallino sound so serious.

"Lay it on me."

"The police looked very closely at two other suspects."

"Who?"

Fallino paused, cleared his throat. "Naturally, the police

questioned the last people to see the victim. It seems your son Josh was one of them. Per Hinton, he had both motive and opportunity, so they looked at him pretty hard."

"Motive? *What* motive?"

"Hinton was vague, wouldn't give me details, but it seems there was some bad blood. Josh say anything to you about it?"

"All I know is Brady was hitting on Josh's girlfriend, and it wasn't going over well."

"That's Colleen O'Keefe?"

"Right. Josh has been dating her for a few months."

"She was the other main suspect. Apparently, the last one to see him alive."

"So what happened? Why didn't the police arrest Josh or Colleen?" The idea of his son being suspected of murder turned Ferd's stomach. His father being accused was one thing —it was uncomfortable and worrying and could certainly affect his plans for election. But *Josh*? All the rest seemed unimportant when weighed against his son's freedom.

"They got back the fingerprint results, matched them with your dad's prints. Then he tried to use Brady's credit card at Safeway on Market Street, so they arrested your father instead."

"Where do we go from here?"

"Not sure there's much more to be done. I'm going to be honest with you Ferd—it's not looking too good for your father."

"I still have a hard time believing he *killed* Brady. Robbed him, maybe. But stabbing a man to death? It just doesn't play."

"You want me to dig deeper, I will. But you may not like what I find."

"Let me think about it."

In the study, Ferd waited while Sonya finished a phone call. He sat on the twin-size bed across from the desk, glancing at the wall where he had hung framed dust covers of Sonya's favorite children's and young adults' books, including ones by

Beverly Cleary, R.L. Stine, and J.K. Rowling. Seeing his face, his wife made her excuses and hung up the phone.

Sonya turned in her desk chair. "Talk to me."

"I heard back from Barry. The police are sure they've got their man, and with good reason. He's in big trouble, Sonya." He summarized what the investigator had told him.

"I'm sorry, honey. I know you were hoping for better news."

"There's something else."

"What?"

"Until my father's arrest, Josh was a prime suspect." Ferd felt a twinge of sadness just saying the words.

"*Josh?*" Her volume rose a decibel. "Whatever for?"

"He was one of the last people to see Brady alive. And the police think he had motive."

"Because Brady was harassing Josh's girlfriend? That's insane!"

"I agree. Josh wouldn't hurt a soul, never mind kill someone."

"Oh, Ferd, I don't like this."

"Neither do I." He paused, thinking. "I feel like I should do something to get to the bottom of this."

"What do you mean? What could you do?"

"What Claire suggested. I could investigate. Make sure my father's not being railroaded."

"I thought that's why you hired Barry."

"It is, but I feel . . . *responsible*. Especially with Josh under suspicion."

"We talked about this." Her voice now had an edge to it.

"I know."

"You can't risk your judgeship, Ferd. They could even remove you from the bench for poking around. You've got to be smart about this."

"I realize that Sonya, but I can't just sit around while this thing plays out. I've got to *do* something."

"Ferd, what if you find out your father's innocent? I can't believe I'm even saying this, but wouldn't that just turn the focus back on Josh? We both know he's innocent, but why put him through it? It could affect the rest of his life, just being a suspect."

"That's why I think I should investigate myself. That way we have options. If someone else goes digging . . ."

There was a deep silence while Sonya stared back at him, her mouth forming a grim line of dissent. "I'm not going to say this again, Ferd. *Stay out of it*. I mean it." In all their years together, she had never talked to Ferd so firmly. It made him more than a little afraid of her.

FERD CLIMBED into his Lexus and hit the freeway, driving south toward San Jose. A drive would always clear his mind. After ten minutes of listening to his own chaotic thoughts, he turned on the stereo to drown them out, cranking the volume. Santana's *Supernatural* blared through the speakers, the guitar solos filling the car, and for a moment, Ferd felt like he could actually breathe. Near San Bruno, traffic stalled nearly to a stop, so he pulled off the freeway and drove to the reservoir where he parked and sat staring at the water. He pulled out his phone and called Fallino, who failed to answer. Ferd left a message, asking him to call back as soon as possible, then did a quick Google search. Finding what he was looking for, he started the car and headed back north, knowing Sonya would be furious if she knew what he was planning. He tried telling himself it was because he was in the area, that it was just a matter of convenience, but in his heart he knew he was crossing her line in the sand.

The Brady residence was in a planned development in Pacifica, a cozy little coastal town just south of San Francisco. Known for its excellent surfing beaches, Pacifica seemed an odd choice for a high-tech executive, most of whom preferred Los Altos or Menlo Park farther down the Peninsula. Although there were some nice neighborhoods in Pacifica, most would consider the small city middle class, at best. Ferd made his way along the curving streets to a grand home built in what Ferd recognized as the New England style, austere white with black shutters on the windows. He parked in front of the house, got out, and rang the bell, not entirely sure what he was doing there. There was no answer; he rang again and followed it with a knock, but got the same result. He had outlined in his mind exactly what he'd ask Ms. Brady: did her husband have any enemies? Ferd hoped to find *someone* the cops might be interested in that he wasn't related to. Satisfied no one was home, he got back in his car.

Sonya was waiting for him at the front door, her hands on her hips. "Ferd, what's going on? Where have you been?"

"Let me get in the door, at least." He entered the house and closed the door, taking his time shrugging out of his jacket. One look at Sonya's face told him her patience was wearing thin. "I left a message with Barry; he hasn't returned my call yet."

"You didn't answer my question." She folded her arms across her chest.

"I was driving by Pacifica, so I stopped by the Brady house."

"You stopped by the *widow's* house? Less than a week after her husband was murdered? Have you totally lost your mind?"

Ferd hung his head, sheepish. "No one answered."

"Lucky for you. I hope you've gotten it out of your system." She started up the stairs but stopped mid-way and turned. "When are you going back to work?"

"Next week."

"Not soon enough, if you ask me."

7

The bed was cold, and Sonya colder, when Ferd climbed under the covers. Lying on her side with her back to him, as far from him as possible, Sonya gave him a terse "Good night," as he settled under the blankets. He lay with his eyes fixed on the ceiling, contemplating all that had happened in the past week. He was wired, unable to shut off his mind. His gaze fixed on a sketch of Josh hanging beside the bed, one drawn by Sonya's artist uncle. Josh: his only child. Living proof that Ferd was nothing like his own father. Thinking about his son made him think about Dwight, and his emotions shifted from resentment to affection for the father he had known for only twelve years. It was a wonder he could have *any* affection for the man at all, but it was there, just the same.

In the morning he woke to the sound of his phone ringing on the nightstand. It was Curtis Rodda, his campaign manager. "Judge Pitt! How the hell are ya?"

Ferd held the phone away from his ear. "Curt, I've been meaning to call you."

"Yeah, the shit's really hit the fan. Can we meet?"

"You got time today?"

"Now's good."

"See you soon."

Rodda's temporary office was located in a storefront on West Portal Avenue across from the Wells Fargo and doubled as Ferd's campaign headquarters. When Ferd arrived, two young female volunteers were busy sorting signs, flyers, and bumper stickers on tables arrayed at the front of the modest space. Rodda jumped up from his desk in the back. "Judge, it's good to see you. Come, take a seat." Ferd's frame dwarfed that of the shorter, thinner man when he reached across the desk to shake his hand. The campaign manager was no bigger than a teenager, but it didn't seem to hinder him. Ferd sat down in a foldout chair by Rodda's desk. Across its surface, The Chronicle lay open to a story about Ferd's father.

"Your father is in some deep shit. Which means *you're* in some deep shit," Rodda said, rubbing a pitted chin. In fact, Rodda's entire face was pitted, the result of severe acne as a teen. His appearance wasn't improved by the thinning black hair combed over a massive bald spot on the crown of his head, and Ferd thought it was no surprise the man was single. San Francisco was not overly kind to unattractive men. Perhaps that was why he was so obsessed with work.

"Tell me something I don't know," Ferd said.

Rodda hissed through his teeth as he shook his head back and forth. "It sucks, I'm tellin' ya."

"You didn't ask me here just to tell me *that*, did you?"

With a quick shrug of his shoulders, Rodda lifted his hands up slightly. "Here's the thing. I've been following the narrative. The news media take is all the same—vague, polite, careful. But social media? Whole other story. A lot of people think you should drop out of the race until your father's case is over."

Ferd stared at him, his mouth open. "They can't be serious. The election's next month. The case could take *years*. Am I just supposed to put my entire life on hold?"

"Hey, I'm just the messenger. Thought you should know what's being said. Can of worms officially *open*, and all that."

"You don't agree with these people, do you?"

"Are you kiddin'? You're my man, for better or worse. You know that." He moved a pile of papers from one side of his desk to the other, his hands suddenly busy.

Ferd felt a pang of unease in his chest. "But?"

Rodda laid his hands flat on the paper-covered desk, rose his gaze to meet Ferd's. "*But*... Campaign contributions have slowed a *shitload* since your father's arrest."

"It's only been a few days."

"I gotta look down the road. And to be honest, I don't like where this road is heading."

"Any suggestions?"

"You gotta get out there and in front of this thing, Ferd. Condemn your father's conduct. Distance yourself from him as much as possible. From what I've read, you haven't seen him in decades, so that should be goddamn easy. Play the 'deadbeat dad, made a success of my life in spite of him' drum for all it's worth."

"You want me to throw my father to the wolves? Abandon him?"

The shrug again. "Did it to you, didn't he?" When Ferd didn't answer, he pressed on. "You want to win this election, or not?"

"I don't see how this situation could help Smedley. She's *defending* him, for Christ's sake."

"She's just doing her job. Not the same as being the only son of an accused murderer."

This was exactly what Ferd had been so worried about–his father's wretched life being the downfall of his own. But there was another angle they hadn't considered. "What if Smedley's *not* doing her job?"

"How do you mean?"

"We both know it would help her chances in the election if my father were convicted. What if that's exactly what she's planning?"

"You mean lose the case on purpose?"

"I wouldn't put it past her."

Rodda scratched his forehead. "Doesn't she have a conflict of interest?"

"Not in the classic sense, though we could make a strong case that her interests are not the same as her client's."

Rodda jumped up, knocking his chair backwards to the floor. "That's it! We hammer home her conflict, paint her as an opportunist."

"How?"

"We'll start with social media, put our volunteers to work on Facebook, Tik Tok, Instagram, all the platforms. Ferd, you're a goddamn genius!"

ON THE WALK HOME, spurred by Rodda's warnings, Ferd decided to put Barry Fallino into overdrive. He dialed the investigator's cell number as he crossed Portola. After several rings, he answered. "Barry, I left you a message yesterday."

Fallino's voice was raspy and low. "Sorry. I'm in the hospital."

"What happened?"

"Heart attack. I'll be here for a while."

"Geez, I'm sorry."

"I was working in my garage, got an old Porsche I fiddle with. Sharp pain on the left side of my chest. Knocked me to the floor."

"Jesus, Barry."

"Yeah. Good thing Margie was working in the garden and heard me fall. She called 911 right away." He coughed loudly. "Sorry I can't help with your father's case."

"Don't worry about it. I'll figure something out. Do you know when you'll get released from the hospital?"

"I'll be here another week or so."

"I'll check on you then. Get well, okay?"

Ferd paced the kitchen floor. With Fallino out of commission, he had a choice: let the case run its course, leaving his father at the mercy of Smedley, or investigate himself. He could always hire a different investigator, an argument he knew Sonya would make, but there was no one else he trusted (an excuse he knew she wouldn't accept). The key was finding someone who had a real motive to kill Brady. The police could get so focused on one suspect, they often overlooked others. He would wait a few more days before trying again at the Brady house—Sonya was right about that, at least. The widow would need time to grieve. But there were other things he could do, in the meantime.

8

Without telling Sonya, Ferd set out for the Blue Arms Hotel on Jones Street. He wondered about the people who lived in such hotels, called SROs for Single Room Occupancy. Most guests – tenants, really – were down-and-out-types. Ferd had stayed in one on Eddy Street when he was in college as part of his sociology course. It was $25 a night. The room was about eight feet by ten feet with a twin bed, chair, and table with a hot plate. There was a single bathroom for each floor. At night he could hear screaming coming from the next-door room, see prostitutes walking the hallways. In the morning he had to wait in line for thirty minutes to use the bathroom. His fellow tenants were scruffy old men, a few younger ones who looked like druggies, and a purple-haired woman with her breasts protruding from a low-cut blouse. It was an experience that Ferd hoped never to repeat. One positive result of his stay was he vowed never to run out of money and be forced into such a lifestyle.

Trying to avoid notice in the rough and tumble Tenderloin, he dressed casually in khaki slacks and a black windbreaker. He found a parking space a block from the hotel and when he exited his car had to kick aside a pile of trash, including a few syringes. As he walked from his car, he had to steer clear of human feces on the sidewalk. Parking on the street brought more stress since there was always the risk of a break-in, a frequent crime in San Francisco. He could've parked at the Sutter-Stockton garage and walked several blocks, but he decided to risk a break-in rather than spend more time in the Tenderloin than absolutely necessary.

He rang the bell to the hotel and a female voice came over the intercom.

"Can I help you?" She sounded annoyed and suspicious. Ferd guessed she was watching him through the video surveillance system.

"I'd like to speak to the manager," he said in his deepest courtroom voice, thinking that would command respect.

"Who the hell are you?"

So much for respect. "Look, can we speak face-to-face instead of over this blasted intercom? I just have a few questions about the murder that happened near here."

"First door on the right," she said as a buzzer went off unlocking the door.

Stepping inside, Ferd noticed a musty odor, probably emanating from the stained dark yellow carpet, which immediately made him sneeze. Standing to his right at the door to the manager's office was a short pink-haired woman wearing blue jeans and a checkered shirt. "You're probably allergic to a place like this," she said. "Not the greatest working conditions but it pays the bills. You from the police? I told the officers who came out for the video everything I know."

Ferdinand was unsure whether he should shake hands and decided against it. "No, I'm not from the police but I have a personal interest in the case. Can we sit down?"

She hesitated then waved him inside. About ten feet square, the office was a mess, a jumble of papers strewn about the cracked oak desk, on the chair facing the desk, and on the bookcase. Ferd immediately felt claustrophobic and waited patiently while she removed a pile of magazines from the chair.

"Have a seat." She sat down in the chair behind the desk. "Name's Joanie Merced; I'm the manager of this fine establishment."

"Well, Ms. Merced, here's the thing: I'm investigating the murder for my own personal reasons."

She looked toward the ceiling then snapped her fingers. "That's right. You're the son? I saw your picture in the paper. You're a judge, right?"

Ferd winced, but nodded.

"But I thought the guy was homeless? You being a judge and all, I suppose you could take him in. Am I missing something?"

"It's a long story. I understand you have video from the night of the murder and wonder if you would be so kind as to show it to me."

"That's all you want, to see the video?"

"Unless, of course, you have more to offer."

"I was here that night. Had some paperwork to catch up on so I worked late." She pointed to the piles of paper. "As you can see, I still haven't made much progress. Anyway, I was leaving work and noticed this guy lying on the sidewalk. There was blood pouring out of his neck. I used my scarf to stop the bleeding. Brand new. Silk, too, from the Goodwill on South Van Ness. Cost me sixteen bucks. Wrecked now. And it didn't do any good. Then I called 911. The cops got here in less than a minute."

Ferdinand nodded, impressed that Merced had taken such quick action. "Did the victim say anything?"

"He didn't say your father stabbed him, if that's what you're worried about."

Ferdinand noticed that she hadn't answered his question. "So he said nothing?"

"Correct, Your Honor. Let's play the video." She searched her desk, pushing papers aside, and came up with a DVD. "I made a few copies," she said as she inserted the DVD into the player. A black-and-white screen appeared with two different camera angles. "Here," Merced said, pointing to the angle on the right. "This is where you can see it best."

Ferdinand leaned forward, waiting for something to happen. Then a man, tall, hatless, and thin, appeared from the right of the screen, stumbling and falling to the sidewalk. A few seconds later, another person came onto the screen. This person was shorter, wearing a Giants baseball cap and dark pants and jacket, and reached down and grabbed something from the victim's jacket pocket. The person was not facing the camera but turned briefly showing a profile for a split second. There was no audio. Was that his father? The height and weight seemed to match but Ferd couldn't discern any facial features. Then the video showed Merced exit the hotel two to three minutes later and walk in the same direction.

"You want to see any more?" Merced asked.

"No, that's enough," Ferd said. "But can you reverse it a bit to just after the one in the baseball cap appears?" Merced clicked on the video, reversing it, then paused.

"Is here okay?"

Pulling out his smartphone, Ferd said, "Let me take a screen shot."

Ferdinand took the shot and stared at the image. He held out his phone, turned the photo upside down. Because of the cap, the facial features were completely in shadow, indistinguishable. The video alone was not enough to sink his father. But he still didn't know what to do about the other evidence: his father's fingerprints on the knife and wallet and his use of the victim's credit card.

. . .

NEXT FERD VISITED every business establishment within a two-block radius of the Blue Arms Hotel, hoping to find more video surveillance from the night of the murder. In recent years, the homeless problem had gotten out of control with pup tents springing up on sidewalks crowded with society's outcasts. He had to maneuver around a few to enter most of the businesses.

His visits to the first nine businesses brought no results. A few refused to talk to him, not wanting to get involved. Several did not have a video surveillance system. To anyone who gave him the time of day, he showed them his father's booking photo from the newspaper and the web page with Brady's photo to see if anyone recognized them. One person, the proprietor of the Sunnydale Market, a corner convenience store a block from the Blue Arms, recognized Ferd's father.

"I've seen him around a lot," the man said in a strong Arabic accent. "Shops here sometimes but mostly he's just harassing people on the streets, what they call an aggressive panhandler."

"How has he appeared?"

"Drunk, usually. Ranting about Allah knows what. Never made any sense to me."

Although this was not a surprise, Ferdinand still felt disappointed that his father's life had sunk so low. He looked around the store and pointed to a screen behind the counter showing four different areas of the store. "Do you have video from last Thursday?"

"The cops asked me and I gave a copy to them."

"Can I see it?"

The proprietor looked at him, squinting as wrinkles appeared in his pock-marked face. "Don't know if I should do that. What's your interest in this case?"

"Let's just say I have a personal interest." The proprietor apparently had not read the news about Ferd. He showed no sign of recognition.

"I don't think so."

"Look," Ferd said, leaning closer and lowering his voice. "The defendant is my father. I'm just trying to figure out what the hell happened."

Ferd handed him his phone which was open to the color photo of Dwight from the newspaper. "I do see some resemblance."

"So can I see the video?"

The proprietor nodded and inserted a DVD into a player, fast-forwarding to the time of the murder.

"Go back to an hour before the murder, say 6:30." Ferdinand wanted to see if either party paid a visit to the store.

The proprietor rewound the video then pressed "play." After a few minutes with no one recognizable appearing, Ferd suggested he fast forward. He did so and forty-five minutes into the video Ferd saw a man enter the store. "Stop there," he said. "Now go slow motion." They watched a man stop by the beer refrigerator and pick out a quart bottle. "I think that's who I'm looking for. Go back a little and pause it." The image was in color and much clearer than on the hotel video. "The time is 1915," he said. "That's fifteen minutes before the murder." He then took out his cell phone and photographed the screenshot.

"How does that help?"

"The clothing is similar. The person on the hotel video also was wearing a dark jacket. But what's most important is this guy's not wearing a baseball cap."

Ferdinand left the store pleased he'd made some progress. Although his father could have put the baseball cap on before the murder, it seemed unlikely a drunk homeless man could have thought that far ahead, especially when the murder did not seem planned.

A few doors down from the convenience store was the Promenade Bar where Josh and Colleen had met Brady. He found the interior to be sterile, shiny silver stools circling small round aluminum tables. The lighting was bright and behind the bar was a young woman wearing a 49ers tee-shirt from which her biceps bulged. Ferd was impressed with her athletic build and especially the broad smile she flashed when he approached.

"Good afternoon, sir. I'm afraid we're not open yet."

Ferd returned her smile. "I'm not here to drink, just to get some information. There was a stabbing last Thursday in front of the Blue Arms Hotel." She eyed him suspiciously.

Before she could ask anything, he pulled out his phone showing his father's booking photo and handed it to her. "Ever seen this man before?"

She nodded. "He hangs around out front sometimes. I've had to call the police a few times because he hassles my customers."

"Ever see him wearing a Giants' cap?"

She shook her head. "Can't say I have."

Ferd showed her Brady's photo from the same article. "This is the guy who was stabbed. He died the next day."

"Sorry, I wasn't working then. You should talk to Conor. But he's gone out of town for the weekend."

"When's he scheduled next?"

"Monday. He'll be here around six o'clock."

9

When Ferd got home, he knew there'd be hell to pay and he was right. As soon as he opened the front door, Sonya stood by the doorway to the study, hands on hips, yelling downstairs. "Ferdinand! Come upstairs."

He glanced up the stairs, hesitant, and slowly ascended. He stood in front of Sonya like a student before a scolding teacher. "Look," he said, "I know my father's arrest has rattled you."

"No, you're wrong. It's not that at all. It's your involvement. For the life of me, I can't understand why you're doing this."

"Barry had a heart attack."

That slowed her down. "I'm sorry to hear that." She paused for a moment. "So that's your excuse: your investigator is out of commission."

"Sonya, hon', it's a good excuse. I also met with Curtis. He thinks my father's arrest could be a big problem for me."

"That's what this is about: your election? Seems to me if you keep this up, you'll be out of a job anyway."

Ferd's attention was diverted as he thought of the Commission on Judicial Performance, the body that could remove him from the bench for ethics violations. "You know it's more than that. Besides, what's the difference if I interview witnesses as opposed to an investigator I hired? I could get in trouble either way."

"That sounds like you're rationalizing. So what have you been up to today?"

"I went to the Tenderloin, watched some video, and talked to witnesses. I learned that the killer wore a Giants' cap, but my father was not wearing one shortly before the murder."

"Uh, huh. And what do you plan to do with this information?"

"Once I gather enough evidence, hopefully proving my father's innocence, I'll take it to the district attorney."

"Really, that's your plan? And what about your job? Or have you forgotten that you're a judge?"

It seemed the more Ferd said, the angrier Sonya became. He didn't know how to appease her. "No, I haven't forgotten."

Sonya swung back around toward her desk, the interrogation apparently over. Ferd went downstairs and turned on the television, but soon grew bored. He called Claire and she picked up right away. "Twice in one week I hear from you," she said as she pulled into her garage. "Must be important."

"Just wanted to fill you in on our parents."

"Parents, plural?"

"Yeah. I visited Ma. She took the news of Dad's arrest pretty hard. I didn't realize how much she cared for the guy."

"My God, that was so long ago. She should be over him."

"Especially since he didn't pay any alimony or child support after the divorce. Ma was hung out to dry." Ferd rested his feet on the ottoman. "You want an update on our father?"

"You're really investigating the case?" She exited the car and made her way to the house.

"You didn't think I'd take your suggestion?"

"It's not that," she said quickly. "It's just that I've put that man out of my mind for so long I imagined you'd done the same. Not that I doubted you'd follow up." She dropped her purse on the kitchen table, poured herself a gin and tonic, and sat down.

Ferdinand wondered at Claire's tone; she sounded worried. "Dad was in the area of the murder and his fingerprints were found on the victim's wallet and a partial on the murder weapon."

"Oh, my. That's not good."

"I also learned that Josh met with Brady shortly before his murder."

"Josh? You're not saying my godson was involved." She placed her drink glass on the table.

"No, no. Just that he's a potential witness at the trial."

"You made me nervous for a second there. What will you do if you find the murderer was someone else?"

Ferdinand thought for a moment. "Give the evidence to the district attorney, try to convince her to drop the charges."

"It's hard, isn't it? Wanting to get back at him for what he did? I know the few times I think about him I just want him to rot in hell. I don't really care what happens to him."

"I'm trying to control my resentment. I don't want him to have that kind of power over me."

"That's very forward-thinking on your part, Ferd. I'm surprised."

"You didn't think I was that enlightened?"

"Oh, you're enlightened alright. Too enlightened for your own good."

Ferdinand sensed she was holding back something. "What're you thinking?"

"Just that the more we crack open our father's life the more nervous I get. I was comfortable knowing little about him, the mystery man. Now I'm afraid the more I learn the more I'll despise him and that's hard to imagine."

"You hate him that much?"

"More than you know."

"Wasn't he a good father to you for twelve years?"

"He was present; that's the best I can say." She sipped her drink. "In the end he pretended to be interested in my life, but I don't think he knew what to do with a pre-pubescent daughter. I was starting to notice boys, wear makeup, shop for clothes. If it weren't for Ma, I would've been lost."

"That's funny because I thought Dad paid more attention to you. He was always complimenting your looks, your smarts, your athletic ability. I have to admit I was a little jealous."

That seemed to rile Claire, who gazed toward the ceiling. "What're you talking about? He let you get away with murder. You'd be late for dinner and he'd say nothing, making sure your food stayed warm. One time you and Bobby Griffin were horsing around in the living room and knocked over his vintage record player. Busted it into pieces. And he barely raised his voice. 'You boys have to be more careful' was all he said."

Ferdinand thought back to his old friend. The last he'd heard Bobby Griffin was doing time in San Quentin for assault, his life in shambles. They'd grown up in the same neighborhood, attended the same schools. How did Ferd's life turn out so different?

"How is it," Ferd asked, "that we've gotten this far in life without therapy?"

"Speak for yourself. I've had more than my share of therapy."

This surprised Ferdinand; Claire had never talked about this before.

"You can't go through three marriages and not see a therapist."

"How much has Dad been discussed?"

Claire hesitated. She squeezed the phone tightly and stood

up, knocking over her drink, which was nearly empty. "More than you know. I better get going."

"Sorry. I didn't mean to upset you."

"You didn't," she said softly. "He did."

IF HE WERE GOING to investigate, Ferd decided, he had to go all in. He knew it was a delicate matter to contact the widow, but he felt he had no choice. If anyone knew of Brady's enemies, it would be her. Early the next morning, using his cell phone, he did an internet search and found Brady's home phone number.

"Ms. Brady, my name is Ferdinand Pitt. I'm sorry to bother you at a time like this. But do you have a few moments to talk?"

"Pitt? Isn't your father the one who killed my husband?" Her voice was flat and cold.

"Accused of killing him. That's an important distinction. I need to find out for myself whether it's true. Would you mind terribly if I stopped by your home?"

"Why should I meet with you of all people?"

Ferd inhaled deeply, contemplating how much to tell her. "You should know that I haven't seen my father for thirty-four years. He abandoned the family and, except for a few postcards, never contacted us again. So I don't feel all warm and fuzzy about him to say the least. My only interest is to determine for myself whether he's guilty. If he is, so be it. I'll write him off and never talk to him again."

He waited for Ms. Brady to say something but all he could hear was light breathing. Finally, she said, "I don't like the idea of anyone snooping around my husband's life. But I'm afraid if I say no, you'll snoop anyway. If I say yes, will that put an end to the matter?"

"I'm afraid I can't say that, Ms. Brady. Sure, if you can convince me my father's guilty, then fine. But, frankly, I don't see that happening. So I don't want to mislead you." He paused, awaiting her reaction. There was none, at least no audible one. "All I'm asking for is a half hour of your time."

"I need to talk to my lawyer about that." She sat at the desk in her spacious bedroom and pulled a file from the drawer.

"I don't see why you'd need a lawyer. I'm not the police. But certainly, if you prefer a lawyer be there, that would be fine."

Ferd could hear papers shuffling, as if she were looking for something. "I will call you back. That's the best I can do."

Ferd paced from one end of his house to the other, certain that Ms. Brady would not meet with him after speaking to her lawyer. His investigation would be stymied from the outset. After several minutes, he made a decision.

10

A minute after he rang the bell, Ms. Brady opened the door tentatively, peeking out, and asked, "What can I do for you?"

"I'm Ferdinand Pitt."

"I told you I needed to speak to my lawyer. I left him a message and he hasn't returned my call. So if you don't mind..." She moved to shut the door.

"Hear me out, Ms. Brady. As I said, I have only a few questions then I'll be out of your hair. My only interest is to find out who killed your husband."

She bit her lower lip, contemplating what he'd said. "Why don't you ask your father?" Ferd thought she seemed worried about something.

"I have. He denies it."

She nodded, stared at him for a moment then said, "I must be crazy, but come in."

To his surprise, he smelled alcohol on Ms. Brady's breath, whiskey perhaps, even though it was ten o'clock in the morning. Was she grieving so much she'd turned to alcohol?

She led him to the living room and held out her hand

toward the couch. Ferd sat down. "We may get interrupted if my lawyer, Joe Crockett, calls." Now that he was alerted to her alcohol use, he noticed a slight slur in her voice. Her eyes seemed bloodshot too.

She offered him coffee, which he accepted. He knew Crockett, a San Mateo heavy hitter who'd made a name for himself litigating high-stakes civil as well as criminal cases. Ferd was glad Crockett hadn't answered Ms. Brady's call or he'd never get anything from her. He glanced around the room, noticing the modern décor, a steel-framed glass coffee table, tall narrow lamps, and a four-foot rectangular mirror above the mantle. A bit cold, he thought, deciding that Sonya had done a much better job decorating their home. The only warm decoration was a banner in the corner above an oak bookcase celebrating the Giants' 2010, 2012, and 2014 World Series championships.

After handing Ferd his coffee, Ms. Brady took a seat across from him. Ferd noticed that she was haggard, extremely thin, perhaps from grief. He knew he had to be delicate. He pointed to the banner. "Was your husband a Giants' fan?"

"No, he detested baseball, thought it too slow. I'm the Giants' fan. I have season tickets with my friend Doris. We went to every home game of the three World Series."

He sipped the coffee and got down to business. "Ms. Brady, allow me to offer my condolences for your loss. I don't know if my father is responsible, but I assure you if he is then I hope he gets just punishment. As I said on the phone, my father and I are not close. I just want to find out the truth."

"The police seem to think he's guilty," she said in an accusatory tone. "What makes you think different?"

"All I can say is it's a hunch. My father is not a nice man, but I'm not convinced he's a murderer. I understand your husband was in the Tenderloin the night of his murder for a work meeting."

She bit her lip and looked down. "That's what he said."

"Did you believe him?"

"Mr. – Judge – Pitt, why should I disbelieve my husband?" Suddenly tension filled the room. Ferdinand realized he had struck a nerve, guessing that she knew more than she was admitting.

"Obviously, I didn't know your husband, but it does seem strange that he had a meeting in the Tenderloin."

"I've been all over this with the police who, by the way, searched my house from top to bottom. They found nothing incriminating and, as far as I know, nothing helpful to their investigation." She looked away as if in deep thought, then continued. "My husband was an adventurous man. When we traveled to foreign countries, he would always want to see the poorest neighborhoods. He refused to prejudge people, especially the poor, who he saw as deserving respect rather than scorn. So, no, it was not strange that he went to the Tenderloin. In fact, our favorite Vietnamese restaurant is there so we went frequently. Also, a new bar called the Promenade with appetizers to die for. My husband and I went there a couple of weeks ago."

Ferdinand realized that he had misjudged Patrick Brady, assuming he was another cold and distant high-techer. There was obviously more substance to him. "What else can you tell me about Patrick?"

"He loved his job and worked very hard to make CAPSLOCK a success. He believed the company could change the world as much as Apple and Microsoft did. His team loved him and he regularly met with them. I would say he was a workaholic except he did have other interests."

"Such as?"

"He was on the alumni board at Stanford, volunteered as a mentor at 826 Valencia, and donated to many local charities. He was a good man, Judge Pitt, a good man." She sniffled but tried not to cry, tensing her face in the effort.

Ferd sipped his coffee, which by now had turned cold. "Do you know who he was meeting that night?"

She shook her head. "I assumed it was someone on his team, but he didn't say. He did say he was going to the Promenade."

"I know you said he loved his team, but was there ever any hint of dissension? Any arguments? Major disagreements?"

"I'm sure there were but I never heard about them." She gazed toward the ceiling. "Wait, there was one time, about a week ago, when he said he'd argued with an employee. Patrick was very upset about it."

"Did he say what the argument was about?"

She shook her head. "No. He didn't usually get into the details of work matters."

"On the night of his murder, do you know if he was meeting with a male or female?" Ferd wondered if she knew about Colleen.

She moved forward on her seat. "What are you implying?"

Ferdinand put up his hands. "Nothing at all. Just wondering."

"I don't know," she said slowly.

"Ms. Brady, did your husband have any enemies, anyone who hated him so much they'd want to kill him?"

She looked away, shaking her head. "Not that I know of."

Before Ferd could get out the next question, the home phone rang. "I'd better get that."

She walked quickly to the kitchen and answered the phone. Ferd could make out a few words like "judge" and "father" but not much else. After a few minutes, Ms. Brady returned.

"That was Joe Crockett. He's not happy with me and says I shouldn't talk to you. So, I'm afraid, Judge Pitt, this meeting is over."

"I hope we get a chance to talk again," Ferd said, holding out his hand. On the way out he was struck again by how impersonal the home felt. Something was missing. It took him a few minutes but then it hit him. There were no photos of the victim, no loving photos of the couple with their arms around each other. Perhaps the Bradys simply were not interested in photos. Or, possibly, Ms. Brady had removed them after her husband's death.

WHEN FERD ARRIVED HOME, he called Josh, who to his surprise picked up on the first ring. He got right to the point. "Ms. Brady said Patrick had some kind of argument with a co-worker a week or so before his murder. Do you know anything about that?"

There was a long silence before Josh answered. "I can't believe you bothered the grieving widow at a time like this."

"She was fine with it."

"She's probably still in shock. Anyway, I don't know what she was referring to. Patrick got into arguments all the time, including with me."

"So nothing unusual stands out?"

"Not that I know of."

"I have one more favor to ask."

"Dad, I don't know... This just doesn't feel right."

"Let me run with the case for a little while just to satisfy my curiosity."

"What else do you need?"

"I'd like to meet with your team members."

"Why?"

"They all interacted with Brady regularly and may be able to point me in the right direction."

Josh let out a loud sigh. "I hate to get them involved."

"They're already involved. Didn't the police also talk to them?"

"Yeah, but..."

"I don't see the problem then, though I could talk to them without your okay."

"I doubt they'd talk to you unless I encouraged them." Josh let out a loud sigh. "Let me look into it."

After hanging up, Ferd searched the internet for CAPLOCK's company website. He was impressed at how sharp and comprehensive the site was, and felt a twinge of pride seeing Josh's photo and bio on the page showing Brady's team. He bookmarked the page so he had easy access to the team's photos.

11

On Sunday morning Ferd made his way to the jail where the deputy sheriff, a burly guy with a handlebar moustache, welcomed Ferd warmly, perhaps sympathetic to his father's plight. He directed Ferd to the same dull secure room as before and returned in five minutes with Dwight Pitt. After removing Dwight's handcuffs, he left him with Ferd.

Seeing his father again caused Ferd to experience a rush of anger and resentment. Somewhat disarming was his father's expression, smiling, glad to see his son.

"I've been investigating your case, talking to people." Ferd fairly spat the words, causing Dwight to flinch slightly. It almost felt good to see his father like that, unsure and uncomfortable.

"I appreciate that. I really do, though my lawyer disagrees. She thinks you're interfering in her investigation."

"She's done jack shit, I'll tell you that. The police say they've got your fingerprints on the victim's wallet and at least a partial on the murder weapon. Care to explain?"

For a moment Dwight covered his face with his hands.

Then he shook his head, looking at the ceiling. "I'm sorry, son. I wish I could. But my lawyer says not to talk to nobody, and that includes you."

Ferd glared at his father. "Has she mentioned any other potential suspects?" When his father hung his head, Ferd said, "I get it. Attorney-client privilege. But I'm putting my ass on the line for you. Least you could do is offer a little help."

"I'm sorry. I really am." Dwight averted his eyes for a moment, then facing Ferd again, said, "You're a good son."

Ferd grunted in response, then turned away. The man in front of him was no father, which meant Ferd wasn't really his son. But if that was true, why'd he care so much about proving Dwight's innocence? He should just tell his father what he'd learned and leave it at that. He owed him nothing more.

"Speaking of which," Dwight said, "Josh stopped by yesterday. Looks just like you. A fine young man. I bet you're proud of him."

Ferd stiffened, surprised Josh had followed through. "He looks like his mother too, though you wouldn't know that because you've never met Sonya." Ferd couldn't resist taking another jab at his father.

"Josh wanted to know all about my life."

"Did you tell him why you abandoned your family?"

Dwight blushed. "You know I can't go into that."

"You mean, you won't?"

"Are you going to give me more shit?"

Ferd looked his father in the eyes and fought the urge to pile on the shit. "When I was here last time, you were telling me about Janet. What happened to her?"

Dwight looked down, biting his lip, struggling to find the right words. "She died. After the divorce from your mother became final, Janet – her last name was Parker – and I married. No kids; she was...she was sterile. She wanted to adopt but I told her I had no desire to raise another couple's kids. I wanted a child made of my own flesh and blood."

Ferd flinched, thinking of the people he knew who'd been adopted. "How'd she die?"

"Cancer." His voice cracked. "She'd been diagnosed with breast cancer and was depressed for a while, taking anti-depressants, also anti-psychotics since she'd been hearing voices. They would tell her not to trust this or that person, watch out for so-and-so. Paranoid kind of stuff. It got so we had no social life. Everyone was out to get her; they had a private agenda that included hurting her in some way. She couldn't trust anyone."

This information softened Ferdinand a little. "That must've been awful for you."

"The worst I've felt since leaving you and your sister. I was a mess."

"Why'd you return to San Francisco?" *And back into my life,* Ferdinand thought. *Wouldn't it have been better for everyone if you just stayed quietly in New Hampshire?*

"To reunite with my family, if you can believe that. I had nothing else to live for in New Hampshire." He brought his fist to his mouth. "Janet encouraged me to fix the mess I made of my life and look you up. But I didn't have the balls."

"So you screwed up the courage only after getting hooked on the sauce? I'm surprised you made it this far."

"I had big plans. I abandoned my house and mortgage; my 401(k) had a little over fifty thousand dollars. Would've been more but I didn't contribute as much as I should have. I blew through it pretty fast, spent a lot on fancy hotels when I first arrived in San Francisco a couple of months ago. I wandered the streets for weeks before I screwed up enough courage to contact your mother."

"You were in contact with Ma?" Ferd knew none of this and was surprised his mother had said nothing.

"No, I searched online and learned she still lived in the family home. I went there several times but found no one."

"She's in assisted living now. Why'd you want to see her after all these years?"

Dwight hung his head. "I had promised Janet I would. Then when she died, I hit rock bottom. I needed to talk to someone who knew me back then. Before..." He swept his hand to encompass the whole jail and shook visibly. "Just thinking about it makes me want a drink." He stood up and knocked on the door. The deputy opened it as Dwight turned his back toward him and lifted his wrists to be cuffed.

As he left, Ferd remained seated for a moment, staring at the heavy door as it slammed shut behind his father.

AT HOME FERD sat at the kitchen table, sipping coffee with Sonya beside him, both hands grasping her mug. "Can you believe that sonuvabitch actually had me feeling sorry for him?" said Ferd.

"You just can't accept that he's human like the rest of us."

"You might be right. I have a hard time dealing with him. I'm torn between helping him and letting him take the fall."

"Be honest," she said coldly. "You wouldn't be helping him if there weren't something in it for you."

Ferd hung his head, unable to come up with a rebuttal. "I can't put anything past you," he said finally.

"And you never will." She cracked a thin smile.

Josh had never responded to Ferd's request to interview his teammates, so Ferd had emailed them on his own using the email addresses on the company website. None had responded. He took out his phone and said, "I've got to call Josh."

Josh answered after several rings.

"This is your father. Just following up on something." He paused. "I know you're busy, but...okay, I'll hold." Ferd held the phone to his chest and said to Sonya, "Our son's so important he can't take a break to talk to his old man. You'd think he had the most important job in the world."

Ferd turned his attention back to the phone. "Listen, I still need to meet with your teammates. I've emailed them but they haven't responded."

"I know. They told me."

"Did you tell them not to respond?"

Josh ignored his question. "Do you think my co-workers would like you interrogating them? I know how you can get; I've been on the receiving end of your courtroom voice many times. Why should I subject my co-workers to that?"

"They've already spoken to the police. I just want to know what information they have. I promise I'll be gentle. I know this isn't an easy time for anyone."

Josh said he'd think about it and hung up. Ferd held up the phone toward Sonya. "Don't know why he was getting so upset. He obviously doesn't want me poking around."

"He's not the only one. None of us wants you investigating this case."

And that includes my father's attorney, Ferd thought.

As he drove east on Market Street, Ferd tightened his grip on the steering wheel. He knew seemingly everyone disagreed, but he was anxious to move the investigation along. He drove past Castro and turned left into the Safeway parking lot, determined to get as much evidence as possible before he had to return to work. The trouble was he had no information about the cashier who had alerted police to someone using Brady's credit card. So he asked to speak to the store manager, a heavyset thirty-something man with a double chin, named Francisco Hernandez. Ferd said he was investigating the murder, not expressly claiming to be law enforcement, but leaving that impression.

He asked if the cashier was working. Mr. Hernandez said the cashier was on duty, and Ferd could meet with him on his break in ten minutes.

Ferd waited in the manager's office at the front of the store, surveying the photos of employees of the month from the past few months. He wondered if the cashier had received an award for turning in his father.

"Here's Manny Silva," the manager said, appearing suddenly at the doorway. "He's the one who helped Mr. Pitt that night."

With a faint moustache and long uncombed hair, Manny appeared to Ferd to be in his late teens.

"I just want some details. Let's start with how he was dressed."

Manny shrugged. "Like a bum if you want to know the truth. Dirty sweatshirt, dark wrinkled pants. Dark jacket tied around his waist. And he stunk."

"What was he trying to buy?"

"A dozen tubes of Colgate."

Ferd found this strange, wondering what his father would do with so much toothpaste. "Did that seem odd to you?"

"Nah," he said, shaking his head. "I see it all the time. They sell the toothpaste to other homeless people."

"So what made you suspicious?"

"He handed me a credit card. It didn't fit, know what I mean. So I look at the card and notice the name: Patrick Brady. I remembered reading in the Chronicle about the murder in the Tenderloin and that name rang a bell. So I called for the manager."

"That's when I got involved," Hernandez said. "After Manny explained the situation, I called the police. The rest I think you know."

"Did Mr. Pitt say anything while all this was going on?"

Manny answered. "While the cops were cuffing him, he

said, 'What the hell? What's this all about?' Like he didn't know."

"He acted completely innocent," the manager said in a dismissive tone.

"Maybe he is," Ferd said before walking out.

12

A fter giving it much thought, Ferd decided it might not be a bad idea to take a trip to New Hampshire for a few days. He called Claire.

"I'm thinking of going to New Hampshire to look into Dad's life, fill in the gaps, maybe understand him better. Want to go with me?"

She frowned. "You've got to be kidding me! You want me to waste my valuable vacation time on that guy? I don't think so."

Ferd paced the living room. "It would be good for both of us. Come on."

"I don't care about his life. He didn't care about mine; why should I care about his? No thank you."

Ferd hung up, confused at her attitude; he assumed it was only natural to want to know more about your father.

He went upstairs to talk to Sonya. "I'm thinking of going to New Hampshire."

"I'm not going with you," Sonya said. "Not that you invited me."

Ferd realized he had hurt his wife's feelings. She must've

overheard his conversation. "I knew you wouldn't go so I invited Claire. She refused."

"Of course, she refused. She has enough common sense not to get involved. I don't like the idea of your going there alone."

"What? You don't think I can handle a little trip?"

Sonya snapped her fingers. "Why don't you take Josh? It would be good for you two. God knows you both need one."

"I don't know."

"Given your relationship with your own father, I thought you'd want a better one with your son."

"I'm sure he's still annoyed at me for getting involved."

"He's not the only one." She gave him a disapproving look. "But you should call him."

Later that afternoon Ferd screwed up enough courage to call Josh. Not that he was afraid of talking to him; he just didn't like getting rejected. At first, they talked about Josh's meeting with Dwight. "He's got warts like all of us," said Josh.

"Seems to me he's got more than most."

"You're too tough on your father, which I understand, believe me. Not everyone can be a hot shit like you. Don't get me wrong; you've earned everything you got. But don't misjudge your father simply because he's different than you."

Ferd couldn't help smiling. "I wish I were recording what you just said. It would apply equally to you and me."

"What do you mean?"

"Don't tell me you haven't judged me in some way because I'm different than you. You're more thoughtful, analytical. Sometimes I shoot from the hip."

"True, but you can be analytical if you want to. I don't think you'd have been so successful in the law if you weren't analytical."

"I'm proud of your success," Ferd said in a rare display of candor. "You did well at B.U. and got a great job with a strong start-up. You've earned the stock options."

Each was silent for a moment until Josh said, "I have some good news. I was awarded Coder of the Year by the company. All the managers had to vote on it and it's a prestigious award. Just found out on Friday."

"Congratulations, Josh. I'm proud of you. You've really made the most of your position. Does the award come with a pay raise?"

"Not a raise, but substantial stock options as a bonus! Could be life changing."

Ferd marveled at the easy money coming from Silicon Valley. Josh had worked there only one year and already was receiving a potentially life-changing bonus. It made Ferd more than a little jealous.

"I'm proud of you," he repeated. "But here's the real reason I called. I'm thinking of going to New Hampshire, just to learn about your grandfather's life, and would love it if you came with me."

"New Hampshire? Are you shitting me?"

"I know it's inconvenient, but just for a couple of days. We could take the red eye tomorrow night, be there Tuesday morning. What do you say?"

"I don't know. I'm awfully busy."

"You can work on the plane. I know your generation has figured out remote working. We'll be back Wednesday night."

"Well..."

"I'll cover all your expenses and make the reservations."

Ferd walked to the window overlooking the front yard. He stared at the flowers wilting beside the browning lawn, hoping he and Josh would have this time together. They needed it after enduring all the tension from recent events, including the ongoing discord with Sonya.

Finally, Josh said, "Okay, as long as we're back Wednesday night."

"You got it."

. . .

FERD CALLED the airline and booked a red-eye flight to Boston, leaving Monday around 11 p.m. They would arrive at 6:30 a.m. on Tuesday, rent a car, and drive to Manchester.

After making the reservations, Ferd accessed the court's online vacation request form and put in for Tuesday and Wednesday off. He knew Presiding Judge Bradstein wouldn't receive his request until the next day, but was counting on her granting it.

THAT EVENING FERD and Sonya flipped through television channels, going from the local news to *Jeopardy*. Ferd rested his legs on the Ottoman as he shouted out answers to the geography questions. Sonya fired back with answers to the literature questions. As usual, she was way ahead of him. In the middle of a question, Ferd's head snapped toward the front window. "What the hell?" he said.

The loud crash caused Sonya to jump to her feet. "Ferd!" On the thick Oriental carpet ten feet in front of them was a brick wrapped in paper. Broken glass was strewn throughout the room.

Kicking broken glass aside, Ferd ran to the window to try to glimpse the perpetrator. A dark medium-sized sedan was stopped in the street in front of his house. The driver had just closed the door and began driving away. Running out the front door, Ferd screamed, "Get back here, you asshole!" Because of the dark, he was unable to make out the license plate number or the make of the car, which drove down the street out of sight.

Sonya was standing in the doorway holding the brick. She removed the rubber bands around the paper and opened it. She read the note aloud: "'KEEP AWAY FROM THE PATRICK

BRADY MURDER CASE.'" It was printed in upper block black letters.

"I knew it," said Sonya. "What did I tell you?" Ferd reached out to hug her, but she backed away. "Who did this?"

"You've got me, unless...I don't want to guess." Ferd realized he hadn't updated the online forms protecting his home address from public disclosure. Anyone could've looked up his address online.

"We should call the police," said Sonya.

Ferd dialed 911 and they waited for the police. Two uniformed male officers arrived and introduced themselves. Paul Fleming was about six feet six inches tall, stick thin, with thinning blonde hair; his partner Jake Sutter was short and stocky with a thick head of black hair, almost an exact opposite. Ferd summarized what happened, including background on his father's case. Both officers, of course, were familiar with the case.

"Where's the brick?" Fleming asked.

Ferd pointed to the coffee table where he had placed it. "The note's there too."

"You touched the note?" asked Sutter.

"I did, to read it."

"I did too," said Sonya.

"We'll need both of you to come down to the station for fingerprinting."

"Understood," Ferd said.

Wearing latex gloves, Fleming picked up the note and read it. "Who knew you were looking into this case?"

Ferd glanced at Sonya who remained seated on the couch. "A lot of people." As Fleming took notes, Ferd listed everyone he'd talked to about the case: including his father and son, Ms. Brady, the proprietors of various Tenderloin stores, the bartender at the Promenade, Joannie Merced at the Blue Arms, and Safeway employees. He also mentioned that Josh's teammates knew he wanted to interview them.

Fleming frowned. "Any idea who could've done this?"

"I hate to guess; it could've been anyone. I know my father's lawyer Nicole Smedley was not happy with me. She's also running against me in next month's election. We've run an aggressive social media campaign attacking her for having a conflict of interest in my father's case."

"We'll have to follow up with all those folks, starting with Ms. Smedley." While Fleming was questioning Ferd, Sutter was busy photographing the brick, note, and broken window.

"Why would Smedley want you off the case?" asked Fleming.

"She claimed I was interfering in her investigation."

"Doesn't sound likely but we'll certainly question her. Do you have contact info for your son and his teammates?"

Ferd gave him Josh's cell phone number. "Josh'll have his teammates' numbers."

"What about video?" Fleming asked. "Do you or your neighbors have any kind of video system?"

"We don't, but I don't know about neighbors."

"We'll look around."

Sutter finished photographing. "Ms. Pitt, do you have anything to add to your husband's statement?"

"Nothing. He pretty much laid things out."

"In that case, do you both want to follow us to Taraval Station?"

Ferd drove to the station with Sonya silent on the way. After both had submitted to fingerprinting, Ferd asked Fleming what would happen next. "We'll dust the brick and note for prints, see what turns up, then question the folks you mentioned."

"I'd appreciate it if you'd keep me posted."

"I will." He paused as Ferd got up to leave. "It might not be a bad idea for you to leave the detective work to the professionals."

Ferd stopped in front of him. "I won't be intimidated, Officer. This little stunt only tells me I'm onto something." Ferd considered the possibilities: Josh's teammates, especially Colleen; Nicole Smedley; and perhaps the widow.

"Suit yourself, but understand I'll have to report everything to Sergeant Hinton."

ON MONDAY MORNING, Ferd returned to work. In chambers he checked himself out in the mirror with his robe on. He rubbed the fabric, smoothing out the folds, luxuriating in the touch of 100% silk. *It had been worth the extra $300*, he thought, *because a judge should look the part and polyester just wouldn't do*. He adjusted his red silk tie, zipped up the robe, and straightened his shoulders. He liked how the black silk hung on his body, hiding the paunch he had started to develop. His hair had turned partly white with a hint of salt and pepper in his long sideburns. As he walked into the courtroom, he had to suppress a smile, his excitement palpable. He was glad to be back.

At lunchtime Ferd made a few phone calls to make his trip to New Hampshire productive. Just as he was about to take the bench for the afternoon session, Bradstein called.

"Ferd, I got your vacation request. Would've been nice if you gave me some notice."

"Sorry about that, Carol, but it was a last-minute thing. I'm going to New Hampshire with my son. We're hoping to learn about my father's life."

"I see." She paused for a moment. Ferd wondered if she doubted his story. "And can I count on you being in court on Thursday?"

"I'll be here; I promise."

. . .

BY SIX O'CLOCK HE found his way to the Promenade Bar. There were a handful of customers at the bar and a male bartender, a thirty-something white man with a scraggly beard and short hair, who was busy washing glasses.

Ferd leaned across the bar, raising his finger, and ordered a draft Sierra Nevada. When the bartender placed an over-flowing mug on the bar, Ferd said, "You must be Conor."

"Who wants to know?"

Ferd held out his hand to shake. "Ferd."

The bartender shook his hand.

"I was here the other day," Ferd said. "A female bartender told me you were working a week ago Thursday night."

"Yeah, I was. What do you want to know?"

"A man was murdered down the street that night. I'm trying to figure out who did it."

"What's your interest?"

Ferd considered how to answer. He didn't want to lie outright so he fudged the truth. "The family of the defendant asked me to look into it." Ferd showed him his father's photo on his phone. "This is him. Did you happen to see him that night?"

Conor stared at the photo for several seconds. "He looks familiar, but I can't be sure."

Ferd took the phone back, clicked to the CAPSLOCK directory, and enlarged Brady's photo. "How about this one?"

"Oh, yeah. He was here all right. I remember because he was such a shitty tipper. Stiffed me for God knows what reason. Is that the victim?"

"Yes. Did you see him with anyone?" Ferd didn't want to lead him with suggestive questioning.

He stared at the ceiling, thinking. "He was by himself for about fifteen minutes then a guy joined him for a little while. They sat at the table near the entrance. I couldn't hear much of anything they said, except they were arguing. I did hear the other guy mention stock options. It got heated and he was getting really worked up."

"This is important. What did this guy look like?"

"He had that privileged look, patrician nose I think they call it, dressed in a tweed jacket with blue jeans. Caucasian, perhaps early to mid-twenties, thin, clean-shaven."

The bartender turned toward Ferd, who suddenly felt self-conscious. Ferd clicked on Josh's photo. "This look like him?"

Hill glanced down the bar at a patron yelling at him from the other end. "Yup. That's him. Looks like you."

Ferd ignored his comment. "One more photo." He enlarged the photo of Colleen O'Keefe, Josh's girlfriend. "Do you recognize this woman?"

Hill stared at the photo, enlarged it even more using his thumb and index fingers. Again, he looked toward the other end of the bar. "I gotta get back to work." He glanced back at the photo. "She's the one who came in shortly after Mr. Tweed left alone."

"You seem to remember that night well."

"It's not often there's a murder less than a block away. I heard the sirens that night. People were talking about someone being knifed. Scared the shit out of me."

Ferd nodded. "Did you hear anything this woman and the victim said?"

"She said something like, 'It's over.' And I gotta say, she didn't look too happy either."

"Did she leave with the victim?"

"Yup. Do you think she might've killed the guy?"

"Don't know." The crowd had quickly made its way to the bar, boxing Ferd in. Soon he was overwhelmed with people on all sides, the noise level rising substantially. Ferd hurried to his car, feeling uncomfortable about what he had learned.

13

Ferdinand had never been to New Hampshire. He and Sonya had flown to Boston years ago and spent all their time in Massachusetts, primarily Cape Cod. For some reason, New Hampshire was not high on his list of vacation destinations.

After takeoff, Ferd told Josh he had talked to the Promenade bartender who was on duty the night of the murder. "He said you and Brady got in a heated argument."

Josh looked away. "I wouldn't call it heated."

"What would you call it?"

Holding his hands out, palms up, he said, "Stern maybe. Serious."

Ferd nodded, knowing an independent witness's characterization would likely prevail over Josh's. His stomach was churning, thinking perhaps this was why the police had put Josh on their list of suspects.

Tentatively, he raised another issue. "He also said you two were arguing about stock options."

"That was a common subject of discussion, so it might've come up. I don't remember."

"Did it have anything to do with the Coder of the Year award?"

Josh shrugged, furrowing his eyebrows. "Maybe."

"You want to elaborate?"

"Not really."

Ferd wondered why Josh didn't want to discuss this, but decided to let it go for now, though there was one other matter he wanted to address. "He also heard Colleen say something about it being over. Any idea what that was about?"

Josh shrugged. "I'd guess she was saying his harassment had to be over. She wasn't going to take it anymore."

"I see." Ferd decided to change subjects. "I hear the police talked to you about the brick thrown through our window."

"Yeah, and the whole team as well. Who do you think could've done that?"

"I've been racking my brain. Only a handful of people even knew I was looking into the case." In his mind, Ferd recounted those people, still no closer to solving the mystery.

As SOON AS Ferd stepped off the plane at Logan Airport, he shivered. "Damn, it's cold here," he said. A chilly February snowstorm had hit the area. Ferd buttoned his raincoat. He didn't own an overcoat so had opted for the raincoat with a heavy sweater providing protection from the cold. Josh was better prepared: he was wearing the pea coat he'd bought while in college.

"I knew this was a bad idea," Josh said.

"I appreciate your taking time off. I know how busy you are. I also realize you weren't that keen to travel with your father."

"You can be very convincing when you want to be."

They walked through the terminal, picked up a rental car, and made their way toward the Holiday Inn in Manchester. As they drove down the freeway, the snow lightly blanketing the road, Ferd glanced at Josh beside him, glad to have his son with him. They took a couple of family trips every year while he was growing up: a week in Bali, Scandinavian and Mediterranean cruises, national parks. It was difficult for him as an only child. He became attached to his parents, protesting loudly when they would leave him with a babysitter or, when he was older, at the teen club on the cruise ship.

"This is nice," Ferd finally said.

"What?"

"You and me. I know I was so busy building my legal practice that I often neglected you."

"Nah, you did the best you could."

Ferd rolled his window down an inch to let in some air. "Remember when you were a teenager? That was a rough time for us."

"Every kid goes through that, seeing their parents as less than the image they had built up."

"You didn't like that I represented insurance companies instead of the little guy."

"Yeah. You said that everyone, rich or not, deserved legal representation. That's when I learned about contingency fees for the little guy. Almost made me want to go to law school."

"What held you back?"

"You."

"What do you mean?"

"I would've had big shoes to fill. I didn't need that pressure."

Ferd was taken aback; he hadn't realized Josh had even considered law school. He wished he had talked to Josh about it, perhaps alleviating the pressure Ferd didn't know he'd felt. "So you decided to go into coding, a most modern occupation."

"I like it. I can work mostly by myself, analyze issues, problem-solve. It's fun."

"And also lucrative. You're making a lot more money than I did when I started my career."

"If the company ever goes public, my stock options will keep me set for a long time."

"What're the chances of that happening?"

"Hard to say. Brady's death has put everything on hold. We need to replace him, which won't be easy."

After securing an early check-in, they went to the hotel restaurant for breakfast. The server recommended the eggs benedict so that's what both ordered. Ferd sipped his coffee, gazed around the nearly empty restaurant, black booths lining the far wall, silverware neatly positioned beside beige place-mats, and said, "I've set up a meeting for later this morning at Manchester Insurance Company. We'll meet Edward Bryson, manager of workers' compensation claims, and your grandfather's old boss."

"How'd you get Bryson to meet with us?"

"Seems your grandfather was a good employee for decades, so he had some goodwill."

Josh nodded, picking at his eggs. After a moment of silence, he said, "I didn't mention this the other day, but I found Gramps to be a sweet old man."

"Gramps? Really?" Ferd held his fork in midair, suddenly shocked to hear Josh refer to his grandfather by this affectionate name.

"He wanted to know all about my life."

Ferd dropped the fork on his plate where it bounced and clattered onto the table. "I'd hardly call someone who abandoned his family a 'sweet old man.'"

"He's changed from when you were a kid."

"Did he tell you why he left his family?"

"He said he had a nervous breakdown and couldn't handle the pressure of being a husband and father. He got treatment in New Hampshire and turned his life around. Then his wife died and he fell into a spiral of alcohol abuse."

That was a bit more than he'd told Ferd. "Do you plan on seeing him again?"

"Of course. He's my grandfather."

"Did you tell your grandmother you visited him?" Ferd drained his coffee.

Josh shook his head. "Somehow I didn't think she'd understand."

MANCHESTER INSURANCE COMPANY was located downtown on Hanover Street, a few blocks from Elm. Ferd found parking easily, a far different experience than in San Francisco. The building was three stories high, made of tan brick with red awnings over the four front-facing windows on the ground floor. The receptionist welcomed them as if they were regular customers, smiling broadly and offering coffee and water. She had dirty blonde hair with blue tips that would have fit in well in San Francisco. She seated them at the oak conference table and after a few minutes a short chubby man with mutton chops walked in.

"Hi, I'm Edward Bryson." His handshake challenged Ferd's own iron-like grip. "What can I do for you, Mr. Pitt, and," turning toward Josh, "Mr. Pitt?"

Ferd got right to the point. "Appreciate your meeting with us, especially on such short notice. My son and I are on a fact-finding mission about my father Dwight Pitt. He's fallen on some hard times and is currently in jail on murder charges. I was hoping you could fill in some gaps in his life."

"I'm sorry to hear that. I liked your father, which was not always easy since he could be a difficult personality."

"How so?"

"He was prone to sulking when things didn't go his way. Would stop communicating."

Thinking that also described his son and maybe even

himself, Ferd stole a glance at Josh, who was listening intently. "Can you give us some examples?"

"Usually, it was about a claim he wanted to deny. He had a very suspicious attitude, which is generally a plus for claims, but occasionally I would overrule him. He didn't take kindly to that."

"How long did you work with him?"

"For about sixteen years. He was with the company maybe a decade and a half before me so he was far more experienced than I was." He gave Ferd a curious look. "Strange but he never mentioned having a son."

"Or a daughter?"

"Not at all. He always said he didn't want kids. I'm surprised."

"Just wondering," Josh interjected. "What did you like about him?"

Bryson shifted in his seat as if this were a hard question to answer. "I should preface this answer with a caveat. I liked his dry sense of humor, his integrity, his quiet determination until about the last few months of his employment."

"Then what happened?" asked Josh.

"His wife died and he went to pieces. Drank excessively, came to work stinking of alcohol. Then he got involved in a workers' comp scam where workers would stage an accident in the workplace and claim devastating injuries. Found out Dwight was taking a cut of their payments so I had no choice but to fire his ass."

Josh and Ferd looked at each other, neither saying anything. Ferd was not surprised; his father had talked about his wife's death. What was surprising was his father had engaged in criminal activity: insurance fraud. "Were any criminal charges filed?" he asked.

"In light of Dwight's three decades of service, almost

without a blemish, the company agreed not to press charges if he repaid the money."

"Did he?" Ferd asked.

"About half. Then he took off, still owing forty grand. I didn't know where he went until you called. That's one reason I agreed to meet with you, but from your description of his circumstances it sounds like the company won't recoup its losses."

"Highly unlikely," Ferd said.

Bryson pushed his seat back. "I'm afraid I've got to get back to work."

"Can I ask you one more thing?"

"Sure." He leaned over the table.

"His wife Janet: did you know her?"

"Oh, yeah. She worked in underwriting on a different floor but, sure, we'd run into each other all the time. She was the opposite of Dwight: comfortable with people, quick to laugh, and an engaging conversationalist, at least up to the last year or so when she seemed down, not as talkative. But everyone liked her. We were all saddened when she died."

"What do you know of her family?"

"Not much, except she was a local girl, from Hillsboro I believe. Had a brother who moved into the family home when the parents died. She and Dwight seemed like a happy couple, though I found it strange they never had kids. Dwight claimed he was too busy at work for kids. His job was his life, which is a sad statement, but most likely true."

By the time the meeting had concluded it was close to the lunch hour so, at the receptionist's recommendation, they walked a block to the Hanover Chop House. Ferd wanted to check in with Officer Fleming. He hadn't talked to him since the night the brick came through the window. He told Josh to go in ahead of him while he called Fleming at Taraval Station.

"Just wondering how the investigation's going."

"Judge Pitt, I'm afraid I can't talk about it. My orders are to direct all inquiries to Sergeant Hinton."

"I see."

"She's running the investigation into the Brady murder so she wants to handle this too. Let me give you her direct number." Ferd wrote down the number.

"Thanks, Officer, I appreciate what you've done so far."

Ferd immediately called the sergeant who did not pick up. He left a voicemail message, wondering aloud on the recording if the brick and note changed Hinton's view of his father's case.

Ferd went into the restaurant, which was dark, and found Josh sitting at a maroon leather booth in back. "No news," he told Josh. "For some reason the police are being closed-mouthed."

"Maybe they've got a suspect."

"I doubt it; they would've told me something by now."

After ordering their meals, a veggie burger for Josh and grilled lamb chops for Ferd, Josh said, "Tell me what you think about what we learned today."

"I don't know what to think. My father's not only a potential murderer; he's also a thief."

Josh stared at him for a moment and said, "That's not my takeaway at all. He comes across as a tortured soul who suffered an unspeakable loss and turned to crime only because of that condition."

"You're more forgiving than I am. He never mentioned his children. It's as if he erased us from his memory. Why would he do that?"

"Good question. Maybe it was too painful to talk about."

"I bet." Ferd wondered how Josh could be so forgiving of his grandfather but not his father. It was easy to have a soft spot for someone you never knew, who was never a part of your life, especially someone you built up in your mind as a free spirit.

Ferd decided it might be a good time to bring up a touchy subject. "Can I ask you something?"

"Sure."

"I really need to talk to your co-workers."

Josh sighed. "The police were pretty aggressive when they questioned us. As I said before, I hate to subject my co-workers to that again."

"I'll be as gentle as possible; I promise."

Crossing his arms, Josh leaned back, clearly not pleased. "I thought this was a social trip about Gramps."

"Look, all I'm asking is for you to give your co-workers the green light to speak to me. You know I tried reaching them on my own."

The waiter brought their meals and refilled their water glasses. They picked at their food, their appetites seemingly gone, mostly in silence. Josh stared at his father for several seconds until Ferd raised his eyebrows. Finally, Josh said, "I see you're trying to help Gramps, which I appreciate. I'll tell the team to cooperate as soon as we get back."

"That's great," Ferd said, putting down his fork. "What I'd like to do next is track down Janet's brother. You're the techie in the family. Use that smartphone to find a guy named Parker in Hillsboro."

14

Hillsboro was just forty-five minutes from Manchester. While Ferd drove the rented Hyundai sedan, Josh searched for Janet's brother on his smartphone and located two male Parkers in Hillsboro. They decided to stop first at the house on Bear Hill Road. A black pickup truck was parked in the driveway. Ferd rang the bell and a young woman with a kerchief wrapped around her head answered. She seemed to be in the midst of housecleaning. "Sorry to bother you, Miss," Ferd said. "I'm trying to locate the brother of Janet Parker. He wouldn't happen to live here, would he?"

She folded her arms, holding the door slightly ajar, obviously suspicious. She stared at Josh in the front seat. "And what is it you want with him?"

"Janet Parker was my father's wife. I have reason to believe her brother may have some information on my father. I flew out from San Francisco to investigate."

"You're a long way from home."

"It's a long story. Any information you could provide would be much appreciated."

She opened the door a few inches more, relaxing a bit. "You've got the wrong Parker. You want David Parker. He works at the auto parts store on West Main. You can't miss it."

AT THE AUTO PARTS STORE, which was strangely located next to a traditional white New England Congregational church, Ferd and Josh both went inside. A sixty-something man wearing a checkered shirt and blue jeans stood behind the counter, which was strewn with huge notebooks containing photos of auto parts on plastic sheets.

"Hi," Ferd said. "I'm looking for David Parker."

The man put his hands on the counter and leaned toward Ferd. "You found him."

Ferd then explained why he and Josh were there. He was interrupted a couple of times by customers who were in urgent need of parts. When he finished, Parker said, "That's an incredible story. So you're Dwight's son. I'm not surprised he wound up on the street. My sister was the only reason he remained partly sane."

"You didn't like my father?"

"I didn't dislike him is the best I can say. He just seemed to have no spark; he lived for work. I couldn't understand what Janet saw in him."

"Do you know why they never had kids?" Josh asked.

"Couldn't. Janet was barren, or at least that's the story they told. But I will say that he took good care of Janet. He fawned over her."

Standing at the counter listening to Parker, Ferd started putting together a picture of his father as an undistinguished, nondescript drone, a man who unlike Ferd would never make his mark on the world. He was isolated, single-minded, and not particularly interesting. With a sense of satisfaction, Ferd thought his father was nothing like him. Ferd had always believed that his life had to mean something. He had to engage in meaningful work, resolving disputes, preventing fraud. But he also wanted to do well, to make enough money that he didn't have to scrounge like his mother did, borrowing twenties from his paper route receipts. She would sit at the kitchen table with a pair of scissors and the Sunday newspaper and clip every coupon she could find. Her life was constantly unsettled, always desperate and anxious.

Ferd decided he couldn't leave Parker without asking about a sensitive topic. "And how about her death? How did my father take that?"

Parker lowered his eyes. "He was devastated; we all were. We knew she was sick, but didn't realize how much."

"Was there an autopsy?" asked Ferd.

"There was. No question it was cancer, though there were rumors Dwight was responsible."

"Why would people say that about my father?"

Parker shrugged. "You know how people are, always looking for the seamy side of life. Dwight had no reason to want Janet dead. I know for a fact he loved her. That's why he started drinking, got himself fired, then left the state. I assumed he went to California, but he never said goodbye. Just disappeared."

"Sounds familiar," Ferd said, stealing a glance at Josh. "And what happened to the family home?"

"He left it with all the furniture there. I managed to sell or donate the furniture, but the house is in foreclosure. Dwight has about sixty days to fix things."

"I wouldn't count on it," said Ferd.

"Is there anyone you think we should talk to – friends, acquaintances – who might be able to help us?" asked Josh.

"They didn't have many friends... Wait, there was someone. A guy in Manchester Dwight went to ballgames with. His name's Walt Brown. Yeah, that's it. I believe he's a fireman at the central station."

FERD AND JOSH made it back to Manchester in no time and quickly found the fire station on Merrimack Street, a white two-story building with red-brick columns. Ferd parked by the flag-pole and proceeded to the door on the left, which was unlocked. They climbed the stairs to the second floor. The lone desk was empty, but a man approached, asking if he could help them.

"We're looking for Walt Brown," Ferd said.

"For me to wake him up, it better be important." He looked across the room where there were several bunkbeds.

Ferd explained who they were and the purpose of their visit. "If you wouldn't mind waking him," Josh added. "We're in town only a few days."

Five minutes later a man approached wearing yellow over-alls with a white tee-shirt. He had a thick white moustache and thinning white hair. Approaching Ferd, he held out his hand. "Walt Brown."

Ferd shook his hand, introducing himself and Josh. He explained the purpose of the visit.

"So you're Dwight's boy? He never mentioned having a son. Haven't seen that sonuvagun in months. He was in a bad way after Janet died. We went to a Celtics game a few weeks after-wards and he hardly cheered even though we were kicking some Laker butt. I gotta say, though, he downed quite a few beers. Good thing I was driving because he was totally shitfaced."

"Did you see him often?" asked Josh.

"Couple of times a month we'd go to a ballgame some-where. We met at church a few years ago. I was an usher and he was a lector. Good man. He had a quiet voice usually but when he got on the altar his voice boomed. Filled the church, St. Anne-Augustin's. Father O'Neill picked him every year to read at the Christmas and Easter Masses." He shuffled his feet.

Ferd was surprised his father went to church at all since he didn't raise his children to be religious. The only times Ferd would see the inside of a church were at Easter and Christmas and it was his mother who brought him. He glanced at Josh then asked, "Did you think he had a drinking problem?"

Brown shook his head. "As I say, got worse after Janet died. Mostly beer with whiskey chasers. Before that, he'd have the occasional beer, but nothing excessive."

"Anything else you can tell us about his life or his character?" asked Josh.

Brown looked toward the ceiling, thinking. "He had a temper, that's for sure. I've seen him confront guys in bars he thought had disrespected him. One time a guy stepped in front of him at the bar and Dwight grabbed him by the shoulders, spun him around, and tossed him to the floor. Didn't say a word. I thought there'd be a brawl, but people got between them until things calmed down. I asked Dwight why he'd reacted so strongly. He said he couldn't stand people acting as if he were invisible. Seemed to me he had a bit of a sensitive ego, if you know what I mean."

Folding his arms, Josh got a serious look on his face. "I'm wondering if he ever talked about his life in San Francisco."

"He was pretty close-mouthed," Brown said, shaking his head. "He was private that way. All I knew is that he had come from California – didn't even know it was San Francisco – and things hadn't gone well there. It was like he had a big secret he didn't want to talk about.""Thanks for your time," Ferd said. He and Josh started walking away when Brown called out.

"Do me a favor, will ya. Tell Dwight I'm praying for him."

. . .

AFTER LEAVING THE FIREHOUSE, they began to drive to the hotel when Ferd's phone rang. The screen on the dashboard flashed the incoming phone number, which Ferd recognized as Sergeant Hinton's.

"Sergeant, thanks so much for returning my call."

"Sorry it wasn't sooner. We were waiting for the fingerprint analysis."

"Anything there? I should say you're on speaker with my son Josh in the car."

"Oh, hello Josh. We spoke recently." She paused. "So we came up blank. No prints other than yours and Sonya's on either the brick or the note."

"And what about your interviews of those who knew of my investigation?"

She exhaled deeply. "We've talked to everyone, including Josh's teammates. Everyone denies involvement in the incident. In fact, the widow threatened to sue us and you for harassing her. She called her lawyer while the officers were there. He shut down the interview."

"Not surprising."

"And there was no video evidence from your neighbors. No one saw anything suspicious."

"So where does that leave things?"

"Well, there are some on the force who've floated the idea that you staged the brick incident so we'd take another look at your father's case."

"You're shitting me!" Ferd tensed, clutching the steering wheel.

"I'm not saying I believe that, but I wanted you to know."

"That's preposterous!" He tried to gather himself. "Isn't it obvious someone wants me off the case?"

"You mean: besides the police?"

"Well, someone's worried what I'd find."

"All I can say is be very careful about interfering in a police investigation."

"Tell me what other suspects you've looked at and maybe I'd reconsider."

"You know I can't do that."

"Then I have nothing further to discuss."

BY THE TIME they arrived at the hotel, it was close to dinnertime, so they decided to eat a quick meal. Afterwards Ferd laid on his bed, still fuming at what Hinton had said, but taking stock of the picture of his father that began to emerge in his mind. He seemed to have lived a normal, rather bland life before Janet died. He was a worker bee, dedicated to his job, without many outside interests. Ferd wondered what had attracted Janet to him. He wasn't the sharing type, mostly keeping to himself.

Wide awake, his body tense, he quietly changed into his workout clothes and took the elevator down to the exercise room in the basement. Three TVs showed ESPN, the volume turned off. As Ferd climbed on the elliptical machine and punched in his program, he glanced at the Top Ten. Inspired by the great plays, he moved quickly and began sweating, the whir of the machine the only sound. *Could my father's alcoholism be related to whatever drove him away from his family thirty-four years ago? Or was the drinking problem just because of the death of his wife?* After thirty minutes of exercise, pondering his family life, he felt he'd learned a bit about his father, though most of that was not particularly positive. Perhaps the more he learned the more empathetic he'd become. At least that's what he hoped.

15

At breakfast the next morning Ferd shared these thoughts with Josh, who was pleased his father had let some empathy seep into the shell he had constructed about Dwight. "You're not as stodgy as I thought," he said.

"Stodgy? Why the hell would you think I was stodgy?" Ferd spread cream cheese on his poppyseed bagel, took a bite. "'Stodgy' means 'dull and uninteresting.'"

"I meant more in the sense of old-fashioned and traditional. You don't exactly keep up with the latest technology, though I was impressed when you got a smart phone. You worked at the same office for decades. You haven't made any new friends in God knows how long. And you listen only to music from the 60s and 70s."

"Well, that's because all the music since then sucks."

"How would you even know?"

"I've heard rap and hip hop. I can't believe anyone would listen to that crap."

Josh smiled as he stirred his coffee. "See. That's what I

mean. You listen to a few rap songs and then condemn them all."

Ferd took another bite of his bagel then wiped his mouth with the paper napkin. "I was surprised to learn your grandfather was so religious. I left a message for Father O'Neill at the rectory that we'd stop by after morning Mass."

"You raised me without any religion. Who would've guessed that we come from a family of devout Catholics?"

"You were lucky you got accepted to Lowell. If not, you would've gone to Saint Ignatius and gotten more religion than you'd know what to do with."

"I know. I had many friends from S.I. I often wonder how I would've turned out if I'd had religion. But that wasn't going to come from you."

It had been years since Ferd had talked religion with Josh. Ferd had flirted with Catholicism at various times, even joining the Saint Thomas More Society at one point early in his career. He and Sonya attended Mass at Christmas and Easter for a few years after they were married but gradually slipped away from the church. Josh was baptized but never confirmed. By the time he was in grammar school, they had stopped attending church completely. After the molestation scandals, Ferd had decided that the Catholic Church was too corrupt for him to be a part of. As a result, Ferd abandoned the idea of God altogether and became a devout atheist.

"Perhaps you would've chosen a different field of study and work. One thing I like about the Catholic Church is they preach service to others. Many lawyers and doctors are products of a Catholic education."

"Are you saying I'm in a selfish, soulless line of work?"

Ferd smiled, purposely not answering. He contemplated his own path, which was much different than Josh's. Although he had attended public school, Ferd had been driven from an early age, deciding in high school that he would go into the law. After reading a biography of Clarence Darrow and Harper Lee's classic *To Kill A Mockingbird*, Ferd decided he wanted to be like Darrow and Atticus Finch and defend the poor and the powerless. That's what drove him throughout college and law school, but when it came time to actually practice law Ferd went in a different direction. No longer did the defense of accused criminals seem like the ideal practice. The more exposure Ferd had to law, the more he concluded that criminal defendants were generally guilty, if not of the charges levied against them then certainly other criminal conduct. In his third year, he had briefly looked into clerking at the public defender's office but as he dug into the nature of the practice, he became disillusioned. When private firms interviewed prospective associates on campus, Ferd was drawn to the big corporate firms, who paid the highest salaries and offered the most generous benefits. All they required in return was that you work like a slave for six or seven years before being considered for partnership. But Ferd wanted trial experience, so he spent a few years at the district attorney's office. When he had the requisite experience, he jumped for the pot at the end of the rainbow and accepted a generous offer from Pickwick & Erving. After nearly two decades of practice, his financial future secure, his itch for public service returned so he applied for the bench.

They finished breakfast and drove to Saint Anne-Saint Augustin's Church, about two miles away. The red-brick church fit in well with the area. If the green steeple were eliminated, the building could have passed for one of the city's old red-brick mills. Ferd parked on the street and they walked to the rectory.

Father O'Neill had just finished the 8:30 Mass and was still hyped up about his homily. "I was on a roll," he said. "Preaching sacrifice on earth so you can enjoy eternal salvation in heaven. This area has gone through some tough economic times so people have had their faith tested. I try to keep their souls on track, but it's not easy." He shook hands with Ferd and Josh and pointed them toward the conference room which had stained glass windows on one side. "But you gentlemen didn't come here to hear me preach. You say you're related to Dwight Pitt?"

"I'm his son," said Ferd, sitting down. "And Josh is his grandson. We're in town to get a better picture of his life." Ferd then related his history with Dwight, including the murder charges.

Father O'Neill rubbed his bald head and said, "Dwight never struck me as a violent man. He was a regular churchgoer and the best lector we had. That man could make you believe whatever came out of his mouth. A true gift. But he was troubled by Janet's death. Who wouldn't be?"

"What can you tell us about Janet?" asked Josh.

"She came to church with Dwight but wasn't active in the parish in any other way. I tried to get her to volunteer for Saturday night bingo but she wasn't interested. Toward the end she was always tired. And sniffling. It seemed every time I saw her she was holding tissue and wiping her nose. Things got worse, of course, as the cancer progressed."

"How was Dwight after Janet's death?" asked Ferd.

"As you might expect. He tried to put up a solid front and continued reading at Mass but his voice had lost its impact, a flat monotone with no pep. He wasn't the same. But when he disappeared, we were all surprised. He didn't say goodbye to anyone as far as I know."

"Were there any rumors about why he left?" asked Josh, who was leaning back in his seat.

"You might imagine that a parish can be a hotbed of rumors. I hate gossip and it pains me to repeat it."

"Anything, no matter how far-fetched, would be helpful," said Ferd.

Father O'Neill leaned forward, his arms extended on top of the table. "Since you're family, I suppose there's no harm." He lowered his voice. "There were rumors he had something to do with Janet's death."

"How so?" asked Ferd.

Shrugging, Father O'Neill said, "I don't know. It just sounded like an ugly rumor to me."

"I thought she died of cancer," said Josh.

"Well, that's the official story. But people talked as if Dwight had somehow killed her. I didn't put much faith in rumors. Janet was dying of cancer; God knows she was in a lot of pain."

FERD AND JOSH had enough time for one more meeting before their afternoon flight. They decided to drive to the Chief Medical Examiner's Office in Concord. On the way Ferd received a call, which he answered through the car's speaker system.

"Judge, this is Curt Rodda. How the hell are you?"

"Okay. I'm in New Hampshire with my son Josh. You're on speaker."

Rodda exhaled heavily. "Hello, Josh. Good to meet you by phone." After Josh returned his greeting, he said, "I was just calling to check in. You gotta let me know when you leave town. We have some events coming up."

"It was a last-minute thing. How's the social media campaign playing out?"

"Like a dream. People are questioning Smedley's ethics big time. Contributions have started to increase as well."

"What can I do to make sure that continues?"

"Do what you're doing now: laying low." Rodda coughed

into the phone. "Sorry about that. Got a peanut stuck in my throat. Do me a favor and keep in touch."

Ferd smiled. If Rodda had his way, he thought, he'd talk to Ferd every day. "Of course. Got to run. We're almost there."

At the front desk of the medical examiner's office, the male receptionist, a young Black man with long dreadlocks, the first Black person they had seen in New Hampshire, handed them a form to fill out. "You're lucky," he said. "We're slow today so I can handle this now."

The form asked for the decedent's dates of birth and death. Ferd asked Josh to call David Parker to get this information while Ferd completed the form. Ferd puzzled over the section asking about his relationship with the decedent. For a moment, he was stumped then realized that Janet Parker in fact was his step-mother so he wrote "step-son." He checked the boxes for autopsy, investigation, and toxicology reports. When Josh returned with the dates, Ferd filled those in then signed the form and handed it to the receptionist. Ten minutes later they walked out of the office holding the three reports, totaling sixteen pages.

"You read these while I drive to the airport," Ferd told Josh.

As Ferd entered the interstate, Josh thumbed through the reports. "It says Dwight came home and found her in bed, not breathing. Cause of death is metastatic cancer."

"So the rumors were bullshit," said Ferd.

Josh flipped through the autopsy report. "It says extensive lesions were found on her breasts. Determined to be cancerous. The cancer had spread to her lymph nodes and pancreas."

No doubt Janet had suffered greatly during her last days, thought Ferd, *and Dwight had watched her steady downfall. Perhaps it was no surprise that he had descended into alcoholism.* Ferd gripped the wheel tightly as snow fell around him. He let up on the gas, concerned with skidding as he thought about the new life his father had made for himself in New Hampshire. It didn't seem to be a distinguished life, but it was a life nonetheless. He had reinvented himself in a new state, maintaining steady employment, finding a wife, and getting married. And his second marriage, though childless, had by all accounts been successful, until the unfortunate end.

16

On Thursday, at the noon lunch break, Ferd checked his personal emails. He had finally heard from Josh's three teammates. The trip to New Hampshire must've been successful in bringing Josh and Ferd closer since Josh had convinced his team to speak to his father. All agreed to meet with him offsite at a Starbucks near the company headquarters in Mountain View. After a few more emails back and forth, they settled on a schedule later that evening, one meeting right after the other.

Besides Josh and Brady, the team consisted of James Ellison, Sa'Quan Williams, and Colleen O'Keefe. If he could develop reasonable doubt in his father's case, he would tell the district attorney directly. Screw Smedley. He wouldn't give her the satisfaction of a successful defense. If his father's charges got dropped, it would be because of Ferd. Smedley would have nothing to do with it. His ego would tolerate no less.

Before leaving court, Ferd studied the photos of the three team members on the company website so he would recognize them. He called Sonya and left a message that he'd be late for dinner then fought the traffic on southbound 101 to Mountain View.

Sitting at a table near the cash register, James Ellison was engrossed in a paperback book. At first Ferd didn't recognize him since he was looking down, his bald dome reflecting the artificial lighting. Ferd walked right past him before retracing his steps.

"James?"

"Yes. Judge Pitt?"

"Please call me Ferd. Thank you for meeting with me." Ferd excused himself to order a coffee, then sat in a chair directly across the table. "Tell me, James, how long have you worked at CAPSLOCK?"

"A long time. About three years."

"You're a veteran." Ferd couldn't help wondering about the current generation, skipping from job to job after a year or two. There was no loyalty anymore, either from the employee or the employer. By contrast, he had been with the same law firm his entire career, except for a few years stint at the district attorney's office. But the law had changed too with large firms paying huge salaries to baby lawyers who couldn't find their way to the courthouse never mind try a case to a jury. Associates were less inclined to follow the partner track, preferring to try a new firm rather than put in the required hours.

"So you must like it," Ferd added.

"Most of the time. It can be a grind though. Sometimes we work until ten or eleven at night, especially when there's a new product launch. I don't like that."

Ellison had a high-pitched voice and talked without moving his lips as if afraid a bug would fly in his mouth. To Ferd, he seemed a perfect fit for a coding position.

"How was it working for Brady?"

"Mostly good."

"So tell me the good part first."

"He was smart, focused, driven. A real company man. I learned a lot from him."

"How about the bad part?"

"Have you met Colleen yet?"

"No. Later today."

"She's an attractive woman. You'll see. Brady thought so too and didn't mind telling her so. 'Isn't that a lovely blouse?' he'd say. And 'You fill it out so well.'"

"You're saying he was harassing her?"

"Harassment means unwelcome conduct, right?"

"Are you saying Colleen welcomed the comments?"

"Well, she never told him to stop. I pulled her aside a week or so before Pat got killed and told her she didn't have to take that shit. She told me to mind my own business. So I guess she liked it."

Ferd knew from his legal practice that a silent victim was not necessarily one who welcomed the comments. There were a lot of reasons a woman would keep quiet, fear of retaliation being the most common.

"Do you know if Pat and Colleen ever saw each other outside of work?"

Ellison shrugged. "They had lunch together once in a while, but other than that I don't really know, though I often wondered why she let him touch her."

"He touched her?"

"Yeah. He'd put his hand on her shoulder, touch her arm while talking to her. It seemed too familiar. But an affair, now that would explain things."

"Are you saying you never suspected an affair?"

"Maybe I just didn't want to believe it. I suppose I had a bit of a crush on her myself."

"Were you aware Colleen and Josh were dating?"

His eyes bugged out. "No one said so directly, but I kinda suspected."

"Why is that?"

"Well…"

Ferd wondered what Ellison was holding back. He was obviously reluctant to say more.

"You can speak frankly," said Ferd.

"Josh noticed Patrick hitting on Colleen and walked by my cubicle." Ellison looked away. "He was pissed and said, 'I'm going to get even with that fucker.'"

Ferd was stunned. This was not welcome news. "Did Josh say anything else?"

"That's it."

Ferd tensed, not happy with what he was hearing. It was bad enough that the police thought Josh had a motive and opportunity to kill Brady; now he had made a threat and there was a witness to confirm it. Although he could understand why the police might view the threat differently, he knew Josh didn't mean he was going to kill Brady. He could've meant he would report Brady to human resources, or some other minor action. But Josh hadn't disclosed this threat to Ferd, which caused Ferd to worry even more.

"Did you tell the police all this?"

Ellison nodded. "That Friday the police spent the day interviewing the whole team. Everything I've told you, I told the police."

"Did they say that Josh was a suspect?"

"Josh? Heavens no, just that they were gathering information."

Ellison looked at his phone, stood up, and grabbed the book he was reading. "I hope this was helpful but I've got to go."

Ferd nodded, thanked him for his time, and glanced at the cover of Ellison's book. It was a Danielle Steel novel.

. . .

FERD SAT AT THE TABLE, scanning his emails, when Sa'Quan Williams entered the cafe. He looked exactly like his photo on the company website. His long hair, replete with red, yellow, and green beads, hung down the back of his neck.

He walked right over to Ferd. "Judge Pitt?" He reached and shook Ferd's hand, nearly crushing him.

"How'd you know?"

Williams surveyed the café. "Easy. You're the oldest dude here."

Ferd smiled. While Williams ordered a coffee, Ferd rubbed his right hand which ached from the handshake. Rarely had Ferd met someone who matched his grip.

"I should also say you look like Josh," Williams said, sitting down.

"Except for the bits of grey hair."

"True. So how can I help?"

"I'm trying to figure out if my father killed Brady. First, what can you tell me about Patrick and Colleen?"

"I didn't know there was a 'Patrick and Colleen.'"

"Pat met Colleen at a bar shortly before he was murdered."

"Whoa!" He sat up straight. "That's news to me. She and Pat had a strange relationship, for sure, but I damn well didn't know they saw each other outside of work."

"What do you mean by 'strange relationship?'"

"Lot of flirting. Pat was more familiar with her than the rest of the team. Different than your typical boss/subordinate relationship."

"Did you ever sense that she resented his attention?"

"Only when Josh was nearby. I don't think Josh was all that happy with Pat."

"Did he ever say anything?"

"Not to me *per se*. But I did notice him getting red and angry when Colleen and Pat were flirting."

"How did Pat and Josh get along otherwise?"

Williams shrugged. "Business-like though I got the feeling they didn't like each other. I do know that Josh was disappointed Pat wouldn't support him for Coder of the Year. In fact, if Pat hadn't died, I would've gotten the award."

Ferd was taken aback. "How do you know that?"

"Pat told me. His vote was the deciding one."

"I understand stock options went with the award."

"Damn right! Pat's death probably cost me close to seven figures."

"What?" Ferd was stunned.

"You heard me."

"That's astounding." His son could be a rich young man.

Ferd couldn't put out of his mind what James Ellison had told him about Josh threatening Brady. "Did you ever hear Josh threaten Brady in any way?"

Williams shrugged. "Don't know about a threat. But after Patrick told Josh he wouldn't support him for Coder of the Year, Josh said, 'You'll be sorry.' Patrick said, 'Are you threatening me?' and all Josh said was, 'You heard me.'"

"I assume you told the police about this." No wonder Josh was considered a suspect, Ferd thought.

"Yeah. They were quite keen to learn about threats."

Ferd thanked Sa'Quan for his candor and waited, anxious and dismayed, for Colleen.

COLLEEN O'KEEFE ENTERED THE CAFÉ, spotted Ferd in back, and waived to him. Ferd stood up to greet her. A striking woman, she was in her mid-twenties, tall and thin with short black hair and a fair complexion. Before sitting down, she ordered an iced macchiato. Josh had told Ferd that Colleen started working for CAPSLOCK shortly after him. She was a couple of years older than Josh and had earned a master's degree in computer science from Cal Poly.

"So you're Josh's dad," she said, sitting down with her drink. "He told me his father was a judge, but he didn't say anything about private investigator."

"A temporary responsibility, I assure you. I appreciate your meeting with me."

"Work has been difficult since Pat was killed. We all miss him so much. What can I help you with?"

"Tell me a bit about him. What kind of a boss was he?"

"Demanding but hands on." Ferd couldn't help but think of the double meaning. "He wouldn't hesitate to sit down and show us exactly how to code. I learned so much from him." Clearly, she had a better impression of Brady than Josh did. Ferd wanted to probe more deeply but – in deference to Josh – without using his courtroom voice. There was no point intimidating this young woman.

"I understand you were with Pat just before his murder."

Her jaw dropped as if she were going to answer but she hesitated, her eyes watering. She looked down, then sipped her drink. "I'm sorry. I still can't believe it. As I said, he was a wonderful boss." She grabbed her drink and again began sucking on the straw. "That night I asked to meet with him to talk about some stuff."

"What kind of stuff?"

"Well, not sure how to say this." She blinked a few times as Ferd kept his gaze on her. He was assessing her credibility as he had countless witnesses as both an attorney and judge. Ferd had developed a knack for weeding out the liars. He could sense dissembling simply from the tone of voice and facial expression. If asked to dissect this skill, he could not elaborate. The tells changed with each person. But he knew a liar when he saw one. Now with Colleen O'Keefe, Ferd saw the same: the woman was either outright lying or holding back the full truth.

She continued. "He was acting too familiar with me at work. Josh didn't like it one bit, which I don't blame him for at all.

Patrick had to run some errands in San Francisco so suggested we meet at the Promenade. I didn't realize it at the time, but Josh overheard us talking. That's why he got to the Promenade before me."

"So what did Patrick have to say?"

"He said he thought he was in love with me and wanted to know if I felt the same way."

"Before then, did he ever give any hint there were problems in his marriage?"

She hesitated, rubbing her eye with her index finger. "He confided in me that there were some problems. His wife wasn't as affectionate as he would've liked. She was a bit of a cold fish is how he put it."

"What did you say to him when he told you he loved you?"

"I told him I was flattered but I was with Josh. He was not happy. We walked out together. When I said goodbye, he pulled me toward him and kissed me full on the lips. I was embarrassed; there were people on the sidewalk. I didn't know what to do. This was my boss! Then he said, 'Let me know if you change your mind.' I never saw him again."

"Did you tell Josh about the kiss?"

"I called him right away. I was so stunned. He was not happy, kept cursing Patrick." Ferd did not like where this was going, though he wondered why O'Keefe was so open with him. *Was she trying to make him suspicious of Josh to divert attention from herself?*

"How about the police? Did you tell them about the kiss?"

She shook her head. "Didn't seem relevant. Besides, I didn't want to hurt his wife. She's already been through enough."

"What about your call to Josh? Did you mention that to the police?"

She looked down for a moment. "Nope. Why should I?"

. . .

ONCE FERD GOT HOME, he went straight to the study to tell Sonya what he had learned. She was working on her laptop, concentrating so much she didn't hear Ferd come up the stairs. When he knocked on the open door, she said, without looking up, "Your dinner's in the oven. Probably dried out by now." She finished typing before looking at him. "Where've you been?"

"Talking to Josh's team."

Sonya swung around and faced him, her jaw clenched. "You're kidding me! On your first day back at work?"

"I told you I had a few loose ends to tie up."

"Ferd, I guess you don't care what your wife thinks. You'll just go ahead and do whatever you damn well want, to hell with the consequences."

Ferd leaned against the door jamb. "Sonya, be reasonable."

"I am being reasonable. Don't forget the brick was thrown through *our* window."

"Okay, I won't bother you with what I learned." He started to walk away.

"Wait! You're not getting off that easy. Give it to me."

He had to be careful how he phrased this information, not wanting to add to her worries. But he had to tell her; she had a right to know.

"They say Josh threatened Brady. Twice. His teammates also told the police."

"So he threatened Brady. How does that connect him to the murder?"

"It doesn't – necessarily."

"What're you saying?" She stood up to face him, her neck and jaw muscles bulging. "Are you saying our son's a murderer? Ferd, how could you?"

"Sonya!"

"I won't have my son even being suspected of such a thing."

"I didn't say that at all. I'm just laying out the evidence."

"Just like a lawyer, huh?"

"No, just like the *police*. You've got to admit it looks bad. Josh was angry at Brady for hitting on Colleen. Brady retaliated by threatening to deny him Coder of the Year. The award included stock options worth close to a million dollars!"

Sonya took a step back as if wanting to distance herself from her husband. She shook her head. "No, it's not true! Your father's the guilty one here, not our son! Josh is not a murderer!" Her voice cracked. "He's not! I tell you he's not!" She stepped forward and before Ferd could respond, reached back and slapped him across the face. Hard. She had never hit him before.

Ferd grabbed her shoulders. "I agree with you: there's no way Josh killed Brady."

She ignored him. "So you think your father is guilty?"

"I-I don't know."

"This is the last straw. I want you done with this investigation. Now! Do you understand?"

"I do; I really do."

But in the back of his mind was a recurring thought: that his father might go to prison for a crime he didn't commit. That summarized Ferd's conundrum: either keep uncovering evidence potentially implicating his son or let his father take the rap. Could he possibly implicate the son he had raised and loved? Or could he let the father he resented, the one who had abandoned his family, go to prison? At first blush, the answer seemed obvious. Screw his father. What difference would it make if another homeless alcoholic went to prison? The world would be a better place. It would be worse to send a young man with a bright future to prison. Josh had much to contribute to society; he was on the verge of greater success in his work. His life would be over if he were convicted. But it went against all of Ferd's beliefs, his ethics, his own training to let an innocent man get convicted. It was wrong; there was no question about it. But Josh was his son; that had to count for something.

17

That night Ferd slept fitfully, constantly visualizing Brady's murder. He saw the faceless killer, the Giants' fan, wearing a Giants cap, lunge toward Brady, knife in hand, and slash him across the throat. The killer stood over him as blood flowed from Brady's neck. Soon air bubbles floated on the blood as Brady made a guttural gurgling sound. The killer reached down and patted Brady's jacket for his wallet, removing it from the left inside pocket. The killer turned and walked away quickly, head down with the brim of the cap hiding the killer's face.

Then Ferd saw Josh behind bars, wearing all orange, a pained expression on his face. Ferd had betrayed his son, condemned him to a life in prison. Josh refused to talk to his father. "I don't have a father," he said repeatedly, an expression Ferd had often used. For thirty-four years of his life, it was the truth. He didn't have a father. Now Dwight Pitt was back in his life, a shadowy figure, having lived an uneventful life. A failure.

When Ferd awoke, something was bothering him. *How could he condemn his father, possibly an innocent man, to a life in prison?* An idea came to him; there just might be a way to get his father off without turning police attention toward Josh. It was a longshot but certainly worth a try. As he was leaving for work, he told Sonya, "I know how to help my father without implicating Josh."

From her seat at the kitchen table, Sonya glared at him.

"Hear me out: I'm going to meet with the district attorney."

"What will that accomplish?"

"I'll point out all the holes in the prosecution case."

"Don't you think his lawyer, Ms. Smedley, has already done that?" She was not happy he was still pushing to get his father off.

"Knowing her, I doubt it. But don't worry: I won't mention Josh."

ON THE DRIVE to the Hall of Justice, Ferd called District Attorney Stephanie Fong and left a message saying he wanted to meet after work. As he took breaks from his calendar during the day, he checked his cell phone, hoping for a return call. When he hadn't heard anything by the end of the day, he decided to visit his mother. She was sitting in the lounge chair reading *People* magazine. Irish music was playing on the stereo. *"I have four green fields, one of them's in bondage. In stranger's hands, they tried to take it from me."*

"Are you still listening to that rebel music?" Ferd placed the Diet Coke he had bought her on the table beside the chair.

"Have a problem with that?"

Ferd laughed. His mother had always played Irish music, usually rowdy rebel or drinking songs. She had stacks of CDs from the Dubliners, Wolftones, and other Irish groups. In her younger days, her taste was more tame, often directed to Bing Crosby, who was not a favorite of Ferd. Bing was too mellow, boring even, with no edge to his music. Ferd was glad when his mother got hooked on the rowdy songs when he was in high school.

He sat down on the couch. "I just got back from New Hampshire."

"Why in God's name would you go there?"

"To get to know my father."

"Mother of God."

"It was cold, but productive. Seems your ex-husband lived a mostly peaceful life."

He told her about Dwight's fraudulent insurance scheme. "His wife had just died. Seems she had breast cancer. Dad hasn't been the same since."

"That's a sad story."

"One strange thing: he never mentioned having children. His brother-in-law, his best friend, his boss all thought he was childless. It was as if Claire and I didn't exist."

"And why should that surprise you? Didn't he ignore you completely after he left?"

"Yeah. I guess I was more disappointed than surprised." Ferd wondered why he had felt anything at all but realized there was a void inside him where his father should have been. Perhaps after all those years without him, Ferd hoped his father was at least thinking of him, wishing him the best.

His mother sipped her soda, looking down at the magazine in her lap. She seemed to go somewhere else, perhaps thinking of better times with Dwight. "So how does all this help your murder investigation?"

"I don't know that it does, but it gives me a better perspective on the old man. He's not quite the ogre I had made out. But I got nowhere on the essential question of why he deserted his family in San Francisco."

She continued sipping her soda. Ferd knew from experience she wouldn't contribute any information on his father's departure and she didn't disappoint. "I'd say you'd better ask him. And maybe ask him why he never acknowledged you and your sister."

"I have asked him, but he hasn't given me a satisfactory answer. And you don't seem to want to answer either. So I guess I'll try him again." He stood up to leave.

"You're going to jail?"

"That a statement or a question?"

"A question of course." His mother held her hand up to her face, trying to stifle a laugh.

18

It was close to nine o'clock the next day when Ferd arrived at the jail. The deputy quickly retrieved his father. They exchanged greetings then Ferd wasted no time getting down to business. "I don't have much time, but I wanted to let you know I just got back from New Hampshire. Talked to some people you know."

"Is that right? So what have you found out?"

"You never told anyone you had children. Why was that?"

Dwight closed his eyes, lowering his head. "Ahhh... I was starting a new life."

"So you just forgot about the old one, the family you had left behind?"

"What can I say?"

Ferd couldn't believe his father was so nonchalant about his children. "Tell me why you left."

"Your mother knows. Why not ask her?"

"I did. She said to ask you."

"I'm afraid it has to come from your mother."

Ferd bit his lip, furious with this response. *Why wouldn't his parents share this information with him? What could be so horrible that they'd want to keep it from their children?* He considered walking out but knew that would accomplish nothing.

"You're both being ridiculous." He paused. "I read Janet's autopsy report. She was a sick woman. The cancer had really spread."

Dwight nodded.

"Apparently people thought you had something to do with her death."

"What the fuck?"

"Just a rumor floating around."

"That's fucking ridiculous." His tone was dismissive, outraged. Ferd looked at him closely, searching for the tells of a liar. He was satisfied his father was being truthful.

"I met your old boss. He said you were fired for committing insurance fraud."

Dwight shook his head as if trying to dispel this idea from his mind. "I was in a bad place."

"Seems like you went from a bad place to a worse one."

"That wasn't the plan. I just had to get away."

"I also met your brother-in-law."

"How is Dave?"

"Didn't seem like you two were particularly close."

"We weren't. He always acted like the big brother, criticizing Janet's choices in life, thinking he knew better. Jesus Christ, the guy works at an auto parts store."

"How about Walt Brown and Father O'Neil? You had some friends back there."

"Not many. I was never one for socializing. Walt's a good guy. He kept me sane right after Janet died. And the good Father... I like him. I wasn't deeply into the Catholic thing, but I liked reading the Bible at church."

"Are you reading it in here?"

Dwight frowned. "I can't get any books in here. I sit in my

cell all day and all night, letting time slide by. One good thing is I feel better. At least jail is good for sobering up."

"Glad to hear it." Ferd looked away, thinking of how to phrase the next series of questions. "I want to go back to the night of the murder. I know your lawyer won't let you talk details but tell me this: were you too drunk to remember what happened?"

Dwight shook his head back and forth. "Was I drunk that night? Yeah. So what? I got drunk every night, and most days too."

"Do you remember seeing Brady at the Promenade?"

"Have I been to that bar? I don't usually hang out in bars."

"They said you hung out front sometimes."

"Might have. But all I've seen of Brady is his photo in the Chronicle."

"I saw a video of you at the corner store a little while before the murder. So you were in the area."

"Yeah, so what? A thousand other people probably were there too."

"Not at that time of night in that location."

"Okay. What do you want me to say? I didn't kill the guy, period."

Ferd got up to leave but remembered one last subject. "Oh, what happened to your house in Manchester? I hear it's in foreclosure."

"Yeah, I stopped making payments when I left."

"Maybe I can help you out with that."

Dwight smiled. "I'm touched that you'd do that."

"But only if these charges are dismissed." He almost shook his father's hand goodbye but thought better of it. As the deputy opened the door and Ferd walked through, he came upon Nicole Smedley, and tension filled his body. "Why, Judge Pitt, I was just going to check on my client."

"He's doing better, no thanks to you."

"What do you mean?"

"With the evidence against him, there's no reason these charges shouldn't be dismissed."

Smedley shuffled her feet, looking down. "I realize he's your father but don't tell me how to handle my case. All the evidence will come out at the prelim. I suspect Dwight will walk."

Ferd wondered what Smedley was referring to but held his tongue. He hated the sound of her voice. Everything about Smedley bugged him: her dismissive tone, sense of superiority, arrogant attitude.

"In the meantime," she said, looking toward the room where Dwight waited, "I'd appreciate it if you didn't interfere in my case."

Ferdinand didn't like her tone. "I take it you mean my father's case?"

"He may be your father but he's *my* client." She was getting agitated. "I understand you've been talking to the police and witnesses and even viewing video. I don't appreciate your injecting yourself into this case. And for the record, I had nothing to do with the brick being thrown through your window."

"Ms. Smedley, you're out of line." Ferd bit his tongue, not wanting to explode at this presumptuous bitch. He knew that would get him nowhere.

"*I'm* out of line?" She raised the volume just a bit, trying to assert her superiority. "Don't you realize this could undermine your father's defense?"

"I don't know what the hell you're talking about." He had nearly succumbed; her tone had gotten the better of him. He took a deep breath. "If you'd done your job, my father wouldn't be sitting in jail now."

"I am doing my job; I'm preparing his defense. The problem is every time my investigator talks to a witness, she learns that you've already talked to them."

"I don't see the problem, Ms. Smedley."

"The problem, Judge Pitt, is that the witnesses are clamming up, saying they already gave you all the information. They don't want to talk to us."

I can't blame them for not wanting to talk to you, thought Ferdinand. "Perhaps you need another investigator."

Smedley exhaled deeply. "I have a very good investigator. She's been with the office for fourteen years. May I ask what you plan to do with all the information you've gathered?"

"Yes, you may." Ferd let that sit for just a moment before continuing. "I plan on using it to get my father acquitted."

"Then do you mind sharing the information with me?"

It was Ferdinand's turn to exhale deeply. "As soon as I have anything solid, I will give you the utmost consideration."

"I don't like the sound of that." Smedley paused for several seconds, waiting for Ferd's response. When he said nothing, she said, "I'm afraid I'll have to use the nuclear option."

"And that would be?"

"The Commission on Judicial Performance. I don't think they'd take kindly to a judge interfering with a pending case, even if the defendant is your father."

"I'm not afraid of the Commission," Ferd said, though indeed he was getting nervous. The Commission could discipline him and, at worst, remove him from the bench. "Do what you have to do."

19

That's all Ferd needed: a complaint before the Commission, just when his judicial career was getting started. Ferd drove around the city aimlessly, through Union Square to North Beach and Fisherman's Wharf. At the Presidio he pulled over, got out of the car, and stared at the bay and the Golden Gate Bridge. *God, this is a beautiful city,* he thought. *I can't lose sight of that no matter how bleak things seem.*

When Ferd arrived home after wandering, he could hear the television blaring. Sonya was on the couch glued to the TV. She was so engrossed she hadn't heard Ferd come in. He purposely slammed the door to get her attention and she turned sharply toward him.

"Ferd, you've got to watch this. Look, it's that awful woman Smedley."

Ferd took a seat beside his wife and stared at the screen. Nicole Smedley was standing behind a podium outside the Hall of Justice with the public defender and his assistant behind her. "I have called this press conference to disclose a gross abuse of public trust. As many of you know, I am defending Dwight Pitt against very serious charges. My client's son, Judge Ferdinand Pitt, has interfered with my defense of the case by talking to several witnesses, perhaps tainting their potential testimony. I have learned that Judge Pitt has done this on his own without the approval – or indeed the knowledge – of the presiding judge. In taking these actions, Judge Pitt has violated the judicial code of ethics requiring him to maintain impartiality at all times and further prohibiting him from commenting on a pending case. I am calling on the Commission on Judicial Performance to investigate Judge Pitt and instruct him to cease and desist this unethical conduct. If his conduct continues, my client will be denied his constitutional rights to due process and a fair trial."

Ferdinand closed his eyes, not wanting to look at Smedley anymore. Sonya spoke first. "That bitch! How dare she accuse you of being unethical? After all the crap she's pulled during the election, calling you Ferd-the-Nerd and attacking your competence. What nerve!"

Before Ferd could respond, his cell phone rang. He looked at the screen. *Oh my God!* he thought. It was Carol Bradstein. She must've been watching the news conference. Ferd threw the phone on the coffee table as if it were a hot coal, wanting no part of the presiding judge.

Sonya glanced at the phone. "What're you going to do? You can't avoid her forever."

"I know," Ferd said, leaning back and kicking his feet onto the table. "What a fucking mess! And all because of my old man. I wish he'd never come back into my life."

Sonya reached over and held his hand. "Why not put aside all this stuff with your father? You should be focusing on your job as a judge, not running around from here to kingdom come searching for evidence."

"It's not that easy. If the old man's found guilty, I'll be tainted forever."

"You don't know that. What about that public defender who became district attorney? His parents were Weathermen who were involved in a robbery and murder. That didn't seem to hurt his career. Besides, as much as I dislike that woman, shouldn't you let Smedley defend your father?"

Ferd took Sonya's hand in both of hers. "I know I have to deal with Carol." He put her hand down and stood up. "But let me give this more thought."

"Good idea," said Sonya.

But as Ferd walked out of the living room, he slammed his palm against the wall, causing an indentation. He walked from one end of the house to the other and, when that wasn't enough, walked around the block. He knew Bradstein was going to tell him to lay off the case. But he wasn't finished with his investigation. Ferdinand received several more calls from Bradstein that evening before turning off his phone. He didn't even bother checking voicemail.

THE NEXT MORNING, he went outside to get the Chronicle and, as soon as he pulled the newspaper from the plastic bag, noticed his photo on the front page. The headline read: "Judge Interferes with Murder Case." The last thing he wanted to do was read the article, so he threw the paper into the recycling bin. He waited a few minutes, stewing, then pulled the paper from the bin. The article had more quotes from Smedley, but didn't add much to the story on the television.

He turned on his cell phone and noticed several more voicemails from Bradstein. There were also half a dozen calls from Curt Rodda, his campaign manager. He would be pissed Ferd hadn't kept him in the loop about looking into his father's case. Finally, gathering his courage, he decided to return Bradstein's calls first.

"Carol, it's Ferd."

"Well, Judge Pitt," she said, emphasizing *Judge*, "I certainly appreciate your returning my calls." Her tone was definitely angry. "I don't usually call judges off hours, but in this case, I had no choice. You do know why I called?"

Ferdinand didn't like her holier-than-thou attitude but decided to let it slide. He still depended on the presiding judge for his courtroom assignments so he didn't want to alienate her. "Yes, Carol, I saw the news. And let me say that Nicole Smedley exaggerates. Although I have been investigating my father's case, I haven't tainted any witnesses. That's absurd."

"And that's not really the issue now, is it?" Ferd could tell this would be an uphill battle. "You're interfering in an ongoing criminal investigation. That could be considered a crime, let alone a violation of the Canons of Judicial Ethics."

Ferdinand blurted, "Bull—" before catching himself.

"It's not bullshit, Judge Pitt. I'm not in the habit of issuing orders to my colleagues but I want to be clear. I am ordering you to cease this investigation of yours *immediately*. Is that clear?"

Ferdinand paused for a few seconds just to show her he wasn't worried. "I'm afraid I can't do that, Carol. If I leave my father's fate in Smedley's hands, he's doomed."

"Judge Pitt! That's insubordination."

"I don't intend to be insubordinate. I have my reputation to consider."

"As much as you may dislike Smedley," Bradstein said, "I think she's a talented defense lawyer. If your father's innocent, I'm sure she'll be able to convince a jury."

"I don't agree."

Bradstein sighed, clearly exasperated. "I hope you'll use the rest of today to reflect on your behavior and perhaps re-read Rothman's *Judicial Conduct Handbook*. Might do you some good."

Piss off, thought Ferdinand. He had read that book before

taking the bench. It was long, detailed, and boring. If a judge's conduct had to be as restricted as Rothman suggests, he might as well live in a closet. No doubt Rothman would look askance at Ferdinand's conduct in his father's case.

"I will do as you suggest," Ferdinand said, knowing he wouldn't bother with either of her suggestions.

"Unless you cease this ridiculous behavior, I will have no choice but to report this conversation to the Commission."

"Well, I'm ready to take my lumps," Ferdinand said as he hung up, struggling with the urge to toss his phone against the wall.

FERD WATCHED sports on TV the rest of the day, his mind wandering to thoughts of a Commission investigation. So far, his judicial career had been untarnished, and he was determined to keep it that way.

His thoughts were interrupted by his phone ringing. It was Rodda. Ferd answered. "Curt, sorry I didn't get back to you. Once again, the shit's hit the fan."

"I know; that's why I've been calling. Why didn't you tell me you've been investigating your father's case? I could've gotten in front of it to minimize the harm. Now, you're being fried on social media."

"What happened to exposing Smedley's conflict of interest?"

"Yeah, that worked at first. But she's turned things around with her grandstanding press conference. The buzz now is that she's dedicated to defending your father, and you're the one in the way."

Oh, shit, thought Ferd. His head was pounding. It seemed like he was being attacked on all sides. "What do you suggest we do?"

"You've got to lay off your father's case for a while, at least until things blow over."

"You mean leave him in Smedley's hands?"

Rodda grunted. "I know that's not ideal. You've got a few events coming up – the bar association debate in particular; it'd be nice if you could say you're no longer looking into the case."

"What am I supposed to say about my father's guilt or innocence?"

"Tell them he's innocent. That's a pretty safe statement, particularly since his trial is months away."

20

Between Bernstein and Rodda, Ferd thought he couldn't win. He needed a distraction. He yelled upstairs to Sonya. "I'm going to the grocery store. Is there anything you want me to pick up?"

She walked to the top of the stairs. "What're you thinking for dinner?"

"How about I make fettuccine carbonara?"

"Sounds fattening. We'll need a salad."

"I'll get salad fixings too."

Ferd opened the front door, but Sonya asked, "How'd it go with Carol?"

"Not good. She threatened to go to the Commission as well. Then Curt Rodda called. I'm getting it from all sides."

"Maybe you should listen to them. And to me for a change."

"Goodbye, Sonya."

He drove to Lucky's at the Lakeshore Mall and parked in front of the store. He grabbed a cart and made his way to the produce section where he picked out salad fixings. As he put avocados in his cart, he looked behind him since he had a strange feeling someone was watching him. While other shoppers and a couple of workers went about their business, he saw no one suspicious. He scanned the ceiling, thinking there might be surveillance cameras, but saw nothing. At the pasta aisle, he grabbed a bag of fettuccine and placed it in his cart. From the end of the aisle, a female shopper approached, pushing a cart. She was heavily made up, but Ferd was sure he recognized her. As she walked closer, her eyes searching the shelves, he was taken aback. *Could she have been the one watching him?*

"Ms. Brady," he said, "it's good to see you're out and about."

She appeared startled, taking a step back. "Judge Pitt, I didn't think I'd see you again." She was dressed in a colorful skirt and waist-length grey jacket and appeared much better than when Ferd had first met her. She paused and stepped closer to him. "I saw on the TV and in the Chronicle that you're in some trouble."

"It's nothing to be concerned about." Ferd tried not to show surprise at seeing her. After his meeting at her home, he expected he'd never talk to her again. She had been circumspect then, a bit aloof, which Ferd understood completely. He was surprised she had even met with him.

"So does this mean you're ceasing your investigation?" She looked away.

"I haven't completed my investigation, but from what I've learned my father is innocent."

"What makes you say that?" Her eyes focused on Ferd.

"Lots of reasons." Ferd looked around, making sure no one was within earshot. He waited for an older man to walk by. "I'll give you one: the killer wore a Giants cap. My father is on video fifteen minutes before the murder without a cap."

"I thought the video from the Blue Arms showed your father?"

"I don't think so. It could show anyone."

She remained quiet for several seconds. "Where does that leave me?"

"You? What do you mean?"

"How can I go on not knowing who killed my husband?"

Ferd could understand her need for closure, but he had nothing to offer her. "I'm afraid I can't help. But there's one thing you can tell me."

"What could that possibly be?"

Ferd knew he had to be delicate but figured he had nothing to lose. A few shoppers lingered nearby. After they left, he said, "I've learned that your husband met a woman the night he was killed." He paused, awaiting her response. All he heard was a deep inhale and exhale.

Her eyes narrowed and she gritted her teeth. "That's disturbing to say the least."

"Did you have any reason to suspect your husband of having an affair?"

"M-my husband was a good man."

"You didn't answer my question."

"Lots of women were attracted to Patrick. He was handsome, successful, and could be charismatic when he wanted. It wouldn't surprise me if a gold-digger were after him."

"Did Patrick ever say that happened?"

"One time he said there was a woman at work who seemed to have a crush on him."

So Ms. Brady knew about Colleen. Sensing he was getting somewhere, he probed further. "There was one woman on your husband's team: Colleen O'Keefe. Have you ever met her?"

"The shameless hussy? I've met her."

There was an edge to her voice that hadn't been there before.

"Where did you meet?"

"At a company cocktail party celebrating a new software release. Now that you mention it, she was all over Patrick."

"So did you suspect she was interested in him?"

"It was obvious."

"Was he interested in her?"

"Judge Pitt, that's a rude question to ask of a widow." She gripped her cart tightly, which Ferd noticed was empty.

"My apologies, Ms. Brady, but I'm trying to get a complete story of Patrick's last few hours."

"Well, I can't help you. I was home alone watching TV."

He sensed he had touched a nerve. He grabbed ahold of his cart and started walking away. "Take care, Ms. Brady."

"And you too."

After checking out, he put the groceries in the trunk of his car, got in the driver's seat and stared at the front of the store. *Something's fishy here*, he thought. He waited a few minutes until Ms. Brady exited. He thought it odd that she was not carrying anything other than her purse. *Why had she not bought any groceries?*

She walked around the corner near Peet's. Ferd got out of his car and followed her. He wanted to see if she were driving a dark sedan like the one he'd seen outside his house just after the brick went through the window. He jogged to the corner and didn't see her. He thought he'd lost his chance when he heard a car engine start. Ferd ran over and tried to get a look at the driver's face as the car backed out of a parking space. The driver's head was turned, but when she finished backing up, she looked forward. For a moment their eyes locked. Ferd was disappointed that the widow Brady was driving a maroon Cadillac SUV and not the dark sedan he had seen.

21

During the lunch break on Monday, District Attorney Fong's assistant finally called back. With Ferd's gentle urging, she set a meeting for that evening. Having finished his calendar early, Ferd prepared for the meeting as if he were delivering a closing argument: marshalling all the evidence, outlining his presentation, and organizing his thoughts so they would have the most convincing impact. When he arrived at the district attorney's building on Rhode Island Street, the assistant was there to greet him. Her grey hair was pulled back into a tight ponytail. "Judge Pitt?"

"Yes."

"I'm Maddie, Ms. Fong's assistant. Follow me; I'll take you to the main conference room." She led Ferd onto the elevator then down the hall to a large conference room. Already seated around a long gleaming table were Fong, Nellie Ambrose, the line deputy handling Dwight's case, and – to Ferd's dismay – Nicole Smedley.

Ferd stopped in his tracks. "What's she doing here?"

"I felt it was only right that she be included," Fong said. "After all, it is her case."

"She reported me to the Commission."

"You left me no choice," Smedley said.

"And now you want to take advantage of what I've learned?"

Smedley turned toward Fong, looking for help, but she demurred. "Perhaps we could all get down to business," Fong said.

Ferd sat down across from Fong without shaking hands, his fists clenched. He told himself to stay cool and relax; he owed it to his father not to lose his cool. He would just have to put up with Smedley for the time being. He couldn't be thrown off his game. He had to remember all the hours of preparation he had put into this meeting.

He looked across the table at the three women facing him: Fong, a forty-something Asian woman with short black hair and large lips; Ambrose, about Fong's age but Caucasian with long stringy brown hair; and Smedley, the lesbian deputy public defender with attitude.

"Judge Pitt," began Fong, "we all know how difficult this has been for you. No one relishes the idea of a family member being charged with such a serious crime. Having them appear in court in front of you must've been a nightmare. So we appreciate your coming forward and sharing with us what you've learned."

Ferd immediately discerned a weakness in Fong's approach. "Let me begin by correcting something you said: this has not been as difficult on me as you might think. I hadn't seen my father in over thirty years after he abandoned the family. So I have no emotional attachment to him or to these charges. But I know a bogus prosecution when I see one."

"What makes you think this prosecution is bogus?" asked Ambrose with an edge in her voice. No doubt she'd played a significant role in bringing and maintaining the charges.

"Because there's no way you can prove murder beyond a reasonable doubt. My investigation indicates that you'll be lucky to get by a preliminary hearing."

"We're listening," Fong said.

"Let's review the evidence you have against my father: he used Brady's credit card at Safeway, his fingerprints are on the wallet, and a partial print is on the knife. You have no evidence of how he came upon the wallet. You assume he took it from Brady after he supposedly stabbed him, but there's no evidence to support that assumption. More likely he found the wallet in the gutter or a trash can where the real murderer had thrown it. As for the knife, you know as well as I do that a partial print isn't worth squat. I bet your expert will admit the print could belong to dozens of other people. Finally, you have no evidence of any previous contact between them, so what's his motive? Indeed, you have no evidence of any motive except possibly for a robbery."

"That's a pretty good motive," said Ambrose.

"Is it now? My father was an alcoholic, living on the streets. You don't think he had other opportunities to rob people. His priors were for shoplifting and petty theft. No violence whatsoever in his background. So, no, I don't think it's a good motive."

"Doesn't it make sense that your father stabbed Brady because he resisted the robbery?" asked Ambrose.

"Ah, you've got a theory for everything. What you don't have is evidence."

"We appreciate your point of view, Judge Pitt," said Fong, "and will discuss the points you've raised. Is there anything else you want us to know?"

"Yes, as a matter of fact. There's a corner convenience store on Jones Street – the Sunnyside Market I believe it's called. I've looked at the video surveillance footage from the night of the murder." He pulled out his cell phone and scrolled to a photo, holding it up for all to see. "This is my father. Note the time stamp: 19:15, fifteen minutes before the murder." He scrolled to another photo. "And here's the murderer. What's different about these two photos?"

"One's wearing a Giants cap," said Ambrose. "He could've had it in his pocket before."

"Really? And he put it on just to murder Brady? Unlikely. Think you can convince a jury that he put on a baseball cap in the fifteen minutes between the market and the murder? I doubt it. Just doesn't ring true." Ferd paused for effect then dove into his closing. "Before I finish, let me say that it's highly unlikely the video of the murderer shows my father. In fact, the quality's so poor, you can't even tell if it's a man or a woman."

"That's because of the baseball cap," said Ambrose.

"Exactly. The cap obscures the face."

"Is there anything else you want to tell us?" asked Fong.

Ferd thought about Josh and Colleen. "That's enough for now."

For the first time Smedley spoke up. "Are you saying you have more evidence you're not sharing with us?"

Ferd had made a good case for his father's innocence without bringing up the CAPSLOCK connection. "I've said my piece."

"*My* investigator says you've talked to more people than you're letting on," said Smedley. "Do you mind sharing that information with us?"

Ferd glared at her for several seconds, then stood up. Gritting his teeth, he said, "You want to know what the witnesses said? Then do your job and talk to them. Stop using this case as an opportunity to win election to my seat. I'm done." He turned to the prosecutors. "Ms. Fong, Ms. Ambrose, I think I've made a compelling case for dismissal of the charges against my father. When can I expect to hear from you?"

Fong also stood and reached over to shake Ferd's hand. "I'll call you in a few days. Thank you for your time."

Without so much as a glance at Smedley, he said, "Good day, counsel."

FERD WAS STILL STEAMING about Smedley as he drove home on the interstate. He hit the right turn signal as he was approaching the exit. A black sedan appeared behind him at a fast rate of speed, passed him on the left then attempted to cut him off, forcing Ferd to move to the right of the lane. The sedan kept moving over into his lane, forcing him nearly off the road into the cement retaining wall on the edge of the freeway. He was so focused on avoiding a collision that he didn't get a look at the driver. Only by slamming on his brakes did he avoid hitting the wall. The sedan sped off down the interstate.

Shaken, Ferd took the exit and parked, trying to gather himself. After a few minutes of deep breathing to stave off the panic attack brewing in his chest, he dialed Sergeant Hinton. After identifying himself, he said, "Sergeant, someone tried to run me off the road."

"What happened?"

"It was the same car I saw outside my house after the brick incident. It cut me off. I'm sure the driver was trying to push me into a wall." He couldn't stop his voice from shaking.

"Was there any contact between the vehicles?"

"No, I managed to avoid it."

"Did you see the driver?"

"No. I was focused on avoiding a collision."

"How about the license plate?"

Ferd inhaled deeply. "Afraid not."

"That doesn't give us much to go on. You sure it was intentional?"

"Yes, it was goddamn intentional! Someone came after me, Sergeant."

"Do you think this had anything to do with your father's case?"

"If not, it seems like quite a coincidence."

"True. Let me see what I can find out. Maybe there's some video in the area."

"I appreciate that." He paused. "I know you don't believe it, but this incident proves I'm onto something here."

"You think someone's still trying to scare you off the case?"

Ferd rolled his eyes, wondering what it would take for Hinton to accept the obvious. "Exactly."

"I'll certainly take that into consideration."

AT HOME, Ferd explained to Sonya how the meeting went. "I think I made a pretty good case for dismissal."

"I trust you, Ferd. But I'm still worried about Josh. When will you hear from the district attorney?"

"In a few days."

Ferd contemplated not telling Sonya what had happened on the freeway, wanting to avoid worrying her even more, but he decided in the end she should know.

"Are we in danger, Ferd?" She moved closer toward him. "This is out of control. How many times did I tell you to drop this investigation? First, we get a brick through the window, now this..." Her voice was full of venom and her anger bothered Ferd. He stepped back so she couldn't slap him again.

"I know. I called the police and let them know what happened, but I doubt anything will come of it. For the time being, we should be extra cautious."

She turned and walked away from him. Ferd wondered if his marriage could withstand this latest setback.

22

That night Ferd had trouble sleeping, wondering if he were getting paranoid. He had been certain that Ms. Brady was driving the dark sedan after the brick incident, but when he encountered her at the mall, she was driving a maroon SUV. Then a dark sedan tried to run him off the road. *Who could it be?* Ferd was at a loss.

Before he had finished his first cup of coffee, FedEx was at the door with a delivery that required his signature. He looked at the envelope and froze: the Commission on Judicial Performance. He had the sudden thought to refuse signing and give the envelope back to the courier. But he shouldn't have been surprised after all the noise that Smedley had made.

Reluctantly he signed for the delivery and tore open the envelope.

Dear Judge Pitt:

I am writing to inform you that the Commission has received a complaint that you have violated the Canons of Judicial Ethics. I will call you in the next day or so to schedule an interview. You have a right to have an attorney represent you at the interview. If you do hire an attorney, please ask him or her to contact me as soon as possible.

Very truly yours,

Nancy Harper

Investigator

Ferdinand crumpled up the letter and threw it on the floor. "Goddamnit! Of all the ridiculous…"

"What is it?" Sonya yelled from upstairs.

"The Commission wants to interview me. I've got to call Henry."

She walked downstairs, noticed the crumpled-up letter on the floor, then reached down to pick it up. Smoothing out the wrinkles, she read it quickly and handed it to him. "Serves you right," she snarled as she walked back upstairs.

FERD WAS PLEASED to return to his old haunting grounds in the financial district. Early for lunch with his ex-partner Henry Smith, he wandered down Trinity Alley and Belden Lane before arriving at the Yangon Star Restaurant, which opened after he joined the bench. The ambience gave him a sense of relaxation, a giant Buddha figure at the entrance in a calm pose with palms raised upward. Large color photos of gold pagodas and lush Inle Lake adorned the walls. The servers were dressed in traditional longyi, some in bright red and blue and yellow.

"Your Honor!" came a voice from the back. Smith was sitting against the wall with his suit jacket wrapped around the seatback and his sleeves rolled up. "Have a seat," he said, shaking Ferd's hand. "How the hell is the bench?"

Ferd gave him a sideways glance and took his seat. "As if you don't know."

"Come on, Ferd, we got this. How's Sonya?"

"I'm afraid this whole situation has put her through the ringer. And me in the doghouse."

"Your wife is a remarkable woman. Wish I had found someone like her." Smith motioned for the waiter. "Two Tiger beers."

"Better make that one," said Ferd. "No drinking while I'm working."

"Not like private practice, is it?"

An African American man with a completely bald head who had once served in the state senate, Smith was known for dating younger woman, most quite beautiful.

"I may have found the one," Smith said. "Her name's Jiselle Cooper. She works in human resources, makes a good living."

"Can't believe you'd actually settle down."

"Maybe I'm maturing. You'll have to meet her. Let's schedule dinner for the four of us."

"Love to," Ferd said as the waiter placed a bottle of Tiger beer in front of Henry. "But first things first. What can I do about this damn Commission investigation?"

Smith drained half the bottle, picked up the cloth napkin from his lap and wiped his lips. "I made a few calls to some lawyer buddies experienced in these sorts of things. First thing we've got to do is find out which canons they think you violated. Then we pretend to cooperate while delaying as much as we can. The more we delay, the more likely they'll lose interest in your case."

"How the hell do we do that?"

"Hey, I'm a busy trial lawyer. I can't just drop everything to meet with this investigator. I'll keep her on a string, you'll see."

After the waiter took their orders, Smith continued. "Once we finally get to the interview, you'll know exactly how to play this. Ferd, I've got your back on this. I'll be with you every step of the way."

Ferd felt somewhat comforted, knowing Henry had his back. He didn't know if Smith's strategy would work but at that moment delay seemed like a good thing.

"So I can leave it in your hands? You'll contact this Nancy Harper?"

"What I always say to clients: your problem is now my problem. Let me worry about it. I'll do everything I can to solve it."

"And what about your fee. I'm a state employee; I can't afford you anymore."

"We'll work something out, no sweat."

Ferdinand smiled, glad to have Henry on his side. When their meals arrived – Yangon chicken on rice for Ferd and tealeaf salad for Henry – Ferd relaxed and turned his attention to less upsetting matters. "How about those Giants? They're on a winning streak."

They talked sports throughout lunch until the end when Ferd said, "I'm worried about Josh." Looking around to make sure no one was in earshot, Ferd told Smith about Josh's involvement in the Brady case. "The cops said Josh was the prime suspect until they got evidence against my father."

"Damn! You don't think Josh had something to do with the murder?"

"Of course not. He's my son; I know him. But I also know how things look. No question he had motive and opportunity. If Brady hadn't been killed, Josh would've lost stock options worth maybe a million dollars." Ferd told him about Brady harassing Colleen and the meetings at the Promenade.

"Josh is a head-strong young man. But murder? I don't see it."

"I don't either but I'm worried that when they realize the case against my dad won't stick, they'll refocus on Josh."

"So you didn't mention him in your meeting with the DA?"

"I purposely steered clear of him. Somehow, they sensed I was holding back. But now I'm afraid I'll see my loser father set free only to watch Josh get arrested. Lose-lose."

Smith sipped his water and asked, "What about the girlfriend...Colleen?"

"What do you mean?"

"She was the last one to see Brady alive. Isn't she also a suspect? Certainly, she too had both motive and opportunity."

"Well, opportunity maybe, but motive? Harassment and a quick smooch? I don't know." Ferd finished his beer and wiped his mouth. "Anyway, I shouldn't have bothered you with this, but I just had to talk to someone. Sonya's pissed at me for getting involved in the first place. The good news is that my father's probably innocent. I thought Fong might release him, but now I suspect she'll stick to her guns."

"Let's see what happens. In the meantime, you've got to focus on the Commission."

"I hear you."

23

B y Wednesday Ferd had heard nothing from Fong and was getting increasingly upset. He sensed Fong was blowing him off but didn't know why. It shouldn't have taken her that long to reach a decision, especially after the way he had laid everything out. Ferd didn't want to appear overanxious, so he refrained from calling her office, even though it was driving him crazy. All he could do was wait. As a lawyer and a judge, he knew how to evaluate a case and knew the evidence was in his father's favor. From the prosecution's perspective, the case was a loser. Surely Fong could see that. Or maybe she had discovered Josh's connection and was preparing to prosecute him. That was Ferd's greatest fear, that the police and prosecution would do a more thorough job, focus on the CAPSLOCK connection, and go after Josh.

While he was driving home from work, Sergeant Hinton called. "Judge Pitt, I wanted to let you know what I've learned about the freeway incident. We were unable to find any video of the car. I checked DMV records of all the people who knew about your investigation, including your son's team at CAPSLOCK and Denise Brady. Ms. Brady's lawyer even sent us a photo of her car, which is a maroon Cadillac SUV, consistent with the DMV records. The only one with a dark sedan is Colleen O'Keefe, who drives a black Lexus."

Ferd tightened his grip on the steering wheel. "I can't believe Colleen is behind all this."

"We're looking into it. I wanted to check with you before I devote more resources. Are you sure it wasn't just a road rage incident?"

Ferd's initial reaction was to scream at her to do her job, but he bit his tongue. "I didn't do anything while driving to piss anyone off. I'm a careful driver."

"Got it. So we'll keep looking into these two incidents. I'll keep you posted."

A minute after he hung up, his phone rang again. It was Henry Smith.

"Ferd, they want to do the interview next Tuesday. I could delay it a little bit, but I'm telling ya, this investigator is a b —itch."

"It sounds like they're out to get me."

"Nah, it's just business. The Commission has to justify its existence and you're a high-profile case. Let's meet Saturday to prep."

"Can't wait."

STEPHANIE FONG finally called on Thursday morning. Ferd had just arrived in his chambers for the morning break when his cell phone rang. "Judge Pitt," she began, "I apologize for taking so long to get back to you. I've discussed your father's case extensively with my staff and we've decided to proceed with the prosecution. I know that's not the answer you hoped for."

"No, it's not. I'm surprised. Do you really think you can get a conviction with such slim evidence?"

"The prelim is set for next week. We'll let the judge decide if there's probable cause to continue with the case."

"That seems shortsighted. Even if you get by the prelim, you still have to convince a jury of my father's guilt."

"I realize that."

She was obviously holding something back. *Now I get it,* Ferd thought. *Fong is afraid of the adverse publicity if she dismisses the case. She was up for reelection this year and letting politics drive her decision-making. She was also probably concerned about public reaction to her buckling under pressure from a sitting judge.* It seemed to Ferd she was taking the easy way out by dropping the decision onto a judge, undoubtedly a visiting judge since Ferd's colleagues would have to recuse themselves.

"Thank you for getting back to me, Ms. Fong. I will continue to monitor this case closely."

"I'm sure you will, Judge Pitt."

SONYA RETURNED HOME from her hot yoga class still dripping with sweat. "Why are you looking so forlorn? What happened?"

"Bad news. The DA is proceeding with my father's case."

To Ferd's surprise, she looked relieved. He realized why. "This doesn't mean Josh is out of the woods. She could still change her mind down the road."

"What're you going to do now?"

"I'm going to take a couple of vacation days to watch the preliminary hearing. I want to see if they have any evidence they haven't shared yet."

She looked askance at him. "Oh, Ferd," she said, shaking her head, "I wish this whole thing were over."

24

After a grueling practice session on Saturday with Henry, who had prepared Ferd thoroughly, subjecting him to a mock interview and even getting nasty at points, Ferd spent the rest of the weekend researching motions to suppress scheduled for upcoming hearings. He found it hard to concentrate as his thoughts kept returning to the Commission. He had worked hard to establish a sterling reputation in the legal community, both before and after becoming a judge. He hoped he hadn't thrown that out the window by inserting himself in his father's case.

The Commission on Judicial Performance interview was at 4 o'clock on Tuesday at the headquarters in the Civic Center. Ferd had gone through his calendar quickly, finishing the last arraignment at 3:30 before hurrying out the door. Nancy Harper greeted them cordially then led them to a conference room. Sitting at one end was a court reporter, an older man with a thick white moustache. Smith pointed to the reporter.

"I didn't know this interview would be reported. Is that necessary?"

"This is a formal proceeding," Harper said. "We could video it, but I didn't think that was necessary."

Smith glanced at Ferd who, per Smith's previous instructions, maintained an expressionless demeanor. It was hard for Ferd to play the stoic since he typically let people know what he was thinking. Except when he was on the bench, he wasn't the type of person to hold things close to his vest. He prided himself on being frank. But now, he knew, was not the time to let it all hang out.

Harper was tall, thin, in her early forties, with mid-length dirty-blonde hair. She was wearing a dark blue pants-suit with no jewelry. Ferd had researched her online and discovered she was an award-winning plaintiffs lawyer having won Trial-Lawyer-of-the-Year honors from the Consumer Attorneys of California. Years ago, she had applied for the San Mateo bench but – despite being interviewed by the Judicial Nominees Evaluation Commission – had never received an appointment. Ferd figured she joined the Commission on Judicial Performance to work out her frustration at not being appointed by going after sitting judges. If she couldn't join them, she would attack them.

The interview began with background questions regarding Ferd's education and work history. He answered each question directly, not volunteering information. Occasionally Harper paused, waiting for Ferd to elaborate, but he just stared back at her, awaiting the next question. She seemed taken aback by his approach, apparently not used to witnesses acting so cool under pressure. Finally, after twenty minutes, she got to the meat of the matter.

"Is it correct that your father is Dwight Pitt?"

"Yes."

"Did he ever appear in your courtroom?"

"Yes, he did. For arraignment. But I recused myself as soon as I figured out who he was."

Ferd had gone beyond the question, breaking his own rule, just to head off any impression that he had acted improperly.

"Before then, when was the last time you'd seen your father?"

"When I was twelve years old."

"You had no contact with him in all that time?"

"None. He disappeared from my life."

"Do you know why he did that?"

Ferd looked at Smith, waiting for an objection. Picking up the cue, Smith said, "That doesn't seem relevant."

"Well," Harper said, "it's just background."

"I suggest you move on."

Harper frowned but carried on. "Judge Pitt, did you discuss your father's murder case with him?"

"Of course, I did. How could I not?"

Harper ignored his taunting question. "Even though you knew his case was pending and he was represented by the public defender?"

"I talked to him as a son to his father, not as a judge or in any legal capacity."

"And I suppose you thought that made it appropriate?"

"Just a minute," interjected Smith. "Are you suggesting it was somehow *inappropriate*? If so, I'd like to know what ethical canon you're relying on."

"A judge has to avoid the appearance of impropriety, even in circumstances where there's no impropriety. So, Judge Pitt, can you answer my question?"

"May I have it read back?" Ferd asked, turning toward the court reporter.

The reporter looked at Harper for direction. She nodded, giving her approval, and he read back the question, reciting every word slowly as if acting in a Shakespearean play.

Ferd fought back the urge to smile and said simply, "Absolutely."

Harper adjusted some papers before asking, "And did you also think it appropriate to interview witnesses in his case?"

Ferd started to answer but caught himself, realizing this was the key question. He had to think carefully. He was suddenly grateful this interview was not being video recorded, since his hesitation could seem incriminating. Henry interjected, "Objection. Vague as to what you mean by 'witnesses.'"

Without taking her eyes off Ferdinand, Harper said, "I think the judge knows what the term 'witnesses' means."

The room went silent, the only sound being Harper's pen clicking repeatedly. Ferd and Henry had rehearsed just this scenario, hoping to force Harper to give a narrow definition of "witnesses." But she didn't take the bait.

"I spoke to several people," Ferd said finally. "It's an open question as to whether they're witnesses."

"Why don't we do it this way," Harper said. "Tell me everyone you've interviewed about your father's case."

"Joanie Merced, manager of the Blue Arms; the proprietor of a corner store, two bartenders at the Promenade Bar, a clerk at Safeway, proprietors of other establishments around the Blue Arms, the victim's wife Denise Brady, and employees of CAPSLOCK."

Henry made a gurgling sound as if choking on Ferd's answer. But Ferd wasn't worried; he knew he'd have to come clean sooner or later. Better to lay everything on the table.

"What motivated you to interview these people?" asked Harper.

Ferd was glad she steered away from asking specifics about his interviews.

"I thought that was obvious," Ferd said. "I wanted to know if my father was guilty of murder."

"Isn't that his lawyer's job?"

"Nicole Smedley? I had no confidence in her, still don't. If my father's guilty, so be it. He should get what's coming to him.

But I didn't want him to be convicted simply because he has a lousy lawyer."

"Judge Pitt, you've been on the bench for about a year and I assume you've read the Canons of Judicial Ethics."

"Of course."

"Then I would point you to Canon 2: 'A judge shall avoid impropriety and the appearance of impropriety in all of the judge's activities.'"

"I'm familiar with it."

"Then surely you must know that acting as a private investigator in a pending criminal case could create the appearance of impropriety."

Smith turned toward her. "Was that a question?"

Harper ignored him. "Let me ask you this: have you ever been licensed as a private investigator?"

"No, I have not."

"Thank you. Those are all the questions I have right now. I will be in touch with you regarding next steps. Mr. Smith, could I talk to you privately."

"Sure. Ferd, do you mind waiting for me by the elevator?"

FIVE MINUTES LATER, Henry Smith came out. "So what did Harper want to talk about?" Ferd asked.

"You're not going to believe this, but she wants to settle."

"Why should I do that?"

"Worst case scenario is they remove you from the bench. Next is a censure. Harper offered to dismiss the charges if you agree to a public admonishment."

"What's that mean?"

"Everyone will know about the discipline, which could affect you for the election or if you want to be elevated to the court of appeal."

"I don't really care if people know I went to the defense of my father."

"Ferd, trust me, you don't want a public admonishment on your record."

"Are you recommending we reject Harper's offer?"

"Let's play it out a little longer. Maybe she'll agree to a private admonishment. That's probably the best we could hope for anyway."

"Alright, but it sure would be nice to get this over with."

AFTER THE COMMISSION INTERVIEW, Ferd went to the club and put in sixty minutes on the treadmill. He was feeling stressed, unsure whether he had sunk his judicial career. He had told the truth. If the truth sunk him, so be it. But he was relieved Harper hadn't pressed him on the details of his interviews. Otherwise, she would have realized that Josh was a potential suspect.

On the way home, he received a call from his campaign manager. "Judge Pitt, pardon my sorry ass for bothering you, but last I looked you were in the middle of a campaign."

"I apologize, Curt, if I hurt your feelings by not calling."

"My feelings be damned. When I sign on to manage a candidate, I expect to win, but I can't win unless the candidate cooperates. I shouldn't have to learn secondhand about your ethics investigation. What the hell?"

Ferd took a deep breath. He realized Rodda was right. "There's just too much going on: I'm trying to look into my father's case, keep my wife happy, and stay out of trouble. You get the picture? I'm not doing a good job in any of those endeavors."

Rodda continued haranguing Ferd. "Right now, all I care about is the bar association debate next week. We need to carve out some time to prepare."

"That's going to be tough."

"What'll be tough is if you get your clock cleaned by Smedley, which is what'll happen if we don't prepare. You know what they say: if you fail to prepare, then you're preparing to fail."

"I've got my father's prelim this week. I've got to be there."

Rodda exhaled deeply. "If he gets held over for trial, I fear the worst."

"I'm keeping my fingers crossed."

"How about Sunday? The debate's a week from Thursday night so that's cutting it close, but better'n nothing."

"I'll meet you at headquarters at one."

"Oh, in case you were wondering, the latest polls show you and Smedley neck to neck. The debate could put you over the top."

"I get it. Thanks." Before hanging up, Ferd added, "Quick question: what do you think'll happen if I get disciplined?"

"Could that happen?"

"They asked me to agree to a public admonishment."

"Jesus, that would suck."

"You're telling me."

"Delay as much as you can. I'd rather the investigation be open on election day, unless you get vindicated."

"Don't think that's going to happen."

25

Ferd parked in his assigned space in the garage beneath the Hall of Justice. He walked through the tomblike garage toward the stairs and climbed toward the second floor.

At the first-floor landing, he wondered who was covering his department, so he entered the first-floor hallway and stuck his head into the courtroom. It was crowded with attorneys and out-of-custody defendants. One defendant, dressed in orange, stood at defense counsel's table as the judge, a sixty-something man, appeared to be taking a plea. The judge was John McDonald, a former plaintiffs personal injury lawyer who recently had been appointed by the governor. McDonald's usual assignment was in traffic court. Presumably judges pro tem, lawyers who volunteered their time, were filling in on traffic court while Ferd was out for the prelim.

Ferd watched for a few minutes until lawyers began arriving, pulling the door open, so he had to step back. He returned to the stairway and marveled at how decrepit the Hall of Justice was. Built from 1958 to 1960, the building had all the charm of a

Soviet office building and was rapidly falling apart, part of it having been declared unsafe in the event of an earthquake. There was an infamous incident where the toilets had overflowed, sending human waste cascading through the ceiling toward unassuming workers below. Efforts to build a new justice center had been met with bureaucratic delays, funding disputes, and general lack of public will. In the meantime, the Hall would have to do – at least for the courts – even after the district attorney moved to newer, fancier digs on Rhode Island Street. Even now, the building smelled like yesterday's garbage.

On the second floor, Ferd made his way to Department 20, anxious to see who would be presiding over his father's prelim. Because of Ferd, no sitting judges could preside; it had to be a visiting judge from another county. Ferd was pleased to see Cheryl Labarle sitting on the bench. Labarle had formerly presided in Marin County and was a regular fill-in at the Hall. She was known as empathic, bright, and fair, a good draw for his father. Ferd entered the courtroom and sat in the back row, trying to look inconspicuous. He watched one case get continued before the judge called for Dwight Pitt, who was soon brought out from the holding tank. He took a seat next to his lawyer, the inimitable Nicole Smedley, who immediately instructed the bailiff to remove the ankle chains and handcuffs. The bailiff, a fifty-something Latino man who was known for his efficient operation of the court calendar, ignored her. Smedley stood up and addressed the judge.

"Your Honor, I request that the chains be removed from my client. He is neither a safety nor flight risk and it's demeaning for him to be presented in public this way."

"Just a moment, Ms. Smedley," said the judge, who gestured for the bailiff to join her at the bench. They whispered for a few minutes before the bailiff stepped down then picked up the phone by his desk.

"As you know, Ms. Smedley," said the judge, "your client is charged with a serious offense. The bailiff is willing to remove the chains as long as he has backup, which he's calling for now."

"For the record, Your Honor," said deputy district attorney Nellie Ambrose as she rose to her feet, "the People object to removal of the chains. This was a heinous crime by a man known to abuse alcohol and I, personally, don't feel safe with the defendant unchained."

"That's ridiculous," said Smedley. "For one thing, Mr. Pitt is innocent and for another, he's completely sober."

"Counsel, enough. I've made my ruling." She turned toward the doorway. "And here's Deputy O'Hara. She will stand in back of the courtroom. Is there a motion to exclude witnesses?"

"Yes, Your Honor," said Smedley.

She turned around to scan the courtroom and caught Ferd's eyes. He glared at her and she glared right back, their enmity palpable. His father then turned to look at Ferd. Without regard for the seriousness of the proceeding, he gave Ferd a little wave.

"Mr. Pitt," Judge Labarle said, "please turn around. You should be giving this hearing your utmost attention."

"Sorry, Your Honor," Dwight said.

Deputy O'Hara approached Ferd and asked him if he were a witness. As she got a closer look, she realized who he was. "Oh, Judge Pitt, she said. "I'm sorry. Didn't recognize you without your robe."

"No problem. I'm here as a member of the public just to observe."

She nodded and returned to her post behind the defendant. A group of reporters entered the courtroom, lugging iPads and laptops, and sat across the aisle from Ferd. He recognized one as Bob Angelo, the legal affairs reporter for the Chronicle. Ferd had met him a few times many years ago when Angelo interviewed him for high-profile cases Ferd was defending. Angelo glanced over, noticing Ferd, and nodded.

"Your Honor, the People would designate Sergeant Carla Hinton as their investigating officer." Ambrose wanted Hinton to stay in the courtroom to observe the testimony before she took the stand.

"She shall be so designated," said the judge. "Ms. Ambrose, please call your first witness."

"The People call Officer Peter Otis to the stand." Ambrose walked to the back of the courtroom and glanced momentarily at Ferd, before opening the door and returning with Officer Otis, a tall Black man with a Fu Manchu. After the clerk had sworn Otis to tell the truth, Ambrose began.

"Sir, how are you employed?"

"I am a police officer with the San Francisco Police Department."

"And how long have you been a sworn peace officer?"

"Going on seven years."

Ferd realized the import of these preliminary questions. If Otis had worked as a peace officer for at least five years, Ambrose could ask him questions that called for hearsay. If he had been a police officer for less, Ambrose would have to establish that he had particularized training in testifying at preliminary hearings.

"Were you on duty on Friday, January 26th of this year?"

"Yes, I was on patrol with my partner Bob Jorgensen."

"Did you receive a dispatch to report to the Safeway store on Market Street in the City and County of San Francisco?"

"Yes, we did."

"Were you told the purpose of the call?"

"Objection," Smedley said, taking her feet. "Double hearsay."

"Your Honor," Ambrose began, "not for the truth."

"What's its purpose then?" the judge asked.

"To explain the officer's subsequent conduct."

"The testimony will be allowed for that purpose."

"Officer, do you have the question in mind?"

"Could you repeat it?"

"Were you told the purpose of the call to Safeway?"

"Fraudulent use of a credit card."

"And what time did you arrive at Safeway?"

Otis stared at Ambrose blankly. "May I look at my report?"

"Will that refresh your memory?"

"Yes."

"With Her Honor's permission, you may look at your report to refresh your memory then turn the report back over."

Otis complied and looked up.

"Has your memory been refreshed?"

"Yes. It was at 1520. So 3:20 p.m."

"Did you encounter anyone there?"

"The store manager approached us. His name is Francisco Hernandez."

"What did Mr. Hernandez tell you?"

"He said his cashier told him…"

Smedley was on her feet, interrupting. "Double hearsay."

"Again, Your Honor," Ambrose said, "not for the truth of what the cashier said, but to explain Mr. Hernandez's subsequent conduct."

"His subsequent conduct's irrelevant," Smedley said.

"I'll allow it," the judge ruled. "Continue."

"Mr. Hernandez told me his cashier had reported an older gentleman using a credit card in the name of a recent homicide victim. His security guard was with the man in the manager's office."

"Did you talk to this man?"

"Yes."

"Did you ask for ID?"

"Yes, he had none, but he gave me his name."

"What name did he give you?"

"Dwight Pitt."

"Did you verify his name in any way?"

"My partner searched a database of booking records and confirmed the name."

"What had he been arrested for previously?"

"Objection, totally irrelevant," Smedley said. "His arrest record has no bearing on whether there was probable cause to arrest him in this case."

"I agree," the judge ruled. "Objection sustained."

Ferd was surprised that Smedley seemed to know what she was doing. Perhaps he had underestimated her. One thing that didn't surprise him was her dismissive tone, which the judge had let slide so far. The sound of her voice was like chalk on a blackboard to Ferd.

"Officer Otis, do you see the man in the courtroom who identified himself at Safeway as Dwight Pitt?"

"Yes, he's sitting over there at the defense table."

"Can you identify an article of clothing he's wearing?"

"He's dressed in all orange."

"Your Honor, may the record reflect that the witness has identified the defendant?"

"The record will so reflect."

Ambrose flipped through her notes. "Did you interview the defendant?"

"I did. The interview was recorded on my bodyworn camera."

"Before interviewing the defendant, did you read him his Miranda rights?"

"Yes, using the department-issued Miranda card."

"Did he acknowledge understanding his rights?"

"He said he did."

"Did the defendant indicate he wanted to waive his rights?"

"He said he wanted to talk to us."

"Objection," Smedley said, "nonresponsive."

"Sustained."

"Move to strike."

"The answer's stricken," Judge Labarle said. "Next question."

"Officer," Ambrose said, "did the defendant expressly say he was waiving his Miranda rights?"

"Not expressly, no."

"Did he continue talking to you after you'd read him his rights?"

"He did."

"What did he say?"

"Objection, calls for a narrative."

"I'll allow it. Objection overruled."

Ferd leaned forward, anxious to hear what his father had told the police. At Smedley's instruction, Dwight had been tight-lipped in his discussions with Ferd. Now he would finally learn his father's side of the story.

"He said he found Patrick Brady's wallet in a trash can on Jones Street. He removed the credit card and all the cash and left the wallet in the trash can. The first time he tried to use the credit card was at Safeway."

I knew it, Ferd thought. The only thing that made sense was his father finding the wallet somewhere. Ferd wondered why Ambrose had asked such an open-ended question when she must've known the answer wouldn't help her.

"Did he say when he supposedly found the wallet?"

"The night before, on Thursday. So January 25th."

"Did you ask Mr. Pitt about the murder of Patrick Brady?"

"Yes, he denied being involved. He knew nothing about Mr. Brady."

Ambrose sat down. "No further questions."

Smedley turned toward her client and whispered something. They talked for about half a minute when the judge
interrupted.

"Ms. Smedley, do you have any questions of this witness?"

"No questions, Your Honor."

Ambrose next called Officer Robert Jorgensen, a young
Caucasian man with a tattoo sleeve on his right arm. She went
through the same foundational questions with him before
getting to the substance of his testimony. He testified that the
cashier, Manuel Zuniga, told him defendant had tried to
purchase a dozen tubes of Colgate toothpaste with Patrick
Brady's credit card. He recognized Brady's name from the newspaper and alerted his manager, who called the police. Again,
Smedley waived cross-examination.

Ambrose's next witness was Amanda Sokolove, a fingerprint expert. She adjusted the wire-rimmed glasses that hung
halfway down her nose and brushed back the short black hair
which was cut just above her eyes.

"Ms. Sokolove, what is your occupation?" began Ambrose.

"I am employed by the San Francisco Police Department
Crime Lab as a latent print examiner." She spoke in a clear
authoritative voice.

"How long have you been so employed?"

"For roughly nine years."

"What do you do as a latent print examiner?"

"I process crime scenes to collect latent finger and palm
prints. I identify and label latent prints, enhance them using a
variety of photographic and computer equipment, and
compare them to known prints."

"Can you summarize your educational background?"

"Sure. I have a Bachelor of Science degree in Criminal
Justice, Forensics from Northeastern University in Boston and a
Master of Science degree in Criminal Justice from Michigan
State University."

"Before today, have you testified in court as an expert witness on the collection and interpretation of fingerprints?"

"Yes, many."

"How many?"

"At least fifty times."

Ambrose faced the judge. "Your Honor, I would ask that Ms. Sokolove be designated as an expert in fingerprint collection and interpretation."

Judge Labarle asked, "Ms. Smedley, is there any objection?"

"Submitted."

"Ms. Sokolove shall be so designated. Proceed with your questioning, Ms. Ambrose."

Ambrose addressed the witness. "Were you involved in collecting latent prints in this case?"

"Yes."

"Explain your involvement."

"The investigating officers seized a wallet and steak knife from a trash can on Jones Street and logged them into the police property room. I then retrieved them from there."

Ferd's eyes widened. He hadn't known the knife was a steak knife. *Why would the killer be carrying a steak knife?* Ferd wondered.

The witness asked, "Shall I go on?"

"I'll ask another question. When was it you retrieved these items?"

"Let me check my report." She pulled a document from her briefcase. "It would've been January 26th."

"What did you do with this wallet and knife?"

"I sprinkled fingerprint powder on the outer and inner surfaces of the wallet and the blade and handle of the knife."

"Were you able to lift any prints from the wallet?"

"Yes, I lifted two fingerprints from one side of the wallet, and a thumb print from the other side."

"Were you able to compare these prints to any known prints?"

"Yes, for the defendant Dwight Pitt."

"Did you draw any conclusions from this comparison?"

Up to this point, Smedley had been listening quietly. At this last question, however, she jumped up. "Objection, no foundation."

Judge Labarle had been sitting with her head resting on her hand and also awakened. "Lay more foundation," she instructed Ambrose.

"Certainly, your honor. Ms. Sokolove, did you note any distinctive markings on the prints you lifted from the wallet?"

"The two fingerprints on one side of the wallet were made by the right index and middle finger. The print on the other side was made by the right thumb. I compared these three prints to the booking prints taken from the defendant, noting common loops, whorls, and arches. There were at least fifteen common characteristics on each print comparison."

"Based on these comparisons, have you reached an opinion as to whose prints appear on the wallet?"

"I have. They're the defendant's prints."

"Is the location of these three prints on the wallet consistent with defendant holding the wallet in his hand?"

"Of course."

"Have you seen the video of a suspect reaching into the victim's pocket after the stabbing?"

"I have seen that video."

"In your expert opinion, is the location of the prints on the wallet consistent with the defendant reaching into the victim's pocket and lifting the wallet?"

"Just a minute," shouted Smedley. "This witness has no basis for reaching that opinion. It would be pure speculation."

"Agreed," said Judge Labarle. "Sustained."

"But Your Honor..."

"No, Ms. Ambrose. That question goes beyond this witness's area of expertise. Ask your next question."

"One last subject, Ms. Sokolove. Did you obtain any identifiable prints from the steak knife?"

"I was able to locate a partial print of a left index finger on the blade."

"Did you compare this partial print with defendant's left index finger?"

"I did. It was consistent."

"Thank you. Nothing further."

"Let's take a fifteen-minute break," the judge said as she walked off the bench.

Ferd did not want to be put in a situation where he'd have to talk to Smedley, so he left the courtroom and walked to the men's room. To his great surprise he thought Smedley had been doing a decent job so far, and wondered how she would handle the fingerprint evidence which was certainly damaging to his father's defense. This was the key evidence aside from use of the credit card. Ferd thought Ambrose had made a mistake getting the officer to relate what his father had said about finding the wallet in a trash can. She should've left that part out since it gave a perfectly innocent explanation for his possession of the credit card. *But why*, Ferd wondered, *did the murderer throw away the wallet after killing Brady to steal it? That was baffling unless the killer's real motive had nothing to do with robbery and the killer was only pretending robbery was the motive.*

Back in the courtroom, Sokolove resumed the stand and acknowledged she understood she was still under oath. Smedley stood for her cross-examination, moving directly in front of the witness about ten feet away. Ferd thought the judge should've moved her farther away but Judge Labarle said nothing.

"Ms. Sokolove, let's start with the knife. You described the print from the knife as a partial print, correct?"

"Yes, a partial left index finger."

"How many similar features did you find with my client's print?"

"There were seven."

"Is that enough to make a conclusive determination that the print on the knife was made by my client?"

"Not conclusive."

"That partial print could've been made by someone other my client, correct?"

"It's possible."

"That's because other people may share the seven similar features you identified. Isn't that true?"

"Yes, other people could've made that print."

Smedley then switched gears. "Did you find any other prints on the knife, full or partial?"

"No."

"No other prints on the blade?"

"None."

"None on the handle."

"That's correct."

"Did you find that strange?"

"What do you mean?"

"Mr. Brady was stabbed in the neck, presumably by that knife. Wouldn't you expect to find the stabber's prints on the handle?"

"That seems reasonable."

"Yet you're certain there were no other prints on the handle?"

"Objection," Ambrose said softly, not really putting her heart into it. "Asked and answered."

"Sustained."

"Is the absence of prints on the handle consistent with the stabber wiping the handle before throwing it in the trash can?"

"Objection, that's speculation."

"Withdrawn," said Smedley. "Is it also consistent with the stabber wearing gloves?"

"Same objection."

"Objection sustained. Ms. Smedley, move on."

Ferd had to give Smedley credit. By asking questions she knew to be objectionable, she was planting an alternative theory in the judge's mind. Obviously, his father wouldn't have wiped the knife or worn gloves if his partial print was found on it. The more Ferd thought about it the more he admired Smedley's strategy. But she wasn't finished.

"Before I sit down, Ms. Sokolove, I want to ask you about the wallet? Other than my client's prints, did you find any other prints on the wallet?"

"No, I didn't."

"You know that the victim took out his wallet just prior to the stabbing?"

"I'm not sure I know what you mean."

"You're aware the victim was at the Promenade Bar that night?"

"Yes."

"And you know he used his credit card to pay for drinks?"

"I'm not aware of that."

Smedley turned toward the judge. "Your Honor, the defense has subpoenaed Patrick Brady's credit card records from the day of the attack. Your clerk has those records and I would ask that they be released to the defense."

"Any objection, Ms. Ambrose?"

"Well..." she hesitated, seemingly unsure how to respond. "No objection."

The clerk handed the records to Smedley, who flipped through them until she found the one she wanted. "Ms. Sokolove, take a look at defense Exhibit A, a credit card statement for January 25th of this year."

Sokolove took the document and studied it. "I've read it."

"Did you note that the last charge that day was at the Promenade Bar?"

"I did."

"Do you have any explanation for the absence of the victim's prints on his wallet?"

"Someone must've wiped the prints."

"No further questions."

26

F erd skirted the reporters who approached him in the hallway, shouting a terse "No comment" several times, as he hurried toward the stairwell. For the lunch recess, he drove home and in less than fifteen minutes walked into the kitchen where Sonya was busy preparing kale salad with grilled chicken. She insisted he join her and he reluctantly agreed. He couldn't believe Sonya had him eating this shit, but she was concerned about his expanding paunch. So he sucked it up and agreed to eat kale salad even though he thought only about a thick peanut butter and jam sandwich.

"Things are going better for my father than I anticipated," he said after taking a bite of kale. "Smedley's not a *total* idiot, anyway."

"Do you think he'll win?"

"It's hard to tell. The prosecution need only show probable cause that my father stabbed Brady. It's a low burden."

"If he wins the preliminary hearing, will he be released from jail?"

"Oh, yes. As soon as it's over."

"Jesus, what would he do then?"

"He'd go back on the street... Unless we take him in."

"Ferd, are you serious? Take in a suspected murderer and known drunk?"

"I can't let my father go back on the street. After all he's been through."

"He *abandoned* you, Ferd. Your mom, your sister. Remember?"

"I do, but ... his life. He's had a rough time."

Sonya put down her fork. "How can it be safe to have a drunk in the house? I'd have to lock up all the valuables."

"He's not going to rob us."

"How do you know that?"

"He's been sober since he was jailed." Ferd cut up his chicken and took a few bites. He could see that Sonya was displeased, her lips clamped shut in a tight line. After all the bad-mouthing he'd done of his father, he wasn't surprised she didn't want his father living with them. Nor did he blame her. He'd just have to find another place for him to live.

"Why don't I look into getting him into a shelter?" he said.

"I think that's probably wise."

THE PEOPLE CALLED several police officers who reported to the scene of the stabbing to testify about their observations and search of the area, including the trash can. Then Ambrose announced her next witness was Officer Simon Wallace, a video retrieval specialist. A young African American man with close-cropped hair, he had been on force less than six years. He had walked the neighborhood looking for video cameras and located several within a half mile radius of the scene.

"Where were the video cameras you located?"

"There was one at the Blue Arms Hotel, of course, and the convenience store a block away, the Sunnydale Market. I checked each establishment in the area. A few apartment buildings on Sutter Street had cameras but the quality was so poor I didn't find them useful. The only other one with an operative video system was the parking garage on Sutter/Stockton, which was four blocks from the scene."

Ambrose marked a DVD containing the video of the convenience store, which was admitted without objection. She then played the video showing Dwight Pitt entering and exiting the store.

"How many times have you watched this video?"

"At least twenty times."

"Do you recognize the person entering and exiting the store?"

"The video's clear and in color. I believe that's the defendant."

"Did you calibrate the time on this video?"

"Yes, it was a minute slow."

Next Ambrose marked a DVD from the Blue Arms Hotel. "Let's talk about the Blue Arms video. How did you obtain this one?"

"The manager Joanie Merced showed it to me. She was the first person to come to the victim's aid."

"I'm going to put on the DVD for a few seconds." Ambrose played the video, which showed the sidewalk in front of the Blue Arms. "Do you recognize this video?"

"That's the video I obtained from the Blue Arms Hotel. Ms. Merced showed me the cameras pointing to the front entrance and provided me a DVD of the video."

Ambrose then moved the DVD into evidence without objection. She played the video showing Brady stumbling on the sidewalk and the suspect in a Giants baseball cap removing Brady's wallet from his jacket pocket. Ferd stared at the video, wondering who was hiding behind that baseball cap. It couldn't have been his father. It couldn't have been Josh either, Ferd was certain.

"Officer Wallace, do you recognize the person in the hotel video?"

Smedley was on her feet. "Objection, that's pure speculation. The face of this person is not visible at all."

"Let me see the video again," the judge said.

Ambrose replayed the video on the big screen. The judge leaned back, glanced at the defendant and back to the screen. "The objection's sustained."

"No further questions," Ambrose said as if she had expected that ruling.

"I have just a few questions, Officer Wallace." Smedley picked up the DVD with the convenience store video then played the few minutes showing Dwight, the same portion Ferd had watched at the store. He felt a twinge of pride that he had been the one to focus on this video and alert Smedley – although reluctantly – to its relevance.

"Did that video show my client?" asked Smedley.

"It did."

Smedley took a step closer to the witness. "What time did my client exit that store?"

"At 7:15 according to the video, but it was actually 7:16."

"Was he carrying anything?"

"He had what appeared to be a bottle of some kind of alcohol."

"Was my client wearing a Giants cap?"

Wallace shook his head. "No, he wasn't."

"In fact, was he wearing anything on this head?"

"No."

Smedley folded her arms across her chest. "Let's talk about the Blue Arms video. Did you say on direct exam whether you had calibrated the time on that video?"

He shook his head. "I wasn't asked."

"Well, let me ask. Was the time stated on the video accurate?"

"No. The victim first appears in the video at 7:30. I calibrated the time on the video and found it was thirteen minutes fast."

"So you're saying Mr. Brady was actually stabbed at 7:17, not 7:30?"

"Based on my calibration, that is correct."

Smedley paused, placing an index finger on her lips as she pondered the answer. "Let me be sure I've got this right. My client left the Sunnydale Market at 7:16 and Mr. Brady was stabbed at 7:17, so if my client were guilty that means he had one minute to commit this crime. True?"

Officer Wallace looked toward the ceiling, realizing the import of the question. After a moment, he returned his gaze to Smedley. "I would say you're correct."

Ferd tried to picture the area. The distance between the store and the hotel was at least a full block. His father would've had to run, or at least walk at a quick pace, to make it to the hotel in time. And while carrying a bottle of beer. And while placing a baseball cap on his head.

"Thank you, Officer." She returned to counsel table. Ferd thought she was finished with her questioning and grudgingly admired her work. But she wasn't finished.

"Officer, you also mentioned video from the Sutter/Stockton garage, but you weren't asked any questions about that one. Did you view that video?"

"Yes, the manager provided it to me."

"Did you calibrate it?"

The witness nodded. "It was accurate."

"Did you identify any persons of interest in that video?"

Wallace looked over at Ambrose, which set Smedley off. "The prosecutor can't answer for you, Officer. Do you want me to repeat my question?"

"The answer's yes."

"Have you noted in your report the time on the video that this person of interest appears?"

"Yes. It's 7:22 p.m."

"So five minutes after the victim is seen on the Blue Arms video?"

"That's correct."

"Did you walk the area from the Blue Arms to the garage to determine how long it would take?"

"I did. It took me four and a half minutes."

"I'd like to mark this DVD, which contains video from the Sutter/Stockton garage on the date of the incident, as defense Exhibit B."

"Any objection to this video being admitted, Ms. Ambrose?" asked the judge.

"None."

"It shall be admitted."

"I will start the video beginning at 7:20," said Smedley. She played the video for a couple of minutes until a young man, early 20s with a prominent chin and bushy hair walked by. She froze the video as this man faced the camera, zooming in so his face was clearer.

Ferd gasped, causing both lawyers to turn around and gaze at him. A few of the reporters also looked over. He put his fist toward his mouth, trying to control himself.

Smedley continued with her questioning. "Officer Wallace, did you take any steps to identify the young man seen on the screen?"

"Yes, I sent out a bulletin to the department."

"Did anyone respond?"

Wallace looked toward the prosecutor's table and pointed. "Sergeant Hinton did."

"What did she tell you?"

"She identified the subject as someone she interviewed in connection with this case."

"And what is the name of this subject?"

"Joshua Pitt."

All of the reporters now looked at Ferd, who stared at the floor. Even Dwight Pitt turned toward Smedley as if surprised. He didn't look pleased.

"Is that the defendant's grandson?"

"That's what I'm told."

"No further questions."

It was close to 4:30 p.m. and the judge recessed for the day. Again, Ferd immediately left the courtroom, with Bob Angelo trailing him, and hurried to the back stairway. He felt ill that the focus was now on his son. Josh had said he went right to the garage after meeting Brady, but in view of this evidence that didn't seem likely. This hearing was supposed to be about his father, not his son. And why didn't Ambrose object to the video of Josh? What relevance did that have to his father's defense? Ferd suddenly felt a wave of nausea as he realized what Smedley's strategy was.

Ferd drove straight home, afraid to tell Sonya about the hearing. When she asked him how it was going, he told her Smedley was doing a better job than expected. "She's been successful in raising a lot of doubts about the People's case."

"If your father gets off, what does that mean for Josh?"

"We'll have to wait and see."

"Great."

BEFORE GOING TO BED, Ferd thought it prudent that he update Curt Rodda on his father's case. "You're not in bed already, are you?" Ferd asked.

"You kidding me? I rarely hit the hay before midnight. What's up?"

Ferd filled him in on the preliminary hearing. "Tomorrow there should be a ruling. My father actually could get off."

"That would be fuckin' great! Just in time for the election."

"Yeah," Ferd said in a soft voice.

"What's the matter?"

"It's just that Smedley asked some questions today about Josh."

"What the hell for?"

"I didn't mention this, but Josh was a suspect."

Rodda was uncharacteristically quiet. All Ferd could hear was his labored breathing. "From the frying pan into the fire," Rodda said finally. "Is that what you're telling me?"

"I don't think it'll happen, but I thought I should give you a heads up."

"You're making me work for my money. Let me stew on it, okay?"

27

A t the start of the second day of the preliminary hearing, Ambrose announced her final witness: Sergeant Carla Hinton. As Hinton stood up from counsel's table, she glanced to the back of the courtroom where Ferd had taken the same seat as yesterday. The group of reporters now monitoring the hearing had expanded from three or four to six or seven. Ferd noticed Angelo had returned and guessed the others were from the Examiner and the two legal newspapers, the Daily Journal and The Recorder. Suddenly, as Hinton was taking the oath, Angelo walked over to Ferd and handed him a business card.

"Call me when you're ready to talk," Angelo said. "I know how hard this is for you, but you need to get your family's side of the story in the media."

"Thanks, Bob. I don't mind talking to you, but can you help keep those vultures away from me?" He nodded toward the other reporters.

"I'll do what I can, but it's a big story."

Deputy O'Hara walked toward Angelo, shaking her head. "Take a seat, sir, or you'll have to leave the courtroom."

"Sorry," Angelo said.

"You know better than that."

Ferd watched Sergeant Hinton carefully, nervous about her testimony. She projected a professional appearance in a black pinstripe suit with her long black hair tied into a ponytail. He wondered what additional evidence she had.

Ambrose established that Hinton had overseen the investigation into Brady's murder. She had directed officers to interview the Safeway cashier, had reviewed the videotaped interview of Dwight as well as the videos obtained from the Sunnyside Market, the Blue Arms, and the Sutter/Stockton garage, and communicated with the crime lab. None of this was new. Then Ambrose asked if Hinton had personally interviewed any witnesses.

"Yes," Hinton said. "I interviewed the victim's wife Denise Brady at her home in Pacifica."

"What was her demeanor?"

"She was distraught, as you might expect, tearful."

"When was this?"

"The day after the stabbing, so January 26th."

"What did she tell you?"

"She said her husband had a work meeting that night at the Promenade Bar in the Tenderloin. She also said they often went to the Tenderloin to eat at a Vietnamese restaurant."

"When was the last time she communicated with her husband?"

"The afternoon of the 25th. He called to tell her about his meeting and that he wouldn't be home for dinner."

"Did Ms. Brady have any idea who stabbed her husband?"

"She did not. She said her husband got along with everyone. She suspected this was a random act of violence."

"After speaking to Ms. Brady, did you interview anyone else?"

"I interviewed employees of CAPSLOCK, Patrick Brady's employer."

"Where did those interviews take place?"

"At the company headquarters in Mountain View. They were kind enough to provide a private conference room."

"Was anyone with you during the interviews?"

"Yes. Officer Otis."

"Which employees did you interview?"

"Patrick Brady's entire team: James Ellison, Sa'Quan Williams, Colleen O'Keefe, and Joshua Pitt."

Ambrose feigned surprise. "Joshua Pitt? The defendant's grandson?"

"That's correct."

"Let's start with James Ellison. Did you ask him if he knew anything about the victim's whereabouts the night of the stabbing?"

"He didn't know why the victim was in the Tenderloin that night."

"Same question regarding Sa'Quan Williams."

"Same answer. He expressed surprise Brady went to the Tenderloin."

"Same question regarding Colleen O'Keefe." Ambrose sounded bored, her voice flat.

"She said the victim went to the Promenade Bar, which is about a block from the Blue Arms. She met him there."

"Did she say what time she arrived at the bar?"

"Yes, around 7:05 p.m."

"Did she say why she met him there?"

"There was a work issue she wanted to discuss." Sergeant Hinton gazed at the floor.

"Did Joshua Pitt indicate he knew why the victim went to the Tenderloin?"

"Yes, he did. He met Mr. Brady at the Promenade as well."

Ferd was listening intently, awaiting testimony about Brady's sexual harassment.

"What time did he arrive there?"

"He estimated 6:55 p.m." Again, Ferd ran the time frames through his mind. Josh arrived ten minutes before Colleen. If Josh had stayed until shortly before Colleen arrived, he should've been at the garage by about 7:10, not 7:22 as the video showed. *Did he return to the Promenade after getting Colleen's call about the kiss?* Ferd took out his handkerchief and wiped his brow.

Ambrose resumed her questioning. "And did he say what time he left?"

"He claimed he was at the bar for about five minutes."

"No further questions."

Ambrose and Hinton had avoided the issue of sexual harassment, but when Smedley stood up, jutting her chin at the witness, Ferd knew it was coming. "Sergeant, what was discussed between Joshua Pitt and Patrick Brady at the Promenade Bar?"

Hinton glanced in the direction of the reporters as if willing them out of the courtroom. "Mr. Pitt said he talked to Mr. Brady about sexually harassing his girlfriend."

Ferd tensed. He didn't like where this going and was afraid how Josh would react to what would undoubtedly be unfavorable publicity. This preliminary hearing was turning into a shit show.

"And who is his girlfriend?" asked Smedley.

"Colleen O'Keefe."

"The co-worker who also met Mr. Brady that night?"

"That's correct."

"Did you also talk to a bartender at the Promenade?"

"I did. Conor Hill."

"And what did the bartender tell you?"

"He confirmed that Joshua Pitt and Colleen O'Keefe met with the victim separately."

"Did he tell you anything about Mr. Pitt's conversation with the victim?"

Hinton hesitated, thinking. "He said it was heated."

"'Heated.' Is that the word he used?"

"It is."

Smedley walked across the courtroom to get closer to the witness. "Sergeant, have you told us everything you heard from the co-workers?"

"Everything? No, but the complete interviews were recorded."

"I understand. Let's turn to James Ellison. Did he tell you about any threats Joshua Pitt made to Patrick Brady?"

Ferd stared at Hinton, knowing what was coming and powerless to do anything about it.

"Yes, he did." She hesitated and looked at the judge. "May I look at the report to refresh my memory."

"Go ahead," Judge Labarle said. "When you're finished, turn it over."

Hinton studied the report, flipped it over, then looked at Smedley.

"Have you refreshed your memory on what Mr. Ellison said?" asked Smedley.

"I have. He said something to the effect of, 'I'm going to get even with that fucker.'"

"Did he mention what that was in reference to?"

"Yes. It was due to Mr. Brady harassing Ms. O'Keefe."

"When was this statement made?"

"A week or so before the murder."

"Let's turn to Sa'Quan Williams. Did he mention any threat Joshua Pitt made to Mr. Brady?"

This time Hinton didn't seek permission. She looked at her

report without objection from the prosecutor. "Don't know if you'd call this a threat but he told Mr. Brady, 'You'll be sorry.'"

"What was the context in which that statement was made?"

"Apparently Mr. Brady was not going to support him for an award. Coder of the Year I think it was. It carried a stock option award that could have been valued in the seven figures."

"So, Sergeant Hinton, we have evidence that Joshua Pitt had the clear opportunity to murder Patrick Brady. Correct?"

"Looking at the time on the videos, that is correct."

"And he had at least two motives: one, Brady's sexual harassment of Joshua Pitt's girlfriend and, two, his refusal to support Joshua for Coder of the Year. Correct?"

"Yes."

"And yet you chose to arrest my client, who had no motive whatsoever to harm Mr. Brady?"

Hinton grimaced, apparently realizing she had been trapped into a corner. She was saved by Ambrose who objected to the question as argumentative. Smedley didn't wait for the judge's ruling.

"Withdrawn. No further questions."

When she turned to talk to her client, she sought out Ferd's eyes and gave him the smirk that he hated, the self-satisfied, I'm-smarter-than-you smirk. Ferd recoiled, wishing he could escape the courtroom. He had to give Smedley credit though. She had employed the other-dude defense to perfection. And it would suit her purposes in the campaign: if she couldn't smear Ferd with his father being a murderer, she would use his son for the same purpose.

The judge asked Ambrose, "Do the People waive opening argument?"

"Yes, Your Honor."

"Ms. Smedley?"

Smedley stood up and put her hand on Dwight's shoulder as she addressed the judge. "I realize the burden at a preliminary hearing is low, but this case cries out for dismissal. The only evidence the People produced against the defendant Dwight Pitt were my client's fingerprints on the victim's wallet and a partial print on the knife, his attempt to use the victim's credit card at Safeway, and a blurry inconclusive video at the scene of the killing. The fingerprints are consistent with Mr. Pitt's finding and touching Mr. Brady's wallet in a trashcan as he told the police. The partial print on the knife is worthless as a piece of evidence; it could be anyone's. Even if it were Mr. Pitt's print, the same explanation applies: he touched the knife while his hand was in the trash can when he found the wallet.

"The video does not implicate my client at all. It does not show the face of the person involved in the altercation with the victim. In fact, this person is wearing a Giants cap while my client is seen on the convenience store video, without a cap, minutes earlier. To buy the People's case, Your Honor would have to believe my client killed Mr. Brady within a minute after leaving the store. And to do so, he would have had to discard the bottle he had just purchased and placed a baseball cap on his head. It just makes no sense whatsoever.

"Finally, I want to address the elephant in the room: substantial evidence points to someone else as the killer, another man named Pitt. Not Dwight but his grandson Joshua."

Ferd nearly gagged and his eyes bugged out. Hearing Josh accused out loud in a public courtroom was devastating. *I can't believe this is happening.* Ferd glared at Smedley as she continued her argument.

"Yes, Joshua Pitt is more likely the killer than my client. Unlike his grandfather, Joshua had both motive and opportunity. He was in a heated argument with the victim shortly before the killing; Mr. Brady was sexually harassing his girlfriend; and Mr. Brady was going to deny him an award as Coder of the Year, an award that was worth potentially a million dollars. In fact, Joshua Pitt threatened Mr. Brady, telling him on

one occasion he would get even with him, referring to him as a
'fucker,' and on another occasion telling Mr. Brady he would be
sorry for denying him the Coder award. Thus, there is not only
substantial evidence of motive, but there are also threats of
violence."

Objection! Ferd thought. There was no threat of violence.
Smedley was overplaying her hand. To Ferd's dismay, the prosecutor sat silently, not bothering to object.

"Furthermore, video evidence from the Sutter/Stockton
garage shows Joshua in the vicinity of the murder *at the time of
the murder!* So, we now have opportunity. Motive, opportunity,
and threats. Yet the police and prosecutors chose to charge
Dwight Pitt, a homeless alcoholic, with this crime, and gave a
pass to Joshua Pitt, the son of a sitting judge. Shameful! I
submit the only reasonable decision for this court is dismissal
of these charges."

Smedley sat down and looked at her client, apparently
hoping for some congratulations. But Dwight looked away, his
arms folded across his chest. Ferd realized his father had not
authorized Smedley's argument. She had attacked Josh on her
own, probably because Ferd had not kowtowed to her.

Judge Labarle turned to the prosecutor. "Ms. Ambrose,
would you like to respond?"

Ambrose stood up tentatively as if she really didn't want to
respond. She just had her head handed to her, thought Ferd.
She'd better come with her "A" game.

"Thank you, Your Honor," said Ambrose.

"Defense counsel has done an admirable job of trying to
deflect the court's attention from the real issue in this hearing:
whether there is probable cause to hold this defendant –
Dwight Pitt – over for trial. This hearing is not about whether
probable cause exists to hold over Joshua Pitt. I submit that the
evidence presented fully supports holding the defendant over.
He killed Patrick Brady, took his wallet out of his pocket, and

tried to use his credit card. What was his motive for committing this crime? We may never know, but as the court is aware, motive is not part of the People's burden. We don't have to prove any motive."

She's right, thought Ferd. *But every decent trial lawyer knows that motive can persuade a judge or jury.* He shuffled in his seat, trying to get comfortable. Ambrose continued.

"But I would suggest that a drunk, homeless, down-on-his-luck Dwight Pitt probably saw this well-dressed man walking in the Tenderloin, perceived an easy mark, and thought of robbing him. When Patrick resisted, which admittedly must've happened off camera, the defendant turned to violence. He stabbed Patrick across the neck and, when Patrick fell down, incapacitated, the defendant lifted his wallet. We see that on the Blue Arms video. The defendant, disguising himself with a baseball cap pulled low to his eyes, rifled Patrick's pockets. Defendant's fingerprints on the wallet are fully consistent with this conduct. Defense counsel tries to explain away the fingerprints by arguing that defendant found the wallet in a trash can. The evidence does not support this.

"Your Honor, please keep in mind the People's burden of proof at a preliminary hearing: it is probable cause, not beyond a reasonable doubt. Ms. Smedley's entire argument was designed to plant doubt in the court's mind about Dwight Pitt's guilt. But even if the court has doubts about defendant's guilt, that is not enough for dismissal. Based on all the evidence presented, there is a reasonable basis for the court to conclude that defendant committed this heinous crime. The defendant must be held over for trial."

The judge nodded and said, "Thank you, Ms. Ambrose." She shuffled papers on the bench, lining them up neatly. "I have given this matter a great deal of thought, both during the two days of hearing and last night. Ms. Ambrose is certainly right about at least one thing: this hearing is not about Joshua

Pitt. I offer no opinion on the strength or weakness of the evidence against him.

"Turning to the case against the defendant Dwight Pitt, I am struck that the only evidence tying him to the victim is his fingerprints on the wallet and attempted use of the credit card. I give no weight to the partial print on the knife. As the criminologist conceded, that print could have been made by anyone. The video from the Blue Arms Hotel does not help. While the person in the Giants cap could be the defendant, it could be a host of other people. I simply cannot conclude from the video that defendant stabbed Patrick Brady. And it is noteworthy that the much clearer video from the convenience store shows the defendant without a baseball cap only a minute before the stabbing."

Listening intently, Ferd appreciated Judge Labarle's comments and liked where she was going. "The fingerprint and credit card evidence tells us only that the defendant had possession of the victim's wallet at some time after the murder. It tells us nothing about the defendant's alleged participation in the murder. It is a stretch to infer from this evidence that the defendant stabbed Patrick Brady.

"Therefore, as to Count One, an alleged violation of Penal Code section 187, the evidence presented does *not* establish sufficient cause to believe the defendant committed each and every element of that offense. Accordingly, Count One is dismissed. Count Two, the misdemeanor for attempted use of the credit card will be certified and sent to Department 17 for trial."

Smedley again was on her feet. "Your Honor, I would like to address defendant's custody status."

"Go ahead, Ms. Smedley."

"In light of the court's ruling, I would request that my client be released on his own recognizance."

"Any objection, Ms. Ambrose?"

Ambrose looked embarrassed, knowing she couldn't argue to hold Dwight in custody for a misdemeanor attempted theft. "No objection."

"The defendant shall be released from custody on his own recognizance," the judge said just before leaving the bench.

28

Ferd called Sonya on the drive home. "Don't turn on the television."

"Why not?"

"You won't like it."

"Ferd, I'm going to turn on the TV if I want. You know me better than that."

"Don't say I didn't warn you."

By the time he had arrived home, she was in a state, having ignored Ferd's directive. "I knew this would happen with your intermeddling. Why didn't you listen to me, Ferd?"

"Sonya, it's not my fault this happened. It's because of that damn Smedley."

"According to the news, our son is now the prime suspect! How did this happen?"

Ferd reached out to Sonya and held her tightly. Holding her face with both hands, he stared into her eyes. "Josh didn't do this. I'll make sure the truth comes out."

"Haven't you done enough already?"

"I can handle this. Let me call Henry and see what he recommends."

"We have to call Josh."

"I'll call him. You lie down and rest."

"Rest? You go to hell. How can I rest at a time like this? I'm going to call Josh right now." She speed-dialed Josh and waited, staring at Ferd, while being directed to voicemail. "Josh, please call me as soon as you get this. It's urgent!"

After Sonya went to the study to finish a project, Ferd called Henry Smith and summarized what had happened at the prelim. Smith was happy to clear his calendar to meet with Josh. Ferd then called Josh. "I just picked up Mom's message. What's so urgent?"

"You haven't seen the news?"

"I've been buried in meetings."

"The good news is your grandfather was released today. The bad news is that his lawyer fingered you as the murderer."

"What the fuck!"

"It's bullshit, I know, but we've got to get ahead of this. The media has already run the story. Henry's willing to meet with us tomorrow."

"I'm too busy."

"Josh, listen. This is not something you can blow off."

"I've got too much going on."

Ferd slammed his fist down on the kitchen counter. He rarely yelled at his son but this time he couldn't help himself. "You *will* be there at five o'clock. Do you understand? I won't take no for an answer."

Then he called the jail and left his number with the outtake people to give to his father as soon as he was released. Finally, he called a shelter and managed to reserve a bed. He was as tired as he'd ever been. The pressure of having his father accused and his son implicated by Smedley of murder was overwhelming. He turned on the television, but news flashes kept appearing announcing his father's release and the accusations against Josh.

Dwight called just after nine o'clock. Ferd drove back toward the Hall and parked on Seventh Street outside the jail. When he saw Dwight walk from the secure area to the lobby, squinting as if the bright lights were blinding him, he got out and stood by his car. Dwight was wearing the same clothes he was arrested in: dark dirty pants and a dark jacket. When he saw Ferd, he held out his arms and they hugged. It felt strange to be hugging the father he hadn't seen in over thirty years.

"Thank you for picking me up, Ferd. You don't know how much I appreciate this."

"You're welcome. Sorry you had to spend any time in jail." They got in the car and Ferd pulled into the traffic lane.

"What happens now with Josh? I want you to know I had no warning my lawyer was going to do that. I never would've allowed it. She blindsided me."

"I'm not surprised. I'm meeting with Josh and a lawyer tomorrow. We'll try to put a lid on this thing. In the meantime, I've found you a shelter bed at least temporarily."

"I was hoping I could stay with you."

"Not going to happen. We've got too much water under the bridge. Besides, Sonya won't have it. Sorry."

Dwight leaned his head back and closed his eyes. "What a tragedy for you and your family. I've met Josh only a couple of times. Hard to believe he could've killed anyone."

"He didn't; I assure you."

After driving a short distance, Ferd dropped Dwight off in front of the shelter. "They're expecting you. Hang on to my phone number and call me if you need anything." He felt insensitive leaving his father like this, but his thoughts were on his son. Right now, Josh was all that mattered.

THE NEXT AFTERNOON after court Ferd parked downtown and walked over to Smith's office. He hadn't visited the firm since he began working at the court. The receptionist, Charlotte, jumped up when she saw him, causing her long white hair to bounce, and gave him a tight hug. Charlotte was a big-hearted woman whose enthusiasm and competence were well-recognized assets. She had been with the firm for nearly two decades. At salary adjustment time, Ferd always made sure Charlotte received fair compensation.

Smith soon appeared carrying a yellow legal pad. "No Josh yet?"

"He'll be here."

"Are you worried?" Smith took a seat at the head of the table.

"Henry, you should've been in the courtroom. It was awful. That damn Smedley made it seem that Josh was as guilty as sin."

"Hate to bring up another painful subject, but Nancy Harper has been calling me. She wants a response to her settlement proposal."

Ferd stood up and stared out the window. "Henry, the election's coming up. A public admonishment will doom me."

"What should I tell her?"

"Tell her I can't settle before the election. You have my authority to float the idea of a private admonishment."

"She might pull the offer."

"That's a chance we've got to take."

The front door opened and Josh entered the office. He noticed Ferd and Henry through the glass wall, waved at Charlotte, and entered the conference room. Ferd was relieved to see he was more dressed up than usual: black pants, grey sport jacket, and a button-down white shirt. Finally, he was taking this seriously.

"I can't believe this is happening," Josh said, taking a seat across from his father. "Have you seen the noise online?"

"Can't say I have," Ferd said. "There's enough noise on TV and in the papers."

"This is ridiculous. I can't believe I got dragged into this."

"Josh," Henry said, "this is serious business."

"I had nothing to do with Brady's murder. Nothing!"

"Josh, here's the deal," Henry said. "You were in the area at the time of the murder. In fact, you met the victim and got in a heated argument with him. The police call that opportunity. You had an ongoing beef with Brady. You were upset at him because of the way he treated Colleen. He threatened to vote against you for Coder of the Year, costing you perhaps a million dollars. You made at least two comments that could be construed as threats. All that adds up to what the police call motive."

"That's ridiculous."

"Josh," Ferd said, "the police have video of you entering the Sutter/Stockton garage after the stabbing. That's more than fifteen minutes after you left the Promenade. I thought you went directly to the garage."

"For God's sake, that's what this is about? I did walk to the garage, but I was pissed off and wanted to blow off some steam, so I wandered around the Tenderloin and lower Nob Hill."

Ferd and Henry looked at each other as Henry shook his head. Ferd guessed what he was thinking: Josh's story about blowing off steam would never fly in front of a jury. "What about the call from Colleen?" asked Ferd.

"What call?"

Ferd raised an eyebrow. "After she met with Brady?"

"Oh, that. She told me Brady had kissed her."

"Any reason you didn't mention that before?"

"It was nothing!" Josh's voice reached a higher pitch. "I was already pissed off and that just added to it. That's why I was walking off steam." Josh was almost pleading for Ferd to believe him.

"I believe you, son. I do. But the police are going to have another story."

"Here's what I suggest," Henry said, "since the cops know about your involvement, it would be better for you to get ahead of this."

"What're you saying?"

"Rather than wait for the hammer to fall, let's meet with the district attorney. That way we get to control the narrative."

"Won't that put me squarely in the bullseye as a suspect? Why would I want to do that?"

Smith leaned forward and turned toward Josh. "If you're innocent, you've got nothing to worry about."

"Really? My grandfather's supposedly innocent and he was in jail."

He had a point there, thought Ferd. "Let's meet with the district attorney, see what happens," Ferd said. "Henry will be there as your attorney. You don't have to say anything if you don't want to."

"If you want, I could meet with the DA without you," Henry said. "But it would be better if you were there."

Josh stood up, a stricken look on his face. "When?"

"I'll try to set it up for Monday afternoon."

29

The atmosphere around the Pitt house was gloomy all weekend. Sonya barely talked to her husband. Whenever she could, she cast blame on Ferd, claiming he had stirred a hornet's nest by inserting himself in the case, that it was his fault Josh was now in police crosshairs. On Saturday Sonya continued to snap at Ferd so he drove to the club. He worked out harder than ever and dropped a few pounds. While walking on the treadmill, he thought about his relationship with his wife. In twenty-two years of marriage, they had rarely had a serious argument, certainly nothing like the ones that had happened since his father came back into his life. Sure, their communication could've been better. Ferd blamed himself for that; Sonya was a talker, willing to share her feelings. In many ways, they had an old-fashioned marriage: Sonya working from home, cooking most meals, cleaning the house. Ferd's income was always higher while Sonya's was play money. The arrangement seemed to work well.

He reflected on what his life would be like without Sonya. Most of his life had been marked by the absence of his father; he would not allow the rest of his life to be similarly marked by the absence of Sonya. He loved her too much. At times it seemed Sonya had made him choose her over his father, but that was not a fair choice. It was not so much that he wanted his father back in his life; he wanted only to ensure justice was served. If he derived some benefit from his father's being proved innocent, then that was all the better.

When he finished on the treadmill, he felt a slight tightening in his chest. He waited a moment then it was gone. *Nothing to worry about*, he thought, dismissing it.

SONYA WAS LESS testy on Sunday, but still not her usual self. Ferd was glad to take some time away for his meeting with Rodda to prepare for the debate. Rodda had placed a long table against the wall with two folding chairs behind it and one in front. "These are the most uncomfortable chairs we have," Rodda said. "The Bar Association will have padded seats, but I don't want you getting too comfortable. I want your ass to hurt."

"Gee, thanks," said Ferd as he sat in one of the chairs. Rodda sat in the other.

"I'm going to play Smedley," he said, "and be forewarned it's going to get nasty."

A young volunteer took the seat in front of the table. She held a yellow legal pad in her lap. "I'm Natalie," she said. "I'll be asking the questions."

"Nice to meet you, Natalie."

"Judge Pitt," Natalie said, "we'll be starting with you. Your father has just been cleared of murder charges with Ms. Smedley defending him. Do you agree she deserves kudos for the work she did?"

Ferd bit his tongue. He'd be damned if he were going to give Smedley any kudos, not after what she did. "No, I don't. The case never should've gotten that far. If Ms. Smedley had done her job, she would've convinced the DA to drop the charges a lot sooner."

Rodda leaned forward. "If you'd only given me the evidence you uncovered during your unethical investigation, I might've been able to get the charges dismissed."

"Unethical? There was nothing unethical about my investigation. I was a son looking out for his father."

"Ms. Smedley," Natalie said, "would you like to respond to the judge's statements?"

"I certainly would. Need I remind everyone that the judge's campaign attacked me viciously on social media, claiming I was purposely going to lose his father's case. These inflammatory attacks were not only flat out wrong; they were defamatory."

"Please..." said Ferd.

"It's true. Your attacks crossed the line."

"Talk about crossing the line." Ferd turned toward Rodda, getting caught up in the role play. "You're the one who called me Ferd the Nerd."

"Did I hurt your feelings, Judge?" asked Rodda in a sing-song voice.

Ferd jumped up, knocking his chair against the wall. "I've had enough."

"Judge?" Rodda said.

"I need a break." He walked outside, letting the door slam shut behind him. He walked toward the tunnel, steaming. He knew he should've been more composed. All the stress around Josh and Sonya was wearing on him, but he couldn't let it show. After stopping at the bookstore, browsing in the mystery and suspense aisle, his anger began to dissipate. He returned to headquarters.

"Sorry," he said. "The pressure's starting to get to me."

"Judge Pitt," said Rodda, "you've got to focus on being judicial. That means cool under pressure. You would never storm off the bench like that, no matter how much an attorney got under your skin. The public expects more out of you than they do of Smedley. You're a judge; she's only a public defender. You get to be called 'Judge' and 'Your Honor' while she has to go by 'Ms. Smedley.' Always keep that in mind."

"I hear you, Curt. I'll do better."

"I was just getting to the really nasty questions," said Natalie.

"Bring it on then," said Ferd as he resumed his seat beside Rodda.

The practice session went on for another hour. Natalie acted a lot tougher than she looked, pressing Ferd to answer the questions and stop interrupting Smedley. Ferd lost his temper a few more times and Rodda talked him off the ledge. At the end, Rodda told Ferd he did fine. Ferd didn't believe him.

"It'll be tougher live," said Rodda. "You'll have to look at Smedley's smug face, so it'll be hard to stay calm. But you've got to. Remember voters don't share your disdain for her; she's running even with you. As I told you before, this debate could put you over the top. The event starts at six on Thursday but be early. You okay?"

Ferd felt down, as if he had already blown the election. "Oh, just peachy."

30

B y the time Ferd arrived at the district attorney's office, Henry and Josh were already there. They huddled for a few minutes before Stephanie Fong entered with Nellie Ambrose. After the introductions were over and water and coffee served, Fong said, "So, Judge Pitt, tell us why you wanted to meet. I'm curious why your son is here and why he needed to bring a lawyer."

"I'm here to make sure his rights are protected," Henry said. "That's all."

Fong nodded and turned toward Ferd. "As you know, I sat through my father's prelim," Ferd said in a firm voice. "Not surprisingly, the judge did not find probable cause. Smedley's defense, which I thought was totally unnecessary, was to smear my son. I suspect personal animus toward me was involved. You already know that Josh worked with Brady. They didn't get along. Josh felt Brady was hitting on Josh's girlfriend, Colleen O'Keefe, who also worked on the team. Brady was going to deny Josh a large monetary award. Josh told him he'd be sorry." He glanced at Josh. "That all came out at the prelim. What didn't come out was that Josh was going to report Brady to human resources. So his supposed threats were certainly not about Brady's life as Smedley implied."

"We're aware of the dissension between Josh and Brady," Fong said. "We're also aware your son had both motive and opportunity."

Turning toward Josh, who looked down at the table, Ferd said, "Josh didn't kill Brady."

"This is an unusual case," Smith interjected. "If I might, it's true Josh didn't care for Brady but there's no evidence linking him to the murder. Josh met with Brady to convince him to leave Colleen alone. He knew Brady had plans to meet with Colleen that night, so he purposely arrived before her to speak to him."

Ambrose leaned forward and said, "If I'm reading between the lines, what I see is Josh threatening Brady then waiting for him before the murder. Josh stabs him outside the Blue Arms. He takes Brady's wallet to make it look like a robbery, then throws it in a trash can along with the knife as he's running away. But he has the presence of mind to wipe both the wallet and knife of prints."

"I didn't kill Brady!" Josh said.

Henry put his hand up in Josh's face. "Don't say anything. You'll have your chance soon enough."

"So why shouldn't I have Josh arrested right now?" Fong asked.

Ferd and Josh looked at each other. "If you think you've got enough evidence," Ferd said, "go ahead and arrest him. You've already had one public relations disaster. You'd better be prepared for another."

This was the moment Ferd feared. *Would Fong have his son arrested?* When Fong stood up, Ferd thought she was going to call in the police to effect the arrest. But instead, she said, "Give me a few minutes. I want to talk to Nellie before making a decision."

After they'd left, Henry said, "What do you think she'll do?"

"I don't think they'll arrest Josh while Dwight's case is still in the news. They can't risk the negative publicity."

"I feel sick," said Josh. He walked to the trash can and leaned over. He heaved a few times but did not vomit. "Good thing I skipped lunch." Henry refilled his water glass and Josh drank it in one gulp.

Ten minutes later Fong and Ambrose returned. "Judge Pitt," Fong said, "we've discussed this information. I'm not in a position to make any promises. Let me talk to Sergeant Hinton. In the meantime, I suggest Josh stay in the Bay Area."

Josh looked relieved, though he wasn't in the clear yet. He reached for his water glass and raised it to his lips before realizing it was empty.

When Ferd arrived home, he filled in Sonya on the meeting. At first, she was overjoyed Josh wasn't arrested, but Ferd warned her it could still happen. "Are you sure you did the right thing?" she asked.

Ferd didn't like Sonya second-guessing him. "What the hell was I supposed to do?"

"Don't get testy with me. I didn't cause this."

After pouring himself a glass of water, Ferd calmed down. "Neither did I. But I did what I had to do. If Josh gets arrested, so be it."

"How can you be so cavalier about your son being charged with murder?"

"I'm not cavalier, Sonya. I'm realistic. We're in a bad situation right now. There's no getting around that." Ferd's temper was rising again, and he didn't want to continue this conversation for fear of what he'd say. "I'm going upstairs."

"What do you mean you're going upstairs? Your son is about to be arrested for murder and you're going to run away from me? Are you shitting me?" She was getting worked up, ready to take on her husband.

"Sonya, please. There's nothing I can do right now."

"You've already done quite enough I'd say. Perhaps if you hadn't stuck your nose into this case, Josh wouldn't be at risk."

"I don't want to fight. Can I just relax for a little while?" He walked upstairs with Sonya glaring at him.

Just as he lay on the bed, his phone rang. Oh, oh, he thought. He hadn't kept Bradstein informed of the latest developments. "Carol, how are you?"

"I heard you met with the district attorney again, Judge Pitt." Still formal. *Would she ever call him Ferd again?*

"A lot's happened since I last spoke to you."

"I've heard some things through the grapevine. Your family has gone through the ringer. I know what happened at the prelim. I don't see Fong risking another bungled arrest unless she obtains stronger evidence."

"Well, that's what I'm hoping, too, but who knows what Fong will do."

Bradstein was silent for several seconds. "How did your interview with the Commission go?"

"I laid everything on the table. We'll see what happens."

"They interviewed me."

That took Ferd by surprise. He didn't realize the investigation was ongoing. He thought the investigator would file her report then he'd be hit by whatever decision was made. "Anything you can share with me?"

"I told them you acted on your own without my approval."

"That's certainly true."

"I also told them I forbade you to continue. The investigator said she'd determine if you obeyed that order." That was not good news, Ferd knew, particularly regarding his meeting with Fong after Bradstein had issued her order. He could be in bigger trouble than he originally thought.

31

On his way to work in the morning, he placed a call to Henry Smith. "I talked to Carol Bradstein last night." He laid out the gist of his conversation. "So, have you heard anything from the Commission?"

"You know I'd tell you as soon as I heard anything. These things take time. I'm not surprised Harper called Bradstein. She's probably called all the witnesses too, including your friend Smedley."

"Great. I'm sure she'll have nice things to say."

"You can bet she'll take credit for Dwight's release."

"I don't care about that. As much as I hate to say it, she deserves the credit. I couldn't get him released with the same arguments, not including the attacks on Josh."

"You did the best you could. If he's arrested, we'll go full steam at the prosecutor."

"Henry, you're not a criminal defense lawyer."

"I realize that. I've handled some white-collar cases in federal court, but state criminal court is not in my bailiwick. We'll have to bring in a specialist. Someone who knows their way around the Hall of Justice."

"Anyone you'd recommend?"

"My top choice is Angela Simpson. She's tried and won several murder cases."

"Her name rings a bell. I must've seen her around the Hall. Whoever we get, Henry, I want you involved. I trust your judgment. Don't worry about your fee. I'll take care of it. Jesus, the way things are going with the Commission complaint and Josh's situation I might just as well sign over my whole salary to you."

"You didn't get on the bench for the money."

"Let's hope we don't get to that point."

IT HAD BEEN some time since Ferd had last seen Claire so at lunch he called her. They agreed to meet that evening at the Philosopher's Club near the West Portal station. When Ferd arrived, Claire was sitting at a table near the bar, sipping on a glass of red wine. Ferd ordered a draft Sierra Nevada and sat across from her. "How've you been?" he asked.

"I've got my therapist working overtime. He's worried about me. I've talked to him about our father more in the last month than I did for almost thirty-four years. The good news is I've learned to control my anger. You know what they say: if you don't like something and can't change it, then change the way you think about it. My therapist has been preaching that to me for years, but it's taken awhile to sink in."

"We've been through a lot, you and I."

"And what about Josh? I saw the news. Is he in trouble?"

"Josh and I met with the DA, but we're waiting for a decision on whether they'll charge him."

"I shouldn't complain; you've more on your plate than I do."

Throughout their lives, Ferd and Claire had supported each other. Although they weren't as close as they once were, Ferd always helped his twin sister in times of crisis. When they were kids, Ferd would go to her defense when boys teased her. In high school he guided her through the tribulations of dating. And when she went through her three divorces, Ferd was by her side, acting as a sounding board and building up her confidence. She did the same for Ferd too, though truth was he didn't need her as much as she needed him.

She sipped the wine. "You know I've always admired you."

"What're you saying?"

"You're still married to your first wife, your son has a high-paying job in Silicon Valley, and you've had a successful legal career."

"You've done alright too. Your kids are in good colleges. You should be proud."

"I am; I am."

Ferd noticed that Claire had finished her wine, so he waved to the bartender to bring another round. "Are you trying to get your sister drunk?" she asked.

"Like old times maybe?"

She laughed.

When the drinks arrived, they touched glasses. "To our dysfunctional family," Ferd said.

"Aren't all families dysfunctional?"

"Maybe, but ours has taken it to another level."

"Speaking of which, I'd like to see our father now that he's out of jail."

Ferd put down his drink. "Are you sure you're ready for that?"

"My therapist thinks so."

"I saw him a few days ago. He said to say hello to you."

"Really? I wondered if he ever thought of me."

"One good thing about jail was he sobered up, but he's going to need help beating the addiction now that he's out. I found a bed for him at a shelter, but I'm trying to convince Sonya to take him in for a short while."

"Why, Ferd, that's most generous of you."

"Unfortunately, Sonya doesn't see it that way. She's afraid of having a drunk living in her house." He took a long sip of beer. "It'd be nice if our father could support himself. One thing I meant to talk to you about was his old house in New Hampshire. If we could stop the foreclosure then sell the house, he'd have some cash and be able to get back on his feet."

"How're we going to do that?"

"I was hoping I could delegate that little problem to you. I can get you the address if you can do some research, perhaps make some calls, and see if the situation's salvageable."

"I see how it is. Let your sister run with it. You trust me with this?"

"Of course. I know you're a competent paralegal."

"I'll look into it." She finished her wine. "How's Sonya doing with all this?"

"Not good. She blames me for putting Josh in the spotlight."

"She'll come around. You two are solid."

"I don't know. We'll see." Ferd walked over to the bar and paid the check.

"When do you want to see Dad?"

"Any time you can set it up."

"Why don't we meet at Mom's."

"You think she wants to see him?"

"I'll talk to her. Let me work on it."

She stood up and they hugged, tightly, as they'd never hugged before. Ferd realized how much his bond with his twin sister was worth nurturing.

WHEN FERD ARRIVED HOME, he could sense the tension in the house. Sonya was sitting in the study working on her laptop. "Josh called."

"Really? What'd he say?"

"The police called Colleen, but she refused to take the call."

"That's strange. I wonder why they were calling."

"Josh said she's very upset. She knows she can't avoid them forever."

Ferd didn't like this development. It certainly wasn't consistent with Fong not filing charges.

"How'd it go with Claire?" she asked, staring at her screen.

"She's doing better. Lots of therapy as you might expect. She wants to see our father."

"I'm surprised," Sonya said, looking up. "I thought she hated him."

"She does, but she's curious about him." Ferd swallowed. "I know you said no before, but what about letting him stay in Josh's old room until he gets on his feet?"

She put the laptop aside. "I don't think so."

"I thought you were sympathetic to his situation."

"I am but that's a far cry from wanting a drunk living under my own roof. How could we ever relax? We'd be worrying about him stealing our things."

"Hasn't the man been through enough already?"

"Ferd, you're not thinking straight. Seriously, a drunk in *our* house?"

"I thought you had more heart than that."

"Don't go telling me I have no heart. You're the one who despised him even after you knew about his wife's death." Sonya was getting testy. "I'm supposed to let that man stay in my son's room while Josh is on the verge of going to jail?"

"Josh is not going to jail."

"Not yet he isn't, but I have a bad feeling, Ferd. This won't end well."

"We've gone over that already."

Sonya stood up, gritting her teeth. Without responding, she walked down the hallway to the bathroom and slammed the door. Ferd stared at the closed door, wondering how his family would ever recover.

32

Sonya and Ferd agreed to defer any decision on his father until things settled down. For one thing, Sonya had a project due within a week. It was a big launch for a well-known author and Sonya had been working long hours to finish on time. Her recent tension, Ferd soon realized, resulted in part from the stress of her work deadline.

On Wednesday afternoon, Ferd returned to chambers for the break and noticed a voicemail message from Colleen O'Keefe. The message said, "Call me as soon as you get this!" She sounded distressed.

He called her back. "They took him away!" she screamed.

"What're you talking about?"

"Josh! They arrested him a little while ago. Led him out of the office in handcuffs." She seemed on the verge of hyperventilating.

"Colleen, calm down."

"I can't calm down. I knew this would happen. The police came to headquarters earlier today and asked what I talked to Josh about after leaving the Promenade. I had to say I told Josh about Patrick kissing me. It was like they already knew. Oh, my God, I feel so bad!"

"It's not your fault," Ferd said. "I'll go to the jail. Let me handle it."

As soon as he hung up, Ferd called Stephanie Fong. "Why the hell did you arrest my son?"

"Judge Pitt, I had no choice."

"Bullshit! You as much as said you didn't have enough evidence before. What makes you think you do now?"

"Actually, I never said that and, after speaking with Sergeant Hinton, we decided there was enough evidence to make an arrest."

"Is there something I don't know about?"

"I can't comment on that."

Ferd slammed his fist on the desk. He couldn't believe Fong had double-crossed him this way. Why had he trusted her in the first place? He could kick himself. With his father's prosecution, she had proven herself a true politician, concerned more about adverse publicity than achieving justice. She would rather a judge dismissed the case than risk public scorn by doing so herself. The same was true now; she was bowing to public pressure to arrest someone. What a coward! He would remember this. *Just wait.*

Suddenly he realized why the police were asking about Josh talking to Colleen. "Did you execute a search warrant on Josh's cell phone?" *Damnit!* he thought, realizing he had given the police Josh's cell phone number after the brick incident.

"Discovery will be forthcoming. All your questions will be answered then." She paused. "I know how tough this is on you, Judge Pitt."

Thinking of Sonya, he said, "I don't think you do," then hung up.

. . .

HE WAITED until he got home after work before telling Sonya. As expected, the news set her off. She was angry at Ferd for failing to convince the prosecutor not to pursue the case. But her anger was tempered by her sadness for Josh. "My God, what's to become of my boy?"

"This is just another bump in the road," Ferd said. "Josh'll beat these charges."

"Really? And why should I believe anything you tell me?"

"Sonya, we've been through this."

"Oh, you're right. We have. And you can go straight to hell."

FERD WAS EMBARRASSED by all the publicity that his father had brought to his colleagues on the court. With Josh's arrest, that embarrassment would be magnified a thousandfold. So he approached them gingerly, sending the following email: *"As you undoubtedly know, my son has been charged with the murder of Patrick Brady. On his behalf I am considering hiring Angela Simpson as his defense attorney. I would appreciate any information you could provide relating to Ms. Simpson's trial skills, ethics, and track record. Thank you for your understanding."*

He received a half dozen responses, most positive. One said, "Ms. Simpson is the ultimate professional. She treats witnesses and opposing counsel with respect and knows her way around a courtroom. Your son would be in good hands." The only negative response stated, "Keep these comments confidential, but I would tread carefully with Ms. Simpson. In my experience she shapes her client's testimony to fit the defense. Not quite suborning perjury, but still unethical, at least in my view. She will do anything to win."

Ferd was mildly concerned with the ethical issue but knew he had to act quickly. So he called Simpson and made an appointment for the earliest time possible, Thursday at four o'clock. He was pushing it with the debate scheduled for six, but Josh was more important than his reelection.

AFTER DINNER, figuring Josh would've arrived at the jail by now, he drove over there, more distraught than on previous visits. Even though he'd been upset about his father's charges, that was nothing compared to having his only child charged with murder.

By the time he arrived, Josh had completed intake and processing and was in his cell. Although it was unusual to allow a new inmate to have visitors so soon, the deputies made an exception for Ferd. They knew how much he'd been through already with his father. The deputy sheriff led Josh to the meeting room and closed the door. Ferd choked up seeing his son dressed in an orange shirt, orange pants, and even orange shoes. He had a much different reaction from when he first saw Dwight. Then it was primarily shock at seeing his father after so many years. Now it was dismay, sadness, and regret that hit him deep in his gut.

Sitting across from each other, neither said anything for several seconds. Josh stared at the table, tension evident in his face. "I spoke to the district attorney," Ferd said. "She wouldn't say whether she had anything new. But the police know Colleen called you about Brady's kiss."

Josh snapped to attention. "Yeah, so?"

"That was right before Brady was stabbed."

"So they think I ran over, grabbed a knife from somewhere, and stabbed him?"

"Josh, I know this is hard to hear, but it's politics. After Smedley laid out all the evidence against you, Fong had no choice but to authorize an arrest. Otherwise, she would've been crucified in the press."

Looking away, Josh said, "That makes me sick."

"Try to keep the faith. I left a message with Henry Smith about the arrest and will ask him to cover your arraignment. I'll follow up with him when we're done here. In the meantime, be careful what you say to anyone and remember that all phone calls are recorded."

"Are you afraid I'll confess? Don't you believe I'm innocent?"

"Josh, I do believe you're innocent. I know how you were raised. You've never exhibited any violent tendencies. To take a knife and stab someone to death: it's unfathomable. You would never do such a thing. But I'm also aware of how the evidence looks. It's not good. We've already seen how it can be twisted against you, but I'll do whatever I can to get you acquitted." Ferd paused, thinking of Sonya. "Your mother is beside herself. Give her a call."

"I'll call her, but I don't want her visiting me. I couldn't bear to have my mother seeing me like this, Dad. This is traumatic enough as it is."

Ferd understood Josh's reluctance to expose his mother to her orange-clad son. He was glad Josh wanted to spare his mother. If only Ferd could've spared Sonya all the agony she's been going through. He realized that he had a lot of work to do to repair their relationship but knew that would happen only if Josh were acquitted. Despite the Commission on Judicial Performance's ongoing investigation, Ferd would find the truth even if it cost him his career.

"You'll be arraigned tomorrow afternoon. I'm also meeting with a criminal law specialist to help out Henry."

Josh stood up and gave his father an awkward hug. "I appreciate your help. I really do. It's just...I have to wonder if you hadn't probed so much whether all this would've happened."

"You know it would have. Smedley knew everything I did. She brought the whole case against you out in the open."

"Yeah, I guess. I knew there was something about her I didn't like."

ON THE DRIVE HOME, Ferd received a call from Henry. "Sorry to hear about Josh. That district attorney has her head up her ass."

"I'm sure it's just politics. Look, I've got an appointment with Angela Simpson for tomorrow afternoon. Can you handle the arraignment? It's at 1:30."

"I've got it, don't worry."

"You might want to waive the ten-day speedy prelim right so there's time to prep."

"Let's see what Simpson says. I'll set the prelim within ten days, then Josh can waive it later."

"Henry, I can't thank you enough for this."

"This is what friends do."

WHEN FERD GOT HOME, Sonya was asleep. She must've taken a sleeping pill, Ferd thought. Between Josh getting arrested and the prospect of his father living with them, Sonya had been through the ringer. Normally she was a tough woman, a giving, loving, bright woman. Ferd didn't want to lose her.

One way he could lighten her load was having his father stay at the Pitt family home in the Sunset. Ever since their mother had gone into assisted living, Ferd and Claire had debated what to do with the house. At first the plan was to see if she would be in assisted living temporarily. When it became apparent it was permanent, they had decided to sell the house but hadn't gotten around to making arrangements. So the house sat empty. Perhaps Ferd could prevail on his mother to allow Dwight to live there.

After kissing Sonya on the forehead and pulling up her covers, Ferd drove to Daly City to see his mother. It was getting late, but he hadn't talked to her in some time. She was still up, sitting in her lounger watching television. Ferd wondered about her life, how she could stand being so immobile, limited. It was a monotonous existence. She had apparently resigned herself to this life and was making the best of it. *How much longer could she survive?* Each time Ferd saw her he was afraid it would be the last time, leaving him constantly uneasy.

"Ma," Ferd said after she let him in. "How're you feeling?"

"Same as always. Like shit."

"Sorry to hear that." Ferd sat on the couch across from her. "I've met with Dad, and he's been released from jail. That's the good news. But now he needs a place to stay."

She stared at the TV, her breathing quickening. "I know what you're going to ask and the answer's no."

"But Ma, can't you see things from Dad's perspective? He's been through a lot in his life and he needs a break."

"Oh, *he* needs a break? What about leaving me to raise two children on my own? Didn't I deserve a break? Why should I forgive him?"

"I know this is hard on you, but no one's using the house. We'd just have to turn on the power and water. I'll handle all the expense; you won't have to pay anything."

She pulled out the oxygen tube from her nose and turned toward her son. "I'm glad you've forgiven him, though I can't say I understand it. He helped raise you and your sister for twelve years. You'd think he'd have had more of an attachment. Instead, he just walks out. But I won't do him any favors. Forget it."

Ferd realized there was no changing her mind, at least for the moment, so he tried a different approach. "How about I bring him by to see you? Maybe you'd soften if you got to talk to him. What do you say?"

"I don't know if I'm ready for that. I'd probably bite his head off."

"Claire wants to see him so why don't I pick up a pizza and bring him by. I'll check with Claire and call you, okay?"

His mother grumbled and complained but eventually agreed. "That doesn't mean I'll let him live in my house. Understood?"

Ferd nodded, glad to get a concession, albeit a minor one. Now he had to break the bad news and tell her about Josh. He tried being gentle. "There's been a mistake, Ma, and Josh has been arrested. I'm going to get him cleared but I wanted you to know. It'll be on the news."

"My Josh? How can that be? He wouldn't hurt a fly."

"I know. It's terrible."

"Well, you've certainly made my day." She turned up the volume on the TV. "Thanks for stopping by."

WHEN FERD ARRIVED HOME, Sonya was sitting up in bed with the television tuned to the local news. "Judge's son arrested in Tenderloin murder!" the banner announced. The lead news reader was an African American man with a thick moustache that extended down the sides of his mouth, but not quite far enough to be a Fu Manchu. "There's been a shocking development in the Tenderloin murder of a high-tech executive," he announced. "Joshua Pitt, son of Superior Court Judge Ferdinand Pitt and grandson of the original defendant Dwight Pitt, has been charged with the murder. Efforts to reach Judge Pitt have been unsuccessful. Police say young Mr. Pitt murdered Patrick Brady after the two had a work-related dispute at CAPSLOCK, a Silicon Valley software company."

Josh's booking photo, showing him in all his orange finery, flashed on the screen. "Oh, my God!" said Sonya, shielding her eyes. "I can't watch this anymore. Shut it off."

Ferd clicked off the TV. Sonya stared straight ahead. The two sat in silence for several minutes. Finally, Sonya said, "I'm trying to deal with this maturely, but it's not easy. Now everyone in the world knows our son is an accused murderer. I feel so bad for him. How scared he must be!"

"He is scared. I'm sorry you had to see that. Josh didn't want you to see him in orange. Let's try to talk to him tomorrow. I think it would make you feel a lot better."

Sonya nodded and rested her head on Ferd's shoulder. They would've remained that way if the house phone hadn't rung. It was after ten o'clock. Ferd thought a call this late can't be good. He looked at the caller ID. The call was from Pacifica.

"Judge Pitt, when you told me your father was innocent, I didn't expect to learn the murderer was your son." She slurred her words.

"You've seen the news, Ms. Brady."

"Yes, I've seen the news. It's very disturbing to learn about your son." Although she said she was disturbed, her voice, though unsteady, was calm and restrained. Ferd would've expected her to go off on him, to show her anger at Josh, the alleged murderer of her husband.

"He's innocent."

"I've heard that before."

"And it was true before, as it's true now."

"Judge Pitt, why do you suppose your family has become so entwined with mine?"

"I wish I knew the answer to that question. But I assure you, I will not stop looking until I find the actual murderer."

"How do you propose doing that?"

Ferd paused. "I don't really know."

"Do yourself a favor, Judge Pitt, and let it go. From everything I've heard your son is guilty. He had it out for Patrick and was just waiting for the right opportunity."

"You're wrong about that, Ms. Brady. My son's not a murderer."

"I said let it go." She was insistent, her voice low and relaxed.

33

The next day around eight o'clock Ferd received a hand-delivered letter from the Commission. As he tore it open, his worries bubbled to the surface. *Could this be the end of my judicial career?*

Dear Judge Pitt:

I understand that your son was recently charged with the murder of Patrick Brady. I want to reiterate my earlier warnings about your involvement in any investigation of the murder.

I also want to make clear that the Commission's offer of a public admonishment will be withdrawn if the Commission learns of your continued investigation, in which case you will be subject to more serious discipline, including removal from the bench.

Very truly yours,

Nancy Harper

Cc: Henry Smith, Esq.

As if by instinct, without giving it any thought, he again crumpled up the letter and tossed it in the trash. "I will not be intimidated," he said to himself. He thought of Josh. With his son's life at stake, he would do whatever it took to free him, the Commission be damned.

Ferd called the jail. "Hi, this is Ferdinand Pitt. I was wondering if you could get a message to my son Josh."

The female deputy, her voice sounding like the one who had accompanied his father to their first meeting, said, "What kind of message?"

"Just to call home."

"No problem, Judge Pitt."

When Josh called several minutes later, Sonya was working in the study. Ferd heard her phone ringing and joined her. "Yes, I'll accept the call," she said, putting the phone on speaker.

"Mom, it's Josh." Even through the phone's speaker, Josh's voice sounded forlorn, lost, as if he really didn't know who he was.

"Oh, my God. You're on speaker and Dad's here. How're you?"

"Not good. This is no fun. The worst part is I'm bored. Sitting around doing nothing has never been my thing."

"Dad is working on getting you out."

"I'm sure he is." The phone went silent.

Ferd motioned to Sonya to let him speak. "Josh, I don't want to say anything now because this call is being recorded."

"Jesus, what happens next?"

"Henry will stop by to see you this morning, then you'll be arraigned." Ferd paused, then said, "I got a call from Ms. Brady."

"Why'd she call you?"

"I'm not quite sure. She's gone through a lot lately."

"Can you put Mom back on?"

Ferd handed the phone back to Sonya. "Yes, Josh."

"I'm going to be alright. I don't want you worrying about me."

"How can I not worry? You're my only child."

"I know but I'll get through this. It may take some time. I'm sorry."

"You did nothing wrong. It's just an unfortunate set of circumstances."

"I'll call you tomorrow," Josh said. "Love you."

"I love you too, Josh."

"Love you, Josh," added Ferd, but Josh had already hung up. Sonya left the room without saying anything. Ferd stared at the walls. *There must've been something I could've done to prevent this. But I'll be damned if I know what the hell that is.*

SIMPSON'S OFFICE was located on Franklin Street, a few blocks from the Civic Center Courthouse and about a mile from the Hall of Justice. When Ferd began practicing, financial district lawyers looked down on lawyers with offices in Hayes Valley, the low rent part of town, where Franklin Street is. With substantial development resulting in designer shops and trendy restaurants moving into the neighborhood, that elitist view had softened somewhat over the years. But Ferd still clung to his old views and decided that Simpson had better be damn impressive if he were going to hire her.

He found Simpson's office on the third floor of a Victorian house. After ringing the doorbell, he was buzzed inside. The elevator had a "Scheduled for Service" sign on it, so he walked up the stairs to the third floor. He was surprised at how heavily he was breathing when he got to the top. He found Simpson's suite at the end of a narrow hallway and opened the door. Behind a desk sat a heavyset woman with black hair shaved on one side. He didn't recognize her.

"I'm looking for Angela Simpson."

"You found her. Judge Pitt?"

"Why yes." Ferd was taken aback at her appearance, which he didn't anticipate.

"Please take a seat," she said, gesturing. "I guess I'm not quite what you expected."

"I confess I am surprised. I was thinking of someone more...traditional."

"This is avant-garde dyke." She waved her hand from her face to her torso. Ferd noticed a photograph behind the desk showing Simpson and a slim blonde woman with their arms around each other.

"You got some good references from judges as well as my ex-partner Henry Smith."

"Glad to hear it. All I know about the case is what I read in the paper. Seems like the cops had a hard time deciding whether the murderer was your father or son."

"That's true. I suspect politics has played a role here. My son swears he's innocent. And I believe him."

"Of course. Why don't you lay out the evidence for me."

Ferd described all the evidence against Josh, including Brady's harassment of Colleen, filling her in on his complete investigation. "I'm not supposed to be investigating the case, but I can't let my son rot in jail."

"I'm impressed by what you've done."

"Tell me about your experience in murder cases."

"I've handled dozens and tried around twenty in several Bay Area counties."

"What's your trial record?"

"That can be deceptive. But so far, I've won outright acquittals in half. It's not like civil cases where you settle when things look bad. In a murder case, the client is looking at life in prison so it's hard to reach a plea bargain. You're usually arguing about what degree of murder. Sometimes you have a viable self-defense argument."

Ferd knew how difficult defending a murder case was and was impressed that she had obtained so many acquittals. "What about when the defendant flat out denies being the murderer?"

"Those are rare cases. Most times you've got to point to someone else as the murderer. Is there anyone like that here?"

"The police have no other suspects."

She scratched her head, the shaved side, and said, "If the victim had been a woman, the first person the police would've looked at is the husband. Second is the lover. Have the police considered the wife?"

"Not that I know of."

"Tell me about the wife."

"Denise Brady is a thirty-something woman who, it seems, stayed home full time. I've met her a couple of times and talked to her twice by phone. She's understandably invested in how this case turns out."

Simpson made some notes on a yellow legal pad. "Worth digging a little more. And this Colleen? What's her story?"

"She and Josh have been dating for a few months. She's well educated, a few years older."

"Any chance she and Brady were having an affair?"

"She denies it, but who knows?"

"It'd be interesting if they were. She's the last person to see Brady alive."

Ferd realized he had forgotten to mention something. "You should know that someone threw a brick through my living room window with a note warning me not to investigate. Then someone tried to run me off the road. The police have hit a dead end on both incidents, though Colleen drives a similar kind of car as was involved in both."

"What kind of car?"

"A dark sedan."

"That's not much to go on."

"I know."

"My, you've had a tough time. But that certainly suggests you ruffled some feathers." Simpson put down her pen. "I'm interested in helping out your son. Of course, I'd like to meet him."

"Sure, I'll set it up. But let me ask you something. Have you had any State Bar complaints?"

"Not that I know of."

"The reason I ask is I heard from someone that you'll do whatever it takes to win. I like that sentiment but want to be sure you act within the rules of ethics."

Simpson sat up straight. "I never heard of any ethical complaints. I'm aggressive and sometimes men think that equals a bitch. I don't care about that, but I do care if someone is judging me based on my gender and not my work."

Ferd sat back and assessed her before coming to a decision. He liked her. She had substantial experience and seemed to value his opinion. "I'm impressed with you and think you'll do a good job for Josh. But Henry Smith will be working with you. He has nowhere near your level of experience in criminal law but he's a trusted friend and former colleague. Will that be a problem?"

"Is that necessary? Are you sure you want to pay two lawyers?"

"Not really, but I will. At least at the beginning."

"If that's what you want, I'm okay with it."

"Good. I'll tell Henry to call you."

FERD BARELY MADE it to the debate in time. He had cut things too close, meeting with Simpson then driving downtown through rush-hour traffic, and parking at Embarcadero Center One. The garage was nearly full and Ferd had to drive deep into the bowels of the earth before finding a space.

Rodda was not pleased. "I thought I'd have to debate Smedley myself," he said, scowling. "Then the shit would've really hit the fan."

"Well, I made it. Let me get a drink of water."

"There're plastic bottles on the stage and Smedley's already there. No time to waste." He put his hand on Ferd's shoulder and leaned in. "Remember, be judicial at all times."

"Got it." Ferd then climbed the steps toward the stage and greeted Smedley, offering his hand while pasting a fake smile on his face. She also sported a fake smile as she shook his hand, a limp wet shake. Ferd wiped his hand on his jacket and greeted the moderator, the bar association president, a tall grey-haired man with a bright smile named Russ Davis. Ferd knew him by reputation as a competent, ethical legal malpractice lawyer.

Davis approached the microphone, which was positioned to the side of the two candidates. Only he would be standing. Rodda had been right; the chairs were cushioned and very comfortable. Between Ferd and Smedley was a small round table to hold their water bottles. A technician had fitted each with a portable microphone. Ferd gazed at the audience, comprised of local attorneys. There were many public defenders present to show support for Smedley. Ferd knew he didn't have any chance of influencing their votes. But there was also a fair contingent from his old firm, including Henry Smith, who must've recruited staff to attend. Seated in the front row, a few seats away from Smith, were Curt Rodda and Natalie. Ferd was glad to have a few friendly faces so close. He vowed to keep his eyes on them whenever the questioning became tough.

"Ladies and gentlemen," Davis began, "it's time to start our debate between two candidates for the San Francisco Superior Court bench. Please welcome Judge Ferdinand Pitt and deputy public defender Nicole Smedley."

There was scattered applause, a few whistles, and even a few public defenders chanting, "Smedley, Smedley." Davis held up his hand. "Thank you. Please hold any applause until the end of the debate. By lot, Judge Pitt has been chosen to answer the first question." He was holding a stack of index cards and turned toward Ferd.

"Judge Pitt, I know this must be a sensitive topic for you, but we can't ignore the news from the past few days. Your son has been arrested for murder. Are you going to be able to focus on your campaign while these charges are pending?"

Ferd knew there would be a question about Josh, but had hoped it would be later in the debate so he could ease into it. Still, he jumped right on it. "My focus is on my family at this difficult time. Let me say at the outset that my son is innocent of this charge; I'll say no more about it for the time being. Will I be focused also on my campaign? Yes, I will. I love being a judge. I enjoy the support of both prosecutors and defense attorneys because I am fair to both sides. I also enjoy the support of the civil bar even though my career on the bench has been entirely on the criminal side. That is much different than my opponent, who is known as a rabid criminal defense attorney, often skirting the edge of ethical behavior, and has absolutely no civil law experience."

The crowd erupted, at least the ones who supported Ferd. He was gratified to have so many supporters present. He needed the ego boost. Davis raised his hand to quiet the crowd. "It seems only fair to give Ms. Smedley an opportunity to respond to the judge's comments. Ms. Smedley?"

Flouting the debate rules, Smedley stood up and looked down on Ferd. "I am surprised Judge Pitt would even mention ethical behavior, given his conduct in his father's case. There's a reason the Commission on Judicial Performance is investigating him. He is not an ethical person and severely undermined my defense of his father. As to his other comments, I stand on my record as an extremely successful defense attorney. I enjoy support from not only my own colleagues but also from many prosecutors. It's true I have no civil law experience, but I am a fast learner and don't anticipate any issues getting up to speed on civil law."

There was scattered applause, focused on one group on the left side, where Smedley's colleagues had congregated. Ferd was about to stand up to rebut Smedley's comments but noticed Rodda motioning with his hands for Ferd to stay seated.

"Please, ladies and gentlemen," Davis said, "hold your applause or we'll never get to half the questions." He flipped to his next index card. "Ms. Smedley, the next question is for you. As you mentioned, you've had a successful career as a criminal defense attorney. Why have you decided to run for the bench at this time?"

Smedley remained in her seat for this question. "I want to bring some compassion to the bench, an attribute sorely lacking from my opponent, who tends to favor the prosecution. He refuses to release defendants pre-trial when they pose no risk to public safety, in direct defiance of the law. His attitude is to lock them up and throw away the key. I'm much more empathetic to the devastation that incarceration can have on defendants and their families."

Ferd was taken aback by these statements. He never considered himself a pro-prosecution judge, only a fair one. He glanced at Rodda and Natalie who were nodding slightly as if to tell him to go easy. "Once again, Ms. Smedley is mistaken," he said. "I am neither pro-prosecution nor pro-defense. I take each case on its own merits. There are many defendants I've released to home detention with an ankle monitor or mandated treatment for those struggling with addiction. At the same time, I will not risk the safety of the public by releasing a dangerous defendant. The same could not be said of Ms. Smedley."

Ferd was getting into the flow of the debate, more relaxed

than he had been at the practice session. But his mind kept returning to Josh being in jail. He wondered how the murder charge would affect Josh's future even if he were cleared. His stomach sunk and he was suddenly very sad. As a result, he found himself not listening while Smedley was droning on about her extensive experience in treatment courts and how she supposedly single-handedly turned defendants' lives around. He found her typically annoying and self-satisfied, but had no idea how the audience viewed her.

For the last question of the night, Davis returned to the subject with which he'd begun the debate. "Judge Pitt, you've now had the unfortunate experience of having first your father then your son accused of murder. How has that experience affected your work as a judge?"

"Thank you for asking that. Although I believe I was always empathetic to the accused as well as victims, recent events have made me more attuned to the detrimental effects of criminal charges, not just on the accused but on his entire family. These charges have been devastating to me, my sister, my wife, and of course my father and son. I am particularly conscious of the power of the state to uproot lives and tarnish reputations."

The applause was immediate. Ferd was taken aback, unaware how strongly others felt about the charges against his family. Led by Rodda and Natalie, several stood, applauding loudly. Ferd was gratified. The noise drowned out Smedley's attempt to respond.

When Davis signaled an end to the debate, Ferd sought out Henry Smith. After catching Smith's eye, he approached and asked him about Josh's arraignment that afternoon.

"He never looked up," Henry said. "Stared at the floor as the charges were being read, mumbled 'not guilty.' That was it."

"Is the prelim set?"

"Yeah, in ten days."

Ferd wanted to ask more, but Rodda grabbed him by the arm and leaned in. "Great job! I'm proud of you. Very judicial."

Ferd managed a smile, surprised at Rodda's comment. In the whole time they'd worked together, Rodda had never complimented him. Maybe he actually had a chance to win this election after all.

34

W ith the debate over, Ferd returned his attention to the pressing matters of his son in jail and his father in a shelter. Then Presiding Judge Carol Bradstein called to invite him to lunch. They met at Sol's Cafe near the Civic Center Courthouse. Ferd arrived first and sat in a booth in back. Wearing a flowered blouse and black dress pants, Carol waved to Ferd and took a seat across from him.

"You've certainly gone through a lot lately," she said. "I wanted to see how you're doing."

Ferd wondered if she had another agenda. She could've checked on his well-being by phone instead of dragging him to Civic Center.

"Not too good," he said, sipping his water.

"How's your son?"

"Depressed. I want you to know he's innocent."

She held up a hand. "We can't discuss a pending case."

"Fine."

The waiter took their orders. She fiddled with her silverware. "I wanted to meet you in person. To be honest, you don't look well: pale, thin, tense. Can't say I'm surprised."

Maybe she was being genuine, Ferd thought. "I appreciate your concern."

"The California Judges Association has some programs for judges in difficult situations. Why don't you call them?"

"Maybe I will, but right now I'm doing okay, exercising, trying to get enough sleep."

She took a sip of water and looked directly into Ferd's eyes. "The district attorney called me."

Ferd sat back, wondering where this was going. "So why did she call you? To complain?"

"She thought you were getting embroiled in the case."

"Embroiled? Of course, I was getting embroiled. First it was my father, then my son. Who wouldn't get embroiled?"

"I understand. I do. But you're already under investigation by the Commission. I don't want you to make things worse."

"Is that what this is about?"

"I have to follow up on these things. Plus, I haven't seen you in a while, so I figured this was a good time."

Their meals arrived and they ate mostly in silence until the end of lunch. Bradstein told him that a visiting judge would be handling his son's case. "As with your father, your colleagues feel they would have a conflict of interest, and I agree."

"Any idea who it will be?"

"Maybe Judge Labarle again," she said, pausing. "One thing I want to prepare you for: I expect the Commission will discipline you. But I don't know at what level yet."

Ferd bristled, his body tensing. "Thanks, Carol. I must say I didn't expect my career to take such an eventful turn."

SINCE FERD WAS close to downtown anyway and he had a half hour before he had to return to the Hall, he thought he'd stop by Henry's office. After calling to make sure he was in, Ferd drove to the financial district and parked in the same $20-an-hour garage as before. Charlotte welcomed him warmly and led him to Smith's corner office with a view of the Bay Bridge. Ferd and Smith sat at a round oak table next to his desk and below his framed certificates from college and law school. Ferd gazed around the office, his before being appointed to the bench, and felt a twinge of nostalgia. How he had enjoyed the high life as a big-firm partner with all the perks such as an expense account and this corner office. If he had ignored the call to public service, he could've practiced in relative obscurity without having his name and photo plastered all over the Internet and in the local press. Even with family members accused of murder, the story would have less of an impact if he were a mere lawyer in private practice.

"I'm meeting with Angela Simpson this afternoon," Smith said.

"Glad to hear it." Ferd exhaled deeply. "She mentioned that when a wife is killed the police tend to focus on the husband. She thinks we need to look at the wife and maybe Colleen."

"Is there any evidence linking either one to the scene? Any motive?"

Ferd shook his head. "The wife said she was home at the time of the murder. I wonder if her neighbors will back that up. We know Colleen was there."

"I'll talk to Simpson about retaining an investigator."

Ferd grimaced. "Regarding the Commission: I just had lunch with Carol Bradstein and she told me I'm likely to get disciplined, though she didn't know at what level."

"She's speculating."

"Maybe, but she did have a long talk with the investigator."

"Let's deal with that when the time comes." He paused, staring at Ferd. "You look like shit. Let's take your mind off this negativity. How about we set up a couples' dinner? I'd like Jiselle to meet you and Sonya."

"I don't know if Sonya will be up for that."

"Nonsense. Tell her I insisted. Let's do it tonight at Le Vieux Manoir. I'll make reservations for seven o'clock."

"Maybe you're right. I'll talk to Sonya. Both of us could use a break."

But Sonya was even harder to convince than Ferd expected. She flat out refused, saying she was too miserable to socialize. "No, you go," she said. "I appreciate what Henry's doing for Josh, but I can't make small talk right now."

Ferd called Henry and told him Sonya wasn't feeling well. They agreed to get together socially when Josh's case was over.

35

Ferd hadn't talked to his father since dropping him off at the shelter so the next morning he put in a call. "I'm looking for Dwight Pitt."

"Hi, this is Adam Rosen, the manager. Mr. Pitt is no longer staying here."

"What happened?"

"Can I ask who this is?"

"I'm his son."

"I'm sorry to tell you this but he broke the rules. This is a sober-living environment, and he was drunk last night. We had no choice but to ask him to leave."

Ferd closed his eyes, disappointed. "Any idea where he went?"

"He's probably on the street. You might check his old haunts."

Ferd immediately walked into the study where Sonya was working. "I've got a new problem."

"What is it?"

"My father. He relapsed and got kicked out of the shelter. Just what I need."

"I'm sorry to hear that. What're you going to do?"

"I'm going to look for him. But if I find him, do you mind if he stays here?"

"Ferd, we've been through that." She frowned. "And now he's drinking."

Ferd wondered where his wife's empathy had gone.

FERD PARKED in a garage on the edge of the Tenderloin. His only plan was to walk the grimy streets until he found his father. A lot of homeless men hung out on street corners, some playing dice or cards. He walked down Ellis holding his phone in his hand, showing his father's booking photo.

"I'm looking for this man," he said to a group of men sitting on lawn chairs. They glared at him without even checking out the photo. Ferd walked on. He tried this routine several times with varying degrees of interest. One person said he'd seen him a few hours earlier walking up Hyde, so Ferd made his way there. Tents lined Hyde and Turk Streets, a homeless encampment the city had allowed to expand.

Ferd stared at every face he passed, getting angry glares in return. Some said, "What're you staring at?" Ferd apologized and kept walking. He showed the photo to a group standing on the corner. "I seen this dude," a tall thin man said. "He was hanging in a doorway a few blocks away. Yeah, I seen him."

"Can you point me in the right direction?"

The man grinned, showing missing upper and lower teeth. "What's it worth to ya?"

Ferd pulled out his wallet and handed the man a ten-dollar bill. The man shook his head, so Ferd took out another ten and handed it to him. "Okay, walk up Hyde to O'Farrell and take a right. It's on that block there. You can't miss him."

Another man walked up to them, having seen Ferd hand over the bills. "I seen him too," he said, holding out his hand.

This man was huge, six feet five inches and probably 260 pounds. Ferd smiled nervously, walked around him, and hurried up Hyde.

On O'Farrell, Ferd looked in doorways for his father. Halfway down the block he found someone stretched out in the doorway of a closed shop, a blanket covering the entire body, including the head. Ferd bent down. "Excuse me. Sorry to wake you."

The person stirred and sat up. It was his father. His eyes were glassy.

"Ferdinand?"

"Dad, what the hell?"

"Sorry. I blew it. I couldn't stay off the booze."

"How'd you pay for it?"

"I begged for money. Got enough for one pint." He sat up, wrapping the blanket around his shoulders. "Found this blanket on the street." It was filthy and smelled like socks worn for weeks without washing.

"Let's go; you're coming with me."

"They won't let me back into the shelter."

"I know. You can stay with me and Sonya."

"Ferd, I can't do that to your wife."

"You're going into treatment. Let me deal with Sonya."

Despite his calm demeanor, Ferd was nervous as hell about bringing his father home. He knew Sonya would be irate. Although this wasn't the time to upset her, he felt he had no choice. It was either take him home or lose him to the streets.

At home, he told his father to sit at the kitchen table while he spoke to Sonya. After giving him a Diet Coke, Ferd walked upstairs to the study. "My father's downstairs. I found him on the street drunk."

"We talked about this." Sonya was stern.

"Sonya, please. Let him stay for a few days. Until I can find a residential treatment facility."

"What am I supposed to do, work in the office? How can I work with him in the house? I won't be able to relax."

"Sonya, can't you put up with him for *a few days*? I'm not asking for much."

She turned to him, spinning in the desk chair. "Not asking for much? Spare me. You've been pushing my buttons ever since your father was charged. First, you had to determine if he was guilty; now you expect me to allow him into my home."

Ferd realized he had a long way to go to regain her trust. "At least come downstairs and meet him."

Sonya relented and went downstairs. Dwight jumped up when he saw her. "I'm sorry to impose," he said, "but it's good to finally meet you."

"Mr. Pitt, I've heard a lot about you." She extended her hand.

"None of it good, I'm sure."

"That's true." She grabbed a Diet Coke from the refrigerator and sat down beside him. "You've had a rough life, I understand."

Ferd leaned against the counter with his arms crossed.

"That's an understatement, at least lately. For a while there in New Hampshire I was doing fine. My wife Janet and I were reasonably happy; I had a good job. Then the shit hit the fan."

"And you found yourself back in San Francisco charged with murder."

"Thanks to Ferd, that issue has been straightened out."

"Yeah." She glanced at Ferd. "He really straightened that out, didn't he?"

"I'm sorry about Josh. That took me by surprise."

Sonya took a long swig of her soda. "Look, Mr. Pitt, let me be straight with you. When Ferd first suggested you stay with us, I was dead set against it. You know why?"

"I get it. You don't want a drunk in your house."

"Exactly."

"Would it make a difference if I stayed off alcohol while I was here?"

"Wasn't that the same rule you had at the shelter?"

Dwight looked down, embarrassed. "You're right, of course." He paused. "I'll only ask for your understanding this one time. If I screw up, I'll leave and you'll be done with me."

Sonya sipped her Diet Coke then stared at the ceiling, thinking, for over a minute. Finally, she looked at Dwight. "Would you mind going down to the basement while I talk to Ferd? Make yourself comfortable."

After Dwight did as requested, she said, "He can stay here for a little while only, but there are some strict rules. He will sleep on the sofa bed in the basement and will not bring any alcohol into this house. We'll have to lock up the wine in the cabinet. And he will stay sober."

"That's fine," said Ferd, glad his wife's empathy had prevailed.

36

Ferd was pleased Sonya allowed his father to stay. That was one worry he could cross off his list. Now he had to check on Josh. He was concerned about his son's mental well-being and wanted to be sure Josh knew he was still working to free him. He parked near the jail and made his way to the holding area. When Josh approached, Ferd stepped forward to hug him but Josh moved to the side, avoiding him.

"What's the matter?"

"I just don't feel like hugging you right now." He sat down.

"I've been getting a lot of that lately," Ferd said as he sat across from Josh. "Has anything happened?"

"I haven't been raped, if that's what you're asking."

Ferd could sense tension emanating from his son. He was frustrated Josh was in this situation. "What've you been doing with your time?"

Josh stared at him as if that were the stupidest question in the world. "I've been enjoying all the fascinating company. We're so compatible."

Ferd brushed off Josh's sarcasm. "I understand you met Simpson. What do you think?"

"A bit unorthodox, but what do I know? I have to trust your judgment. But I'm glad Mr. Smith will still be involved."

"I'm working on a few leads. I'll get you out of here as soon as I can."

"Take your time. I'm living the life here."

ON THE DRIVE HOME, Ferd received a call from Henry Smith. "Simpson's investigator spoke to the widow's neighbors. One guy remembers Ms. Brady going out the night of the murder but can't say when she came home. He fell asleep in front of the TV."

"What time did she go out?"

"Around 6:30."

"That contradicts her alibi. Why didn't she tell me about that?"

"Maybe she's got something to hide. Or maybe she forgot."

"I doubt that." Ferd considered what to do with this information. "So what's our theory: that she brought a steak knife from her kitchen and planned on killing her husband?"

"Good question. It does seem unlikely, but let's just play it out, see where it goes."

"And what about Colleen? Anything there?"

"She told the investigator she went right to the parking garage after Brady kissed her. And she wasn't happy to be interrogated again. The investigator sniffed around a bit more and got the impression she was closer to Brady than she let on. It's possible she actually had an affair with him. But not much to go on."

"Thanks, Henry. And, oh, try to keep in touch with Josh. He's not doing so well right now."

37

The next morning, as Ferd was preparing to go to work, he received another hand-delivered letter from the Commission. *Here comes the discipline,* Ferd thought, hoping that he wasn't kicked off the bench.

Dear Judge Pitt:

The Commission has received information that you have continued investigating the murder of Patrick Brady. The Commission needs to question you further and has scheduled an appointment for next Thursday at 4 p.m. You may, of course, have counsel present to represent you.

Sincerely,

Nancy Harper

cc: Henry Smith, Esq.

Ferd resisted the urge to throw away the letter, instead placing it in his inside suit pocket. On the drive to court, he called Henry. "Did you see the Commission letter?"

Henry sighed. "I'm available Thursday afternoon so I can't argue for a continuance."

"Yeah, I can make myself available."

"How did they find out?"

"I don't know, but I have my guesses."

"You think Carol Bradstein said something?"

"I wouldn't be surprised. I should've declined her lunch invitation."

FERD'S AFTERNOON calendar was light, so he left work early and made his way to Henry Smith's office to join a defense strategy meeting with Angela Simpson. She started the meeting by summarizing the discovery she had received from the prosecution. "The only surprise is a search warrant served on Verizon," she said.

"For what?" asked Ferd.

"They were looking for call detail records for Josh's cell phone the night of the murder."

"You mean so they could track his location?" asked Henry.

"Exactly."

"Did they get anything?"

"Oh yeah. Verizon produced a spreadsheet of Josh's incoming and outgoing calls in the half hour before and half hour after the murder. Verizon also provided a map pinpointing where the various cell towers were located, and which sector was used. Sectors show the direction of the signal from Josh's phone."

"Jesus, it's incredible what they can do," Ferd said.

"Well," Henry said, "don't keep us in suspense. What did the data show?"

Simpson pulled a pile of papers from her briefcase and spread them on the conference room table. "Mind you the data is of limited value. A cell phone tries to find the strongest signal and proximity to the cell tower is only one factor to consider. Others are line of sight, topography, amount of traffic, and - to a lesser extent - weather. There was an incoming call at 6:45 from the cell tower in Union Square. Another call came in at 7:14

from the same tower, meaning Josh was likely in the same general area then."

"The garage video showed him there at 7:22 so that's not surprising. Do the records show where Josh went after the Promenade?" asked Ferd.

"They're not that precise."

"So we don't know where Josh was at the time of the murder?"

"Only that he was likely in the Union Square area."

"How far is it from the cell tower to the Blue Arms Hotel?"

"Good question. About three hundred yards."

"So where does this leave us?"

"The cell phone records don't really add much to the video evidence. I suspect the police hoped to get more justification to arrest Josh and were waiting for the return on the search warrant. They got the results shortly before the arrest."

"The call at 7:14," Henry said. "Who was it from?"

"The data doesn't tell us that. It provides only the number."

"Let me see the number," said Ferd. He glanced at the records. "That must be the call from Colleen. I suspected the cops executed a search warrant on Josh's cell phone because they questioned her about the call before Josh was arrested."

"Wait. I don't think I've heard about this yet," said Simpson.

Ferd turned toward her. "Colleen called Josh to tell him about Brady's kiss."

Simpson gritted her teeth. "So the police think Josh went looking for him."

"What do we do about the prelim?" he asked.

"We should waive the ten-day right and take it off calendar."

"I agree," Henry said.

"What're we going to do about widow Brady?" asked Ferd.

"What do you mean?" asked Simpson.

"Henry said a neighbor saw her leave home the night of the

murder. Can't we follow up on that? What about getting *her* cell phone records?"

"That's an interesting idea," Henry said.

"I don't know. Her lawyer will likely fight a subpoena duces tecum, assert her right to privacy."

"I'll get you her cell number. She called my home once, so it should be saved on my phone. Worth a try," said Ferd.

"I'll draft the paperwork and get it served," said Henry.

Ferd left the meeting with concern about Josh having to stay in jail for the time being. But he had mixed feelings about the case: worry about the phone call from Colleen but hope that he could find evidence linking Brady's widow to his death. Ferd finally felt like he was at last moving forward with Josh's defense. If they could prove that Denise Brady was in the Tenderloin at the same time as her husband, that would go a long way to proving her guilt, particularly in view of her denying leaving the house. In his gut he felt there was something there. But his gut wouldn't get Josh exonerated; for that, he needed evidence.

THE ELECTION WAS tomorrow so Ferd stopped by campaign headquarters. He had been so busy with his family issues that he hadn't devoted as much time to the campaign as he or Rodda would have liked. Rodda was on the phone so Ferd exchanged small talk with the volunteers, who were getting ready to hand out more flyers to prospective voters. When Rodda hung up, Ferd walked over to his desk.

"Things are buzzing around here," said Ferd. "It's good to see."

"We have a terrific team. The best!" As Ferd sat down, Rodda continued. "Good news. The polls since the debate show you slightly ahead. We've got to work hard tomorrow to get out the word. Can you do some meet-and-greets?"

Ferd shrugged. "I don't know. I've taken so much time off work lately; I can't take the day off."

"At least before work and at lunchtime. Can you commit to that? Come on, Judge, this is for all the marbles."

Ferd nodded. He liked Rodda's enthusiasm. He had steered Ferd through the ups and downs of the campaign, never wavering in his support or optimism. "I'll do everything I can," Ferd said. "I assure you."

I t took some delicate negotiations, but Ferd was able to get all parties' agreement to meet at his mother's place that night. After knocking, Ferd entered first, followed by his father. When Melinda noticed her ex-husband, she stared for a good ten seconds without saying anything. Finally, she said, "Mother of God, I never thought I'd see you again."

"How are you, Melinda?"

"As you can see, I can't breathe so well, and it's getting worse. But from what I hear I'm doing better'n you."

Ferd placed the pizza in the oven to keep it warm. He watched the interaction between his parents, wondering how each would react. Dwight stood about six feet away while Melinda remained seated in her lounger. "For heaven's sake, take a seat. Ferd, get some water for everyone, will you?" There was no attempt by either parent at a kiss or hug. Ferd wasn't surprised.

He grabbed three glasses of water and handed them out.

"Where the hell is your sister?" Melinda asked. "She's always late."

"Ma, that's not true. She'll be here, don't worry."

It was obvious Melinda and Dwight were struggling with how to talk to each other. Ferd tried to help out. "Ma, Dad had a relapse, so now he's staying at my place."

She turned to Dwight, who had taken a seat beside Ferd on the couch. "What're you doing messing around with booze anyway? I never figured you for a drunkard."

"My life took a rough turn. I don't know if Ferd told you, but my wife died. She had cancer. Then I got fired, so I came back to San Francisco. I wanted to see you and the kids. I stopped by the old house and, of course, no one was there."

Melinda shook her head. "Hard to believe my ex-husband's homeless."

"I've got to compliment you, Melinda, on doing such a good job with the kids. Lord knows that wasn't easy to do on your own."

"You knew that when you left." Melinda couldn't hide the bitterness in her voice. "And when you didn't contact us for thirty-four years, except for finalizing the divorce."

Ferd could tell they were feeling each other out, slowly digging out the past, sensitive to each other's privacy. He sipped his water and checked his watch. Claire was ten minutes late. Good thing he had put the pizza in the oven.

Dwight leaned forward, his eyes watering. "I apologize for that, Melinda. I know that doesn't make up for anything, but I truly mean it. I'm a weak man; I couldn't handle things."

A knock came on the door and Claire walked in. "Sorry I'm late, everyone. Well, look who's here. You look as bad as Ferd said."

Dwight stood up. "It's good to see you, Claire. You turned into a beautiful young woman."

Claire removed her jacket and hung it on the back of the wing chair as she sat down. "I'm not beautiful or young anymore. Thirty-four years, Dad. Can you believe I've gone through three marriages? And I never had a father to walk me down the aisle."

Dwight looked down. He was getting it from two sides: Claire and Melinda. Ferd wondered if he would just take it and let the criticism roll over him. But instead, he spoke up. "I'm sorry I wasn't there for you, Claire."

Before things could get out of control, Ferd interrupted. "Why don't I get the pizza? Everyone must be hungry by now." He walked into the kitchen with Claire following.

Speaking in a low voice, Claire said, "I'm trying to hold it together; I really am. If I get too angry, stop me. I need to control my emotions."

"You're doing fine." He placed the pizza on plates and held out a couple for Claire to serve. "I'll get you a glass of water."

They ate the pizza in silence, commenting only on how good it tasted. After they'd had seconds, Dwight announced he had something to say. "I appreciate the three of you joining me today. I know this hasn't been easy on any of you. If you'll let me back in your lives, I'll do my best to make it up to you."

"That's a big ask," Claire said.

"I don't have a life," said Melinda. "And I won't be on this earth much longer anyway."

"I think this is a good first step," said Ferd. "We'll take it slow, let things develop naturally. You can't expect us to erase thirty-four years just like that." He paused then turned toward Melinda, who was hacking loudly. She seemed to be worsening. Ferd waited for his mother to stop coughing before saying, "Ma, now that we have you and Dad together, don't you think it's about time you told us why he left? God knows, you've given me nothing but the run-around."

"Dwight?" Melinda said, looking at him.

"Melinda, it's your story to tell."

Melinda removed her oxygen tube from her nose so she could speak clearly. "Dwight, I have to admit that at one time I thought you were a good man. Loving and kind. Worked hard and supported the family. But then you bailed on us."

"You know why," Dwight said defiantly.

Suddenly Melinda's eyes began tearing up. She took a hit off the oxygen and said, "What the hell. I'm about to depart this hell hole anyway. And you kids have a right to know the truth."

Melinda looked back and forth from Ferd to Claire. "I've got to use the bathroom," she said as she stood up.

While she was gone, Ferd looked at Claire. "Here we go again," he said. "More avoidance." He cleaned up the plates and refilled the water glasses. All three remained silent, anxious to hear what Melinda would say.

When Melinda returned from the bathroom, she asked, "Are you three talking about me?"

"No, Ma," Ferd said.

Claire said, "Ma, stop stalling. Why did Dad leave?"

Melinda started coughing and replaced the oxygen tube. She took several deep breaths, not looking at either her children or her ex-husband. Finally, having caught her breath, she removed the tube. "This is hard for me to say. I was going to take this to my grave, but I see now you have a right to know. Your father found out I had an affair."

"Mom!" Claire said, glancing at Dwight who sat with his eyes downcast.

"So you're saying Dad left his whole family just because of that?" Ferd asked.

"It wasn't because of that. In fact, it was twelve years before he found out."

"How did he find out?" asked Claire.

"He talked about having another child. I didn't want to, but he insisted. So we tried for a few months without success. He wanted me to have fertility tests, but I refused. I knew I was fertile; I had twins twelve years before. So I told him to get tested himself. When the results of his tests came back, he got very upset. His doctor told him that his low sperm count was likely a longstanding problem. Then he asked the doctor how he could have two children with such a low sperm count and the doctor told him to ask me."

"My God! Mom!" said Claire.

"So I had to tell him I'd had an affair with his best friend, Ernie Wilson. Damnit!" she snarled, staring at Dwight. "You were working all the time, so it wasn't all my fault. And it was only the one time, I swear." She turned back to her children. "But I got pregnant with you two."

Ferd stood up and paced, unable to keep still. "Are you saying that this man here is not even our father?"

Melinda replaced the tube, nodding as tears streamed down her cheeks. The effect on her was immediate. The tears soon came faster and faster; her nose began running, blocking the oxygen tube. She had to take out the tube again, blow her nose, wipe her face with a sleeve, and meet her children's stares. They looked at her in disbelief, their lives forever altered by her revelation.

"No wonder you left," said Claire, turning toward Dwight. "One minute you think you have a happy family; the next you discover the family's not even yours."

"Wait a second," Ferd said, his anger rising. He too turned to Dwight. "You raised us as your children for twelve years. How could you just walk out on us?"

Dwight buried his face in his hands. "I'm not proud of it, but I just couldn't handle things. I had to get away." He looked at Melinda. "The whole thing shocked me, that you'd had an affair with Ernie, that I couldn't have children, that Claire and Ferd were not mine. My whole world crashed down around me. I ran; that's all I could do to survive. I know it wasn't courageous or kind or loving. And I wasn't forgiving."

"But Ferd's right," said Claire. "You'd been our father for a dozen years. Don't you think you had some responsibility to Ferd and me?"

"I did," Dwight said, looking at her. "I'm sorry; I truly am. Something came over me when I found out you two weren't really my children. I panicked."

"You're a coward." Claire was not going to cut him any slack. "We were just entering our teens when we could've used a father most. Ma did the best she could, but life would've been a hell of a lot easier if you'd been there."

"Why didn't you tell us this a long time ago?" Ferd asked his mother. "You could've spared us decades of anger and distress."

"Really? I don't think so."

Ferd leaned toward Claire and hugged her. "All those years... All that therapy you went through."

"This is mind-blowing," Claire said, standing up. "I need some time to talk to my therapist and process this. If you'll excuse me..."

Claire left without kissing her mother or acknowledging Dwight.

Turning toward his mother, Ferd said, "This changes every-thing, doesn't it, Ma? Thanks for this bombshell." He too left without kissing his mother goodbye.

On the drive home Ferd and Dwight didn't talk. Each had too much to think about: their past and their future. When they got to the house, Dwight excused himself to go to the basement to sleep. Before heading down the stairs, he said, "I'm sorry, son. I truly am."

"Don't call me that anymore. It's not true."

"Well, I guess you're right." He took a step down then turned toward Ferd. "I'm really sorry about all this."

"You mean about leaving us?"

"That, and not owning up to the truth. It was cowardly on my part."

"You and Ma, both. "

"It made me sick to learn that you and your sister were not mine."

Ferd bristled. "That's where you were wrong." He couldn't help raising his voice.

Dwight's eyes watered. "I'm glad you turned out a better man than I ever was. Goodnight, Ferd."

"Goodnight, Dwight."

Sonya pressed Ferd for what had happened. "My mother finally came clean: Dwight's not my father."

"What're you saying?"

Ferd couldn't hide his irritation. "What could be clearer? Dwight is not my father." He walked to the living room and back, moving as fast as possible to keep his thoughts from overwhelming him. But he couldn't take it out on Sonya. That wouldn't be fair.

"I'm sorry," he said. "I'm still in shock. My mother confessed she had an affair twelve years before my father left."

"So who's your father?"

"Someone named Ernie Wilson. Dwight's best friend. That's all she said. Right now, I don't care about him."

A s he lay in bed on Tuesday morning, Ferd was still processing his mother's revelation, having exchanged several late-night emotional text messages with Claire, who remained angry at their mother.

This was election day. Ferd had planned to campaign at the Glen Park BART station before reporting to work, but before he could get moving was startled by the house phone ringing. He reached across Sonya to answer it.

"Hello."

"Is this Ferdinand Pitt?"

"Yes, who's this?"

"This is Molly. I'm a nurse at St. Philip's."

That shot Ferd awake. "Is my mother alright?"

"I'm afraid not, Mr. Pitt. She was taken to Seton Hospital early this morning. She had significant trouble breathing."

"Molly, do you know what department she's in?"

"Try ICU."

Sonya turned over, awake. "Who was that?"

"St. Phillip's. My mother's in the hospital. I'm going to visit her."

She sat up. "Oh, Ferd. Do you want me to go with you?"

"Not necessary. You've got work to do. I'm going to take the day off. I'll let you know how she's doing. This means I won't be able to campaign."

"Can I help?"

In deference to Sonya's busy schedule, Ferd hadn't asked her to take a direct role in the campaign. "It would be great if you could hand out flyers at Glen Park BART."

She got out of bed. "I'll go there right after I shower."

FERD HURRIED THROUGH HIS SHOWER, dressed, and called Claire, who agreed to meet him at the hospital. He drove to the hospital, a ten-minute trip he made in seven. On the way, he received a call from Curt Rodda. "Curt, I can't talk now. Bit of an emergency."

"No problem. Will call you later."

Ferd found a parking space easily and stayed in his car for a moment to call Judge Bradstein. He wanted to let her know he wouldn't be at work. He was glad he got her voicemail since he really didn't feel like talking to her.

The nurse led him to the ICU where he could see his mother through a glass wall. She was intubated on a ventilator. A few minutes later Claire appeared. She had been crying and her makeup was smeared.

"What's the doctor say?" Claire asked.

"Haven't talked to her yet," said Ferd.

Claire stared through the glass at her mother. "I feel bad about last night. I was so mad at her. God, I hope that's not the last conversation I ever have with her."

Ferd put his arm around her shoulder and pulled her toward him. She sunk into her brother.

A young woman approached them. "Hi, I'm Teresa Cheng,

Melinda's doctor." They introduced themselves and asked about the prognosis.

"It's amazing your mother's been living on her own as long as she has. Her lungs are severely scarred from years of smoking. So the short answer is I don't know, but I'm not confident she'll pull out of this. I'm sorry."

Ferd rubbed his eyes and glanced toward his mother. "How's her oxygen saturation?"

"That's one thing that gives me pause. It's in the high eighties, which isn't bad and surprising, considering how labored her breathing is."

"When will we be able to see her?" asked Claire.

"Not until she gets off the ventilator and there's no telling when that'll be. We've given her a fairly heavy dose of steroids so she's immunocompromised. Check back with me tomorrow."

When Ferd got home, he felt sick, saddened by his mother's condition. Sonya was still at the BART station, but he told Dwight, who had been spending time watching TV in the basement. Dwight sat at the kitchen table with his head on his arms, sobbing, surprising Ferd. He gave him a few minutes alone and went into the living room.

Soon Sonya came home. "How is she?"

He shook his head. "She's on a ventilator. It doesn't look good."

"Come here." She reached out to hug Ferd and they embraced for a few minutes. "I miss our hugs."

"Me too." He blinked back tears. When a chair squeaked against the kitchen floor, both turned to find Dwight standing in the hallway.

"I don't know why this has hit me so hard," said Dwight. "I hadn't seen her for thirty-four years. Maybe it has something to do with Janet's death. The two women I loved gone."

"Don't write Mom off just yet," said Ferd. "She's tougher than you think."

"I'd like to see her."

"We're going back tomorrow night," said Ferd. "Why don't you go with us?"

"That would be great."

FERD WAS unable to focus on the election, but he returned Curt Rodda's call. "Curt, sorry I couldn't talk earlier. My mother was rushed to the hospital."

"Goddamn, that's terrible. Especially today of all days." He paused for a moment. "I wanted to update you on some early exit polls. You're ahead of Smedley by a couple of percentage points. It would really help lock this thing up if you could stop by a few of the neighborhood polling places."

"I don't know. The way I feel now..."

"Judge Pitt...we're in the stretch run. I know it's hard to focus given what's happened to your mother, but being invisible is not an option."

Ferd's head was pounding. He didn't want to think of the election, but he did want to win. It would be a travesty for him to lose his seat after all he'd been through. "Tell you what: I have to vote soon anyway so I'll go to the poll, shake some hands, and hope for the best."

Rodda made a clucking sound. "Try to hit a few. I've mobilized the volunteers to your base on the west side. Remember we have a victory celebration tonight at the St. Francis."

AT THE POLLING place in a public middle school, Ferd introduced himself to an elderly couple on their way to vote. "I'm a superior court judge and am running for reelection."

The fog was thick, dampness everywhere. The woman wore

a light raincoat with the hood up, her husband a windbreaker with a baseball cap. They stopped and seemed to appraise Ferd, looking him up and down. "Barney, I think this is the judge whose son killed that poor tech guy."

"I thought it was his father," Barney said.

"Actually, neither," Ferd said. "My father was charged first, but that case was dismissed so the prosecutor charged my son. They're both innocent."

"Well," the woman said, "I don't think we want a judge with a murderer in the family." She turned toward her husband. "Do we, Barney?"

He took his wife's arm. "Let's go vote, Miriam."

Distraught at their reaction, Ferd cast his vote then returned home, pessimistic about his prospects. He walked slowly, his feet heavy.

THAT NIGHT AROUND TEN O'CLOCK, Ferd made his way to the front of the room at the St. Francis Hotel. Sonya was on his right side, Curt Rodda on his left. He approached the microphone. The crowd of about a hundred supporters suddenly burst into applause. Ferd was touched. He hadn't been feeling a lot of love lately from the electorate.

"Thank you so much. You don't know how much I appreciate your support. This has been a difficult campaign. As you know, first my father then my son was charged with murder. My son remains in jail for a crime he did not commit. Today, to make matters worse, my mother was rushed to the hospital in serious condition. I wasn't going to come here tonight, but my campaign manager Curtis Rodda can be quite persuasive."

Ferd glanced at Rodda and nodded. "We were hoping to announce my victory tonight, but it appears that will be delayed. The latest information we've received is that the election is neck and neck. One minute I'm ahead; the next Nicole

Smedley's ahead. This election will come down to the absentee ballots, which Curt assures me favor us. Let's hope he's right."

Putting his arm around Sonya, he said, "I want to give a special shoutout to my wife, who has been by my side during this troubling time. Thank you, Sonya. I love you."

The crowd cheered then began chanting, "Sonya! Sonya!" Ferd stepped back and waved.

When the crowd noise had died down, Rodda approached the microphone and said, "Let's make sure Judge Pitt knows how you feel about him. Can I get a loud chant of 'Ferd-in-and! Ferd-in-and!'"

The crowd kept up the chant as Ferd and Sonya made their exit. For the first time in a while, at least for a moment, Ferd was feeling good about life.

40

R odda told Ferd he had to be patient, that it would take several days and perhaps even a week to count the absentee ballots. In the meantime, he spent time at the hospital, staring at his mother, whose condition hadn't improved. He had a hard time concentrating on work, worried about losing his seat on the bench, either through the election or a Commission disciplinary ruling.

Ferd called Henry Smith. "Henry, do I really need to go through a second interview with my election in question? Won't they just drop the charges if I lose?"

"Probably not. One scenario is you resign in exchange for a dismissal, but of course that's out of the question."

"How about a private admonishment?" Ferd felt sick just saying that. His stomach clenched. "Have you floated that idea yet?"

"I did, but she hasn't responded. Let me talk to Harper face-to-face after the interview."

· · ·

FERD TOOK his seat across the table from Nancy Harper. Beside him, in the same seat as before, sat Henry Smith.

"Since you already questioned Judge Pitt," said Henry, "I hope this will be brief." Ferd was pleased Henry was taking the offensive, trying to limit the damage this further Commission interview might cause.

"Do you have somewhere else to be?" asked Harper.

Henry couldn't very well claim a conflict in his schedule since he had acceded to this date. "No, but my client has a lot going on."

"We should be finished in no time."

"Great, let's proceed."

The court reporter asked Ferd to raise his right hand and swore him in again. After Ferd said, "I do," Harper commenced with the questioning.

"Judge Pitt, I will be asking you only about events that have transpired since the initial interview so this should be brief. In the time since that interview, have you been in touch with any witnesses related to the murder of Patrick Brady?"

"I have."

"I instructed you not to have contact with any witnesses. Do you recall that?"

"I do."

"So you purposely disregarded my instruction?"

"Well, not quite." Ferd was determined to keep his answers short but wouldn't let Harper steamroll him. "Things changed."

"How so?"

"My son was arrested for the murder."

"I see. So you thought the arrest of your son somehow excused you from following my instruction?"

"Ms. Harper, do you have any children?"

Harper stopped typing in her laptop and glared at Ferd. "That hardly has any bearing on this matter."

"I believe it does. If you had children, you'd realize that a parent would do virtually anything, within the bounds of the law, for his child."

"And that includes risking your judgeship?"

Ferd glanced at Smith, who had refrained from objecting to this point. Smith nodded. They had prepared for just this question.

"I didn't believe I was risking my judgeship. I still find it hard to believe the Commission would even fault me for helping out family members. A judge should not have to decide between fulfilling his duty as a judge and as a son or parent."

"Let's get back on track. Why don't you list for me the witnesses you've spoken to since the first interview."

"Again," Smith interrupted, "objection to the term 'witnesses' as vague and ambiguous."

"I understand the objection," Harper said, "so just tell me everyone you've spoken to regarding Brady's murder since the first interview."

"Sure. Stephanie Fong, Nellie Ambrose, my son, and Denise Brady."

"I recognize those names. Anyone else?"

Smith held up his hand. "'Anyone else' what?"

"Judge Pitt knows what I'm asking."

"I believe I've given you all the appropriate names," Ferd said.

"I'm concerned that you're qualifying your answer," Harper said. "What does 'appropriate' mean?"

Smith started to object but Ferd cut him off. "That goes to Mr. Smith's objection. I've talked about the murder to the people I've mentioned as well as Dwight Pitt, my son's lawyers, my wife, my mother, my sister. See what I mean. I wouldn't consider any of them 'witnesses' except perhaps Dwight."

"I get it. I appreciate your clarifying that."

Harper made a few notes in her laptop. "How many times

have you been in touch with Denise Brady since the first interview?"

"A few."

"What does that mean? Two, three, four?"

Ferd saw a chance to play with her and answered, "Yes."

"Judge Pitt!"

"What? I believe you defined 'a few' accurately."

Harper seemed frustrated. "Oh," Ferd added, "you should know that Ms. Brady initiated the last contact."

"You mean she called you?"

"Exactly."

"Do you know why she called you?"

"She heard of my son's arrest and wanted to convince me of his guilt."

"Why would she want to do that?"

Henry put up his hand. "That calls for speculation."

"It does," said Ferd. "But I have a theory."

"Okay. I'm listening," said Harper.

"She didn't want me investigating her husband's murder."

"Why would that be?"

Smith said, "Objection. Again, calls for speculation."

"But it's pretty solid speculation," said Ferd.

"You can answer," Harper said.

"No," Smith said. "I don't want my client speculating. That would be inappropriate."

Harper closed her laptop. "In that case I have no further questions."

"Let me walk my client to the elevator," Henry said. "Then we should talk."

Outside, Ferd asked Smith why he didn't want him to answer the last question. "What if Harper calls the widow before the police have completed the investigation? I don't want to risk her destroying evidence."

"But she knew about the subpoena of her cell phone records, so what difference does it make?"

"I agree but why take that risk. Call me paranoid but I don't want to take any unnecessary chances on this case."

They shook hands and Henry said, "I'll call you later after I see what Harper says about a private admonishment."

WHILE FERD WAS DRIVING HOME, Smith called. "The good news is Harper didn't reject a private admonishment outright."

"Where does that leave us?"

"She's got to run it by her supervisor. She should have an answer in a few days."

"By then, the absentee ballots will have been counted."

41

The next morning, while resting in chambers, Ferd received a disturbing text from Curt Rodda: "Smedley leading by 200 or so votes, but 1k still to be counted." Ferd clutched his chest, thinking the worst. He returned to the bench, conscious that his days may be limited.

IT DIDN'T TAKE LONG for Denise Brady's lawyer Joe Crockett to challenge the subpoena duces tecum of her cell phone records. Simpson called Ferd to give him the time and department for the hearing. "It's a close one," she said. The Honorable Cheryl Labarle, the same judge who had heard Dwight's prelim, would be presiding.

Ferd arrived at the Hall of Justice shortly before the hearing and made his way to Department 20. Fortunately, he was able to delay his own calendar so he could attend. He sat in back while Henry and Angela sat at counsel table with Josh in chains. It sickened Ferd to see his son chained like a violent criminal. He couldn't help himself and approached counsel table and whispered to Henry to get the chains removed. Henry spoke to the bailiff who phoned the judge in chambers, then refused to remove the chains. Henry turned around to Ferd who held up his hands in a questioning manner. "Only one bailiff available," Henry mouthed.

At the prosecution table sat Nellie Ambrose and Joe Crockett, who looked more distinguished than most criminal defense attorneys Ferd had encountered. He wore a dark pinstriped suit and sported a closely cropped white moustache and goatee. Again, there were reporters in the gallery, Bob Angelo among them. Ferd nodded to Angelo then directed his attention to the bench where Judge Labarle was taking her seat.

After calling the case and hearing the attorneys' appearances, Judge Labarle said, "This matter is on calendar for a motion to quash a subpoena duces tecum filed by Denise Brady, wife of the victim in this case. Mr. Crockett, I have read your moving papers. Would you like to be heard?"

"Yes, Your Honor. This subpoena is a gross invasion of an innocent party's privacy. The defense would have you believe that my client is a suspect in her husband's murder. Nothing could be further from the truth. She is an aggrieved widow, whose grieving period has been unjustifiably interrupted by this subpoena. My client's whereabouts at the time of her husband's murder are undisputed. She was at home waiting for her husband. Her cell phone records are no one's business but her own and we oppose the production of these records in the strongest terms possible."

Ferd was impressed at Crockett's eloquence, though not surprised given his reputation. Judge Labarle turned to the defense side. "Who will be arguing on behalf of the defense?"

"I will, Your Honor," said Simpson, standing up. "As the court well knows, my client is presumed innocent. He is entitled to defend himself to the fullest extent of the law. One way to defend himself is to present third-party culpability evidence, that someone else committed this tragic crime. Through our investigation, we have learned that Ms. Brady lied to the police when she said she was at home the night of January 25th. We have obtained a declaration from a neighbor who swears under penalty of perjury that she left the home at 6:30 that evening, giving her more than sufficient time to drive to the Tenderloin and commit this crime. We submit that her cell phone records will confirm her lies and exonerate my client."

"Thank you, counsel," the judge said. "I have looked at this matter closely and researched the relevant law. This court is required to balance Ms. Brady's right to privacy with the defendant's right, as Ms. Simpson argued, to defend himself to the fullest extent of the law. Certainly, these cell phone records will invade Ms. Brady's right to privacy since they will disclose both incoming and outgoing phone calls and could indicate her general location during the relevant time period. The defense claims they will show that Ms. Brady traveled to the Tenderloin to kill her husband. Defendant has presented no evidence she killed her husband, however, and no motive for her to do so. Defendant relies entirely on the statement of a neighbor who claims to remember Ms. Brady leaving her house and getting in her car at 6:30 the night of the murder. Given the weeks that passed between the murder and his statement, the Court must view his recollection with skepticism. Balancing Ms. Brady's right to privacy with the defendant's right to present a defense, therefore, the court finds that the balance weighs in favor of protecting Ms. Brady's right to privacy. Accordingly, the motion to quash is granted."

Ferd slumped. He had thought that the judge would surely allow them to obtain the cell phone records. Ferd waved off the reporters swarming around him and made his way to the first floor where his own calendar had backed up. He was worried about Josh's future.

. . .

WHEN FERD GOT HOME, he broke the news to Sonya that the judge had granted the motion to quash and they'd have to go in a different direction. She gritted her teeth and asked, "What next?"

"I've got to consult with Josh's lawyers and figure out another angle."

She clenched her fist, and for a moment Ferd thought she was going to strike him. But then she unclenched her fist and placed her hand on his shoulder. "Ferd, I know this has been as tough on you as me. But so help me God, you'd better figure this out. And soon."

42

Ferd stood at the ICU window. His mother looked pale and frail with all the tubes sticking out of her. He told himself she was getting good care, that he had done all he could, when he felt a sharp pain on the left side of his chest that seemed to radiate into his left arm. He clutched his chest. *Must be indigestion*, he thought. But just to be sure, he called his doctor and made an appointment. *I'm forty-six years old. Far too young to have a heart problem.*

Ferd was not happy when his medical care transferred to Dr. Honda. He was content with his previous physician John Palmer, a seventy-year-old with a calm and engaging bedside manner. But Dr. Palmer succumbed to leukemia, a matter of weeks between diagnosis and death. Dr. Honda had bought out Dr. Palmer's practice and Ferd came along with it. He knew he could still change primary care doctors but was too lazy to do the research. He'd seen Dr. Honda only a handful of times. He was young and Ferd didn't have confidence in his medical abilities. And he was awkward, ill at ease conversing with Ferd, particularly after he became a judge. He seemed to hold Ferd in awe, which Ferd didn't mind at all.

Dr. Honda asked him to take off his shirt. "What seems to be the problem?" he asked.

"I've had a lot of stress lately. You may have heard that my son's been accused of murder."

"I did read about that," he said as he placed the stethoscope on Ferd's chest, nodded, then took his pulse. "Your lungs are fine, but your heart rate's a bit high. Let's take your blood pressure." He placed the rubber sleeve around his bicep and squeezed the ball a few times. "One-forty-five over ninety-five. Too high."

He palpated Ferd's neck, chest, and stomach, smiling without saying anything. He had a comforting smile, Ferd thought. He told him about the chest pains.

"You've been through several different life traumas. It's important that you treat yourself appropriately."

"I feel like screaming."

"Then scream."

Ferd looked at him to see if he were serious. Although he felt like screaming, he couldn't do it. Not now, not here. It would be undignified.

"You've got to manage the stress better."

"What can I do?"

"Exercise, walk, go to the gym. Even a little bit helps. But I'm concerned about the chest pains. I'll refer you to a cardiologist. I think you should see Dr. Gleason stat. I'll call him and see when he can see you."

Ferd nodded, nervous that he was escalating his treatment. "How's the heart sound?"

"It sounds fine, but that doesn't mean you didn't have a myocardial infarction or merely angina. We can't take any chances."

He stood up and led Ferd to the door. "I'm hoping there's nothing to worry about."

. . .

FERD CALLED Henry and asked for an update on Josh's case.

"Looks like we'll have to try the case," said Henry.

"Isn't there anything else we can do about Denise Brady?"

"Simpson's investigator is still digging, but without cell phone records we're stumped."

Ferd hung up, feeling as down as he had for some time. Dwight was in the basement watching television while Sonya was working in the study. Ferd decided to do something he hadn't done in ages: go for a run. He put on sweatpants and a long-sleeve tee-shirt and dug his running shoes out of the closet. He wiped off the dust and put them on.

He started out slowly, making his way down Sloat Boulevard, jogging in place at the traffic lights. It was a slight downhill so he ran easily, turned left after a mile and made his way to Lake Merced. His wind got the better of him. So he walked, swinging his arms for momentum. He decided to run clockwise and picked up the pace to a slow jog. He passed several pedestrians and joggers, all of whom seemed attached to cell phones, either listening to music or talking. He hadn't brought his with him and felt naked. *What would we do without cell phones?* He thought of all the applications his phone had: his cell phone knew where he was at all times, at least for those apps with location access enabled, including one that calculated how far he walked or jogged.

As he began jogging more quickly, thinking about cell phones and Judge Labarle's ruling, an idea stuck in his mind. There was more than cell tower triangulation that could locate a cell phone; there was GPS. *Why hadn't I thought of that before?* Desperate now to get home, he picked up the pace, crossed the street, and made his way past Saint Stephen Church. He knew just whom to call, the person who would be instrumental in getting his son released.

He was breathing heavily by the time he got home but without pausing to catch his breath, he placed the call to former client Stan Farmer, general counsel at Google. "Stan, it's Ferd Pitt."

"Judge Pitt, haven't talked to you for a while. How's the bench been treating you?"

"Oh, it's been fine. Listen, Stan, I'm involved in a case now and need your help." He told Stan about Josh's charges. "I remember talking to you one time about Google's geolocation capability. We talked about this briefly during that employment case. If I remember correctly, Google tracks what cell phones are in a particular location at a specific date and time. Am I right?"

"Yeah, we can do that. If I have a street address, I can find the latitude and longitude coordinates and determine the cell phone numbers of any phones in the area at a particular time. It's called Sensorvault. Google tracks you through location history, web and app activity, and device-level location services. We use the data to target ads and test their efficiency. Why do you ask?"

"I need a favor. Can you tell me all the cell phones that were in the area of the Promenade Bar and Blue Arms Hotel in San Francisco on January 25th of this year, say from 6:30 to 7:30 p.m.? That's the time and location of the murder."

"Jesus, Ferd, that's asking a lot. There are privacy concerns. We could be sued."

"I wouldn't ask if it wasn't important."

"I know. It's just...I can't release any data without a search warrant or subpoena."

"The police are unlikely to seek a search warrant. They think they already have the murderer in custody."

"San Francisco police seek Sensorvault data from time to time, but it's unusual. Most police departments aren't that sophisticated. If they requested it in all cases, we'd be overwhelmed. I'd have to hire a bunch of new staff."

"So I'll have my son's team issue a subpoena duces tecum."

"Make sure you define the area narrowly to limit privacy objections. It's called a geofence."

"How long will it take to get the data together?"

"Give me a day or two. I've got to talk to my people. I'll put one of my best on the job: Bailey Johnson. She'll take care of you."

AT THE ENTRANCE to the jail Ferd found Angela Simpson waiting for him. He was supposed to meet her at 4:30 but was fifteen minutes late. Because he had been late to work in the morning, his calendar backed up, a frequent occurrence recently, and went all the way to 4:30. It took him fifteen minutes to sign some orders and walk to the jail.

"Henry's tied up but I wanted to be here," Simpson said. "He's been down since the ruling on the motion to quash."

They were directed to the meeting room where Josh soon appeared. He looked rundown and anxious. "What's next?" he asked.

"I had an idea that might prove the case against Denise Brady," said Ferd.

"I thought that ship had sailed," said Josh.

"There's another angle your father came up with," said Simpson. "It just might work."

"What's that?" asked Josh.

"Every phone has GPS tracking from apps with location enabled," Ferd said. "Your map and restaurant apps, social media, the list goes on and on."

"Everyone knows that," said Josh.

"Well, did you know Google retains location data from these apps?" asked Ferd.

Josh looked puzzled. "So how do you propose getting the GPS data from Google?"

"We'll issue another subpoena duces tecum," said Simpson. "This time on Google."

"What makes you think the judge will allow it?" asked Josh.

"Good question," said Simpson. "This subpoena is far less intrusive than the last one. Denise Brady can't really object since she denies being out of her house at that time anyway. So we have a better chance of getting this one by the judge."

Josh closed his eyes and took a deep breath. "You know what I miss most about being here? You and Mom of course, but I miss working on the computer. I miss staring at a screen, inputting commands, creating software. I guess I really am a nerd. Sitting here day after day staring at the four walls is enough to drive anyone batty."

Ferd could tell that Josh was trying to contain his excitement, afraid to let loose for fear of disappointment. It was the same for Ferd. He had gone through so many ups and downs with this case that he hesitated to get his hopes up. He would remain stoic, both for himself and for Josh.

43

L ater that night the doorbell to Ferd's home rang. Ferd switched on the outside light and looked through the peephole. "What the hell?"

He opened the door to find Curt Rodda standing there, grinning broadly. "We won! We won! I had to tell you in person." They hugged for the first time ever.

"That's great!" Ferd said. "Come in. This calls for a celebratory drink." After letting Rodda inside, Ferd yelled upstairs. "Sonya, we won! Come down and celebrate with us."

Sonya appeared at the top of the stairs. "Ferd, that's wonderful! I'll be right down."

Ferd poured shots of Jameson for him and Rodda and a vodka tonic for Sonya. They sat at the kitchen table sipping their drinks when Rodda said, "Not to put a damper on things but it was a close call."

"How close?" asked Ferd.

"Sixty-four votes."

"Oh, my goodness," said Sonya.

"Smedley has asked for a recount," said Rodda. "So it's not a sure thing yet."

Ferd chugged the rest of his drink, still wondering if his judgeship were secure.

DR. GLEASON APPEARED to be in his mid-seventies, a patch of white hair on top of his head and a full white moustache. He ushered Ferd into the examining room, told him to remove his shirt, listened to his heart, then said he wanted to perform a stress test. With the aid of an assistant, he hooked Ferd up to sensors and had him walk quickly on the treadmill. After nine minutes, Ferd's heart rate had rapidly increased and he had built up a good sweat. Dr. Gleason stopped the treadmill and had Ferd lie down on his left side. He ran a wand covered in gel across his chest.

When he was finished, he said, "The rhythm seems fine. I don't think you had a heart attack. I suspect it was angina, reduced blood flow to the heart. There is coronary artery disease. It's not terrible; less than half blocked."

Ferd stared at the floor. "What does that mean in terms of treatment?"

"Surgery is not necessary, but I'm putting you on low dose aspirin to increase blood flow and Lipitor to decrease your cholesterol level."

"How long will I have to take them?"

"For the rest of your life. You'll be taking one of each before bed."

"I feel like I'm too young for all this."

"It's not unusual for someone your age to have coronary artery disease. It's typically a function of lifestyle, exercise, diet, stress level, that kind of thing."

"I've always had stressful jobs and I didn't exercise as much as I should have."

"Why don't I refer you to a dietician and physical therapist, get you on the right track."

"I appreciate that, Doctor."

"And try to keep stressors to a minimum."

Right, thought Ferd, *that won't happen if I keep working as a judge. And, considering the election recount and the Commission's investigation, that was a big "if."*

FERD WENT to the hospital with Dwight, who was struggling with sobriety, though he hadn't fallen off the wagon. Ferd had found an outpatient program for him that met five days a week. Although Dwight was attending regularly, taking Muni Metro downtown, he confessed to having urges. But he was optimistic about his future.

Claire had thoroughly researched Dwight's foreclosure and learned that the bank had made some mistakes on its notice. The property had not yet been sold so Ferd took steps to enable Dwight to get his house back, hiring a New Hampshire lawyer to put a stop to any sale. Although foreclosures were outside of Ferd's area of legal expertise, he did as much reading as he could on the subject and formulated a strategy to help out Dwight.

Melinda was still on a ventilator and unable to communicate. Staring through the glass wall, Dwight rested his palms and forehead on the glass. "I'm so glad I got to see her at least once more," he said.

"She's not dead yet."

"She always was a tough one. When I confronted her about having an affair, she didn't deny it. 'It was twelve years ago,' she said. As if that was the end of that."

"Tell me," Ferd said, "did you even think of staying and raising Claire and me as your own children?"

Dwight turned to look at him, leaving a moisture mark on the glass. "Do you think your life would've been better if I had?"

"I don't know. My hate and anger at you drove me to work hard, to show I could succeed without a father. Sure, I missed having a strong male figure in my life, but Mom did her best to make up for it. At least when she stopped drinking."

"She had a drinking problem? I hadn't known that."

"Until our later years in high school. Still, she was able to support us when she was drinking. She worked regularly, though she made jack shit, and helped us with homework. She was a good mother."

"I'm glad to hear that. I've had two times in my life when I drank too much: first when I came to New Hampshire and then when I left. I had lost the two women I loved in life and turned to alcohol. It was not pretty."

"Your friend Walt told me you got in some fights."

He stepped away from the wall. "Look at me. Do I look like a fighter? I had whiskey courage; that's all it was."

"Do you think you can beat the drinking problem now?"

"I admit it hasn't been easy." He paused then said, "I've been thinking of something."

"What's that?"

"Before Janet's cancer had metastasized, she confronted me about some old photos I kept in a manila envelope in my closet. She had been cleaning out the closet and noticed the envelope hidden in back."

"What were the photos of?"

"You and Claire."

"You actually kept photos of your children?"

He nodded. "I looked at them every once in a while, wondering how my life had turned out the way it had."

"What did Janet say about them?"

"She got very upset that I had kept that part of my life from her. Betrayed is how she put it." Dwight's voice started cracking. "I tried to defend myself, saying it was too panful to discuss and that's why I lied to her. My, how I deceived her. What was wrong with me?"

"You did what you thought was best."

"No, I was selfish with Janet just as I was selfish with your mother. I suspect my guilt is part of the reason I got hooked so easily on alcohol."

"You have to move forward now."

Dwight put his hand on Ferd's shoulder. "Thanks for hearing me out. And I'm glad you let me stay in the basement. I can moan and groan without disturbing you. I'm determined to beat this thing. I've given you my word."

"The word of an alcoholic is hardly a sure thing."

"True enough. I won't argue with you there."

44

Ferd took the medicine prescribed by Dr. Gleason and for exercise he and Sonya walked around the neighborhood after dinner. He knew he needed to exercise more, so he bought a set of dumbbells that he kept in the garage. Every morning before work he would go to the garage and lift weights, pumping up his biceps and triceps.

Dwight, too, was working on getting healthy, continuing on the road to recovery by attending groups every morning. He had developed a fondness for mystery novels and was reading his way through classic authors such as Robert Parker, Sue Grafton, Dick Francis, and John MacDonald.

Henry and Angela drafted a subpoena duces tecum of Google's Sensorvault data, asking for information only for phones associated with Patrick Brady, Denise Brady, Josh, and Colleen O'Keefe. By doing this, they narrowed the number of people who would be affected, thereby protecting others' right to privacy. They limited the area to one hundred yards in either direction from the Promenade Bar and Blue Arms Hotel, and the time period to one-half hour before and after the murder. Before formally serving the subpoena on Google,

Ferd read it to Stan Farmer who made suggestions to make it airtight.

As expected, the district attorney moved to quash the subpoena. Ferd appeared at the hearing along with Simpson and Henry. To Ferd's surprise, Joe Crockett also appeared. Ambrose argued forcefully, "This subpoena is yet another desperate effort by the defendant to shift blame for this murder. There is absolutely no basis to invade Denise Brady's privacy. I strongly urge the court to quash this subpoena."

Crockett rose, his stocky frame towering over other counsel. "I appear this morning to ensure that Denise Brady's privacy is protected." He turned around and gave Ferd an evil eye. Ferd bit his lip. "As the court found at the last hearing on the cell phone subpoena," Crockett continued, "the defendant has no credible evidence that Ms. Brady was anywhere but home at the time of this murder. I too urge the court to grant the motion to quash."

"Your Honor," Simpson began, "two of the four people named in the subpoena – the defendant and Colleen O'Keefe – have consented to the subpoena. One, Patrick Brady, is deceased. That leaves only one with a privacy interest: Denise Brady. And this subpoena infringes only slightly, if at all, on Ms. Brady's privacy rights. In fact, it shouldn't infringe at all since Ms. Brady insists she wasn't in the area at the time of the murder. We have drafted the geofence narrowly to encompass only the areas of the Promenade Bar and Blue Arms Hotel. Therefore, I would urge the court to deny this motion."

Judge Labarle looked down at her notes. "I have no problem with the subpoena as it relates to three of the four individuals identified," she said. "But I am still concerned with Denise Brady's right to privacy for all the reasons stated in the prior motion. In light of that, I am going to order the Google custodian of records to appear at a hearing on Monday morning. She is to bring with her documents responsive only for the three individuals mentioned –

Joshua Pitt, Patrick Brady, and Colleen O'Keefe – and should be prepared to testify about those documents. After that testimony, I will announce my ruling on whether to release the documents."

Again, Crockett turned around to look at Ferd. This time he was smirking. Ferd did his best not to show the turmoil that roiled inside him. *How could Josh prove Denise Brady guilty without evidence of her presence at the crime scene?* He stood up, ignoring Crockett, and walked toward Josh, who had risen so the bailiff could apply handcuffs. Ferd put his hand on Josh's shoulder only to be told by the bailiff to stand back. No contact was allowed. As Henry started to say something, Ferd turned and hurried out of the courtroom.

"ALL IS NOT LOST," Ferd told Sonya at dinner that night. "If the documents prove Josh was not in the area of the murder, that may be enough for the judge to dismiss the case."

"How confident are you about that?"

Ferd picked at his mashed potatoes. "Well, nothing about this case gives me confidence. The judge seems intent on protecting Denise Brady's privacy no matter what."

Sonya pushed her plate aside. "I appreciate your leveling with me, Ferd. At least there's some hope."

Ferd nodded, placed his hand on Sonya's, and squeezed tightly.

ON MONDAY MORNING, Ferd entered Department 20. "How're you doing, Judge?" asked Bob Angelo.

"I'm feeling pretty good right about now," he lied. "Looking forward to my son being released." In truth, Ferd was as nervous as he'd ever been. Even trying high-stakes cases hadn't made the butterflies flutter in his stomach the way they were now. This hearing would determine whether Josh would be released, a free man, or would languish in custody. He couldn't even believe his son was in jail.

"What makes you think that's going to happen?"

"Just a gut feeling."

"If your son manages to get the case dismissed, will he be suing the city for false imprisonment?"

"I've no comment on that, Bob." *But*, thought Ferd, *that was an interesting idea.*

The bailiff appeared and asked everyone to stand, then announced the judge's presence. Henry and Angela sat with Josh in a repeat of the prior hearing. The People were represented by both Stephanie Fong and Nellie Ambrose. For Fong to appear, Ferd surmised, the district attorney must be worried about this motion. The clerk swore in Bailey Johnson, Google's custodian of records. Johnson, a fresh-faced twenty-something Caucasian woman with bright red hair, held in her hand a copy of the records.

"I asked you to be here, Ms. Johnson," the judge said, "to explain the documents produced by Google in response to the defendant's subpoena duces tecum. What's the name of the program that accumulates this data?"

"It's called Sensorvault."

The judge flipped through the documents. "Let's start with this map. Can you explain what this shows?"

"So per the court's order, we were asked to identify only three separate cell phone numbers in the area of the Promenade Bar and Blue Arms Hotel on January 25th. Let's start with the map of the Promenade Bar. Do you have that?"

"I do."

"Okay, the colored dots correspond to the phone numbers. Red is for Joshua Pitt, Blue is for Colleen O'Keefe, and green for Patrick Brady. Each page identifies the phones in that area at a set time beginning at 1847; the next page is three minutes later etc. until 1947, a half hour after the murder."

"That's 7:47 p.m.?"

"Yes. Let's look first at 6:55 p.m. at the Promenade. You can see green and red dots, indicating that Patrick Brady and Joshua Pitt are there. Three minutes later – the next page – you can see that the red dot is gone but the blue dot has joined the green dot, meaning that O'Keefe has joined Patrick Brady."

"I get that so far. Now turn ahead five pages and tell me what that represents."

"This is at 7:10. There is still a blue dot and a green dot. Three minutes later we see the map with no dots, meaning that all three cell phones have left the area."

Ferd was on the edge of his seat. He was anxious to learn what the other documents revealed.

"Now turn to the map of the Blue Arms Hotel," the judge instructed.

"This picks up a green dot at 7:13, corresponding to Patrick Brady's phone. The same is true at both 7:16 and 7:19. Only the green dot is present."

"Was Joshua Pitt, the red phone, anywhere near the Blue Arms at any of those times?"

"Not according to our records."

Ferd nearly jumped out of his chair. He saw Josh turn to Angela and grin. The reporters all turned to look at Ferd, who was sporting a grin of his own.

"Thank you, Ms. Johnson. Do the People have any questions?"

Fong and Ambrose huddled, discussing their strategy. Finally, Fong said, "Just a few, Your Honor."

Standing up, Fong asked, "Ms. Johnson, does Sensorvault work when a phone is turned off?"

"No, it doesn't. Sensorvault tracks web and app activity so the phone must be powered on."

"In light of that, based on the records you've provided you can't tell if Joshua Pitt were in the area of the Blue Arms Hotel at 7:17 p.m.?"

"No, all I can say is his phone did not return any data. It may have been outside the geofence or turned off."

"No further questions."

The judge looked at Simpson, who was busy flipping through Josh's cell phone location data obtained from the People's search warrant. "Does the defendant have any questions?"

"One moment, Your Honor." She continued flipping.

"Ms. Simpson?"

"Yes. Ms. Johnson, do your records show where Josh Pitt was at 7:10 p.m.?"

"Let's see. Yes, at 7:10 he was near the Blue Arms Hotel."

"Is that the last location you have for him?"

"It is."

"Do your records for 7:13 p.m. show Josh anywhere near the Blue Arms?"

"No, they don't."

"How about 7:17?"

"We have nothing."

"7:19?"

"Nothing."

"I have nothing further, Your Honor," said Simpson.

Before announcing her ruling, the judge gathered all the subpoenaed documents into a manila envelope. "After reviewing the subpoenaed records, as revised by the court, and hearing the testimony of the witness, the court denies the motion to quash and releases the records to the defense."

Her clerk retrieved the envelope and gave it to Simpson, who stood back up. "I have a motion, Your Honor."

"What is your motion?"

"We move to dismiss the complaint in the interests of

justice. Joshua Pitt was nowhere near the scene of the murder. The People speculate that the defendant shut off his phone before the murder, which is preposterous. There is no evidence to support that. In fact, although the court did not allow us to receive Sensorvault records of Denise Brady, the evidence that was presented fully supports the defense theory of the case. Other than the defendant – and his grandfather I might add – the only other suspect floated by the police was Colleen O'Keefe. This evidence shows that although she was the last person – other than the murderer – to be with the victim, she was not present at the time of the murder.

"We know that Patrick Brady was hitting on Colleen O'Keefe. His wife must've suspected something was going on because she followed him that night to the Tenderloin."

Judge Labarle straightened and put out her hand, palm forward. "Wait. That's speculation. You argued the People were speculating and now that's what you're doing."

"But Your Honor, Ms. Brady was clearly waiting outside the Promenade when her husband exited with O'Keefe. After Brady kissed O'Keefe, what the wife would've interpreted as evidence of an affair, she snapped."

"Enough! Are you finished?"

"Well..."

"I don't want to hear about Denise Brady. As I said, that is speculation. But how do you explain the defendant's phone being near the Blue Arms at 7:10 p.m.?"

"That was seven minutes before the stabbing. The most logical explanation is that he walked by the Blue Arms on his way to the Sutter/Stockton garage."

Fong and Ambrose were quiet, each staring at the table. How could they have charged the wrong person for this murder two times? Ferd was enjoying their obvious embarrassment, thinking that Simpson had made her points forcefully, though she might have pushed the judge too far. He knew they would have to eat a substantial amount of crow if the judge dismissed the case but eat it they would.

"Ms. Fong, would the People like to be heard?"

"Briefly, Your Honor. We know from defendant's cell phone records that he was still in the area shortly after the murder. And we know from the Sutter/Stockton garage video that he was in the area at the time of the murder. Just because defendant's phone may have been undetected on Sensorvault doesn't mean he's innocent. Defense counsel suggests it is speculation to suggest defendant turned off his phone. In light of defendant's proficiency with high tech, it is not a stretch to believe defendant knew about Sensorvault, knew he could be tracked by his phone, and deliberately turned off his phone to avoid being tracked." She began to take her seat, then apparently thought better of it.

"And might I add, Your Honor, that the People's burden is probable cause, not beyond a reasonable doubt, at this stage of the proceeding. I submit there is ample probable cause that defendant committed this murder."

Simpson jumped up. "Might I respond, Your Honor."

Judge Labarle waived her back down and gave Fong a stern look. "The court can't maintain this complaint based on speculation, even under a probable cause standard. The interests of justice require that the motion to dismiss be granted. The defendant will be released from custody."

Josh turned around and smiled at Ferd, mouthing "thank you" while his eyes teared up. Henry put his arm on Josh's shoulder. Josh was free. *This nightmare was over*, thought Ferd. *Finally, my family could relax and get back to normal.*

45

Ferd and Sonya settled back into their lives after Josh's release. Ferd and Claire worked together to stop the foreclosure of Dwight's New Hampshire home. They then gave Dwight a choice of moving back there or selling the property and pocketing his equity. To Ferd's surprise, Dwight didn't want to move back. He asked Ferd to invest most of the equity on his behalf and put it into a trust so Dwight wouldn't be tempted to blow it on alcohol. But first he wanted to pay back the $40,000 he had fraudulently obtained from his prior employer. Dwight moved into a halfway house where he was in charge of the kitchen. He still fought urges to drink but had so far remained sober. He wanted to stay in the Bay Area so he could get closer to his "children." For their part, Ferd and Claire were open to welcoming him into their lives.

The election recount dragged on for weeks. Ferd and Rodda were in contact every day, though there weren't really any developments. Finally, Rodda called with the results of the recount. "Are you sitting down?" he asked.

"Don't tell me I lost?"

"Goddamnit, you won! By even more than before: a

hundred and thirty-two votes! You've got another six years on the bench."

"That's great news, Curt." Ferd paused, taking in this latest development. "Pardon me for not being more enthusiastic; I'm still waiting for the Commission decision."

"You'll be fine; trust me."

"Curt, I know I haven't said it enough, but I really appreciate all your work. I couldn't have won it without you."

Rodda laughed. "I hope you still appreciate me after you get my final bill."

A FEW DAYS after the hearing on the motion to quash, Stephanie Fong called Ferd. "I wanted you to know how sorry I am for putting your family through so much misery. After the hearing, the police obtained a search warrant for Denise Brady's Facebook account and found several photos of her wearing a Giants cap identical to the one worn by the killer. With this evidence, another search warrant was issued for her Sensorvault data. We're still awaiting the return on that warrant, but between us, I suspect your theory of the case is accurate."

"Ms. Fong, thank you for the update. I always suspected Ms. Brady hid her hair underneath the Giants cap, then waited outside the Promenade where she witnessed her husband kiss Colleen. They had an argument, which continued to the Blue Arms."

"The only question is where she got the knife," said Fong.

"I doubt she brought it from home, but knowing that area she could've picked it up from the gutter." He paused. "I hope in the future your office is more careful before charging someone with such a serious crime. You have put my family through a terrible ordeal."

"Please accept my apology. Oh, we are also looking at Ms.

Brady for throwing the brick through your window and trying to run you off the road. Stay tuned."

"Can't say I'm surprised."

"I look forward to seeing you on the bench."

"As do I, Ms. Fong."

JUST WHEN HE hoped his life would return to normal, Ferd received the dreaded phone call from Henry Smith. "Ferd, you're going to get a letter from the Commission today."

"Tell me it's good news.

Henry cleared his throat. "Harper relented. She agreed to the private admonishment."

"My God, that's wonderful. I can't believe I'm saying that, Henry; you're a lifesaver."

"For you, Judge, anything. Now you can get your life back to normal."

"Wishful thinking."

THE LETTER CAME in a thick envelope. Ferd tore it open and flipped through the pages of the decision, which started with an overview of all the investigative work Ferd had performed on the Patrick Brady murder. Ferd was surprised at how much they knew, things he hadn't revealed to Harper. They had obviously followed up on the information he had given them. He skipped to the last page which stated the resolution: a private admonishment. Seeing the decision in writing brought a tear to Ferd's eyes. He clutched his hand to his heart and shouted for Sonya.

"Hon', I'm still a judge," he told her as she rushed downstairs. "They've given me a private admonishment, a punishment I can live with. Henry worked his magic."

"Oh, Ferd! That's good news! I'm so glad." She put her arms around him and hugged him tightly."

"This was the final piece. We've got to celebrate. We can actually get our lives back to normal."

She extended her arms, still clutching his shoulders. "Ferd, life with you has never been normal." Then she kissed him on the lips. "Which I'm mostly glad about."

FERD AND SONYA regularly enjoyed a glass of wine or two at dinner, and for several nights in a row toasted to Josh's freedom, thankful to have him back.

Unfortunately, a week after the Commission letter, the hospital called, saying Ferd's mother's condition had worsened. Ferd held a meeting at the hospital with Claire, Josh, Dwight, and Sonya. They stood in the hallway outside the ICU as doctors and nurses passed by at a distance, giving them space. Glancing at his mother, who was motionless, Ferd said, "The doctor has recommended removing the ventilator, but it's a family decision."

"Oh, Ferd," Claire said, "I don't think I can. It's just too awful to think about."

"I know. It's agonizing. The idea of ending the life of the woman who gave me life is overwhelming." He wiped his eyes. "But we can't let her go on like this. There's really no life there. So I vote we remove the ventilator."

He turned toward his sister. "Claire, I need to know you're okay with that."

She looked down, her chest heaving. "I-I agree with you."

"Josh?"

"I feel guilty I haven't seen much of her lately, but in my heart, I know that's the right decision."

"Dwight, I don't know that you're entitled to a vote, but I'll ask anyway."

"I'm just so grateful I was able to see her one more time. You're right – it's not my decision to make."

"Sonya, what do you think?"

She put her arm around Ferd's shoulders and rubbed his back. "I think you're making the right decision. As painful as it is, it's time to let her go."

Ferd nodded and had the nurse page Dr. Cheng, who gave them permission to be by the bedside while the ventilator was removed. Melinda's eyes were closed and her chest rose and fell as the machine breathed for her. Her skin had a waxy appearance as if she had already been embalmed. Ferd leaned in and kissed her on the forehead. "I love you, Mom." Claire and Josh followed him, reciting a similar sentiment.

Even Dwight stepped forward and held Melinda's hand. "You did a terrific job raising Ferdinand and Claire. For that I will be eternally grateful."

Sonya then held Melinda's hand. "Goodbye, Melinda. We're all going to miss you."

With that the respiratory therapist removed the ventilator. Melinda's chest stopped rising and she lay still.

"She's gone," said Ferd.

WITH HIS MOTHER dead and Dwight getting regular treatment, Ferd's thoughts turned to his actual father, Ernie Wilson. *Should I try to contact him?* He was torn between wanting to leave well enough alone and making the acquaintance of his real father. Since discovering that Dwight was not his father, Ferd had essentially switched roles with him and assumed the parenting role. Dwight was dependent on Ferd to provide shelter and treatment. How long would Ferd have to manage his money? He knew he couldn't do so forever; Sonya wouldn't allow it. And he wasn't sure he wanted to. He felt no loyalty to Dwight, only pity for the terrible turns his life had taken. *What would it be like to have a real father back in my life?*

Ferd decided to search for his father. He performed Google and Facebook searches for both Ernie Wilson and Ernest Wilson and came up with thousands of results. Discouraged, he gave up.

In the meantime, Ferd organized a celebration dinner for both Josh and Dwight at Original Joe's of Westlake, making a reservation for eight. He included Henry Smith and Jiselle, a beautiful woman with short black hair, full cheeks, and expressive dark eyes. He also invited Angela Simpson, but she was traveling in South America. Ferd was struck by how bright and cheerful Jiselle seemed, the kind of woman who would light up any room she entered. Sonya wanted to mark the occasion in a concrete way but couldn't find balloons, banners, or greeting cards celebrating dismissal of murder charges. She satisfied herself by ordering carrot cake with two candles and "Freedom: Dwight and Josh" written in orange frosting. Sonya hadn't realized the irony of her color choice until Josh said, "After my stint in jail, orange is not my favorite color."

Josh introduced Colleen to Sonya, who hesitantly hugged her. Ferd knew that Sonya wondered if Colleen was right for Josh and had suspected her of having an affair with Brady. "It's so good to finally meet you," she said stiffly. Colleen also hugged Ferd, thanking him for helping Josh. Dwight and Josh embraced as if they had known each other their whole lives. Perhaps it was the shared experience of spending time in the San Francisco County Jail that brought them together. Henry and Jiselle offered hearty congratulations to both Dwight and Josh. Claire was still sad over Melinda's death, but perked up when dinner was served so as not to drag down the group.

Ferd ordered a bottle of Sonoma Valley cabernet sauvignon for the table and offered a toast. "To justice, finally." Everyone raised a glass, even Dwight. Ferd thought he wouldn't drink the wine but he did, chugging the glass. "Dwight, what are you doing?" Ferd asked.

"A little wine never hurt anyone."

Sonya looked askance at him and Ferd exhaled deeply, realizing Dwight still had a ways to go before he could accept sobriety. An awkward moment which Claire interrupted. "Ferd, you'll be surprised to hear that Neil is thinking about law school." Ferd's nephew was a junior at the University of Oregon, majoring in sustainability.

"Glad to hear it," he said with a sideways glance at Josh. "About time he studied something useful instead of that environmental crap."

"Dad, it's not crap," Josh said. "People have to realize that climate change is real. My generation gets it; if we don't act now, then there will be tragedy."

"I agree," Colleen said. "My brother is an environmental scientist for the EPA. With the current administration cutting back on environmental regulations, his job is in jeopardy. We should all be worried." She turned toward Ferd and lifted her wine glass, sipping it while keeping her eyes on him.

"In any event," Claire said, "Neil was so upset over what happened to Josh that he wants to make a difference, maybe represent the wrongly convicted."

"I think that's admirable," said Sonya.

"And I'll second that," Dwight said, pouring himself another glass of wine.

EPILOGUE

Ferd's heart problems were under control, his energy renewed. Since Dwight struggled with rehab, Ferd found him an inpatient clinic in the East Bay, far from the temptations of the Tenderloin. Josh was doing well at work though he switched teams due to the competition with Sa'Quan. He was still dating Colleen; they were even talking of moving in together.

With Dwight's help, Ferd continued searching for his father Ernie Wilson. Getting back to Facebook, he narrowed his search to anyone named Ernie Wilson and Ernest Wilson in their late 60s who lived in California. There was no guarantee that his father still lived in California, or indeed if he were still alive, but Ferd had run out of choices. He was left with several hundred candidates. That's when Dwight came in handy. He spent hours reviewing each photo to identify his old friend. Of course, he hadn't seen him for over thirty years, but he could at least shorten the list.

Dwight narrowed the list to four men. Ferd Googled each one until he was satisfied he had the right home phone number. He had the same awkward conversation with each one: "Hi, Mr. Wilson, you don't know me, but my name is Ferdinand Pitt."

"Mr. Pitt, what can I do for you?"

"Did you live in San Francisco over thirty years ago?"

"What the hell? Who is this?"

"I'm trying to track down my birth father."

There were typically several seconds of silence. "Who was your mother?"

"Melinda Pitt."

The first three said they never knew anyone with that name. The fourth, though, had a different reaction. "Oh, my goodness, that was some time ago. How is she?"

"I'm afraid she recently passed away." He paused. "She told me you're my father."

"What the...?" The phone went silent. "I'm truly flabbergasted. I never knew Melinda got pregnant by me. We were together only that one time. We ran into each other on the street and stopped for a few drinks. Then we went to my place. Drunken fools we were! This is shocking to tell you the truth."

"I understand, as it was for me."

"Do you have proof?"

"I don't, but it should be a simple matter to get DNA tests. I should tell you that you also have a daughter. Claire and I are twins."

"Are you trying to give an old man a heart attack? Thank God my wife is no longer with us or this would distress her greatly. What is it you want from me?"

"Only to meet you and get acquainted. Claire's not ready to do that yet, but I'm willing to travel to your place and spend some time together. It says here you live in Palm Springs."

"Let me give that some thought."

"Certainly. There's one thing you should know about me."

"What's that?"

"I'm a judge here in San Francisco. I just won the election."

Ferd felt an urge to brag, to make his father proud of him. He knew it was ridiculous, but after all he'd been through, he needed some affirmation.

"Congratulations, Judge Pitt! I like the sound of that."

"So do I."

ACKNOWLEDGMENTS

Beneath the Gavel is the first novel I wrote in third person. It turned into more of a learning experience than I expected. Because the protagonist is based on a short story from my collection, *What If Holden Caulfield Went to Law School?*, I thought the writing would come easily. Nothing could be further from the truth.

Fortunately, I had the assistance of many readers in shaping the novel into publishable form. Thanks to my forever writing group Tom Beatty and Jeff Westmont for their close reading and insightful comments. As usual, I had the assistance of talented editors in finalizing the manuscript. My thanks go to Zoe Quinton, Stacy Robinson of The Next Chapter, and Kerry Stapley, who taught me the intricacies of writing in third person, for which I am eternally grateful.

A special thanks to Ted Hertel, Jr., who reviewed the first several chapters through Mystery Writers of America's critique program. His comments were on point and most helpful.

Finally, I am inspired to continue writing by the encouragement of my friend and fellow writer, Sheldon Siegel, who read and commented on an early version of this manuscript. His generosity and writing talent are amazing.

ABOUT THE AUTHOR

Stephen M. Murphy is a judge in the San Francisco Superior Court and an accomplished author known for his gripping legal thrillers. He graduated from the College of the Holy Cross and the University of San Francisco School of Law before serving as a law clerk in New Hampshire, where his work on a murder trial inspired his first Dutch Francis novel, *Alibi*. His writing, praised for its impeccable plotting and lifelike characters, explores the complexities of the legal system with authenticity and intrigue. *Beneath the Gavel* is his first standalone legal thriller.

www.stephenMmurphy.com